BRADY REMINGTON LANDED ME IN JAIL

TIJAN

Copyright © 2013 Tijan

Cover design by Coffee and Characters

<h1 style="text-align:center">1</h1>

When my phone rang at three in the morning, I wasn't surprised. It was a Friday night, now Saturday morning and I knew that my best friend had gone to a party. He always chose the party. I always chose to stay home for some good sense and a good book. Then the phone rang again and I picked it up before it woke my grandma. Viola wouldn't have been surprised by who was on the other end, but she would've stomped around harder than necessary in her clogs for the rest of the weekend. No one wanted that.

"Brady, I'm sleeping."

"You're a liar, Rayna Cassidy," he tsked me.

I rubbed the grit out of my eyes and scooted up against my headboard. Years had prepared me for what this phone call was going to be. "What'd you do?"

He chuckled. "Let's just say I'm not the one in the hospital, but I am calling from jail. Can you come get me?"

I groaned, even my bones were exhausted. "Who was it this time?"

"Why do you care?"

"Brady."

"Sorry. He's a loser and if I see him again, I'm going to pound him into dust."

"I hope there aren't any police men near you." I thought of another time when a cop had overheard and not taken his threats lightly. Brady had stayed an extra five days with a doubled bail. I had not thought it was cute. He had.

"We get some privacy for these calls now. So are you coming or what? I'm itching for tacos."

"Tacos? Why do we always have to go there?"

"Rayna."

"Yeah, yeah. I'm on it." I grumbled and grinned at the same time. Then I threw back the sheets and my grin vanished. The cold air blasted me, but I threw some clothes on and ignored my sudden chills. With some money stuffed in my back pocket I headed out the window and swung free from the last rung in the ladder to the ground. It was either too late or too early because the dew hadn't come out yet. However, the full moon was out and it highlighted the clothesline while I ducked underneath.

It was a short ten minute drive into Northshire Folk and after I swung through the two streetlights in town, past the closed bar, past Nellie's, I turned into the police station. Two squad cars were positioned at the front, but I knew they parked in the rear too. The main door, which was a glass door with 'The Northshire Folk Police Headquarters' emblazoned on it, jingled my arrival and I looked up to see Deputy Doug come out from the back room. His beige uniform had been pulled out of his pants with the tails in desperate need of an iron. The blonde comb-over had been neglected at some point that evening with thin wisps pointed in every direction except the way they were supposed to go, to the left. Needless to say, they didn't cover the wrinkles that seemed etched into his forehead either.

Deputy Doug had looked better, but I refused to believe it had anything to do with Brady. I told myself I didn't need to start being concerned now. It was hardly a worthwhile weekend for Brady without a trip to jail.

"Hey, Deputy Doug."

He squinted at me. "Rayna, is that you?"

"Can I post bail for him?"

Deputy Doug frowned and the old droop came over his sixty-something shoulders.

My stomach dropped. "What'd he do?"

"It's not what he did, but who." Deputy Doug shook his head and reached for a file. "You want to know who?"

Did I really?

Deputy Doug didn't wait for my response. "Kidrick Stephens."

"What?" I blinked. Kid used to be best friends with Brady, but he moved away two summers ago. He was the male me for Brady. My life became a lot easier when Kidrick left, but... "Wait —Kid's back?"

...and Brady put him in the hospital?

"Yeah, he's back," Deputy Doug huffed as he stamped something official on some papers. "He's back and his daddy is furious and now I have a monster headache. Do you know what's going to happen? Mr. Stephens is going to press charges against Brady and do you know what that means?"

Frank Stephens had been the town's golden boy. He bought most of the town, sold almost all of the businesses, and made millions off the entire exchange. To say that he was pompous and an ass was an understatement.

"He's going to press charges against Brady?" My stomach fell to the floor. Although we all knew this day would come...

Doug banged the papers on the table and aligned them a little too roughly. "And they're going to stick this time. Brady— he ain't...anyways—" He glanced over his shoulders and stopped. "Your boy's coming out now. Don't take him for break-fast this time, Rayna. Take him to get a lawyer because he's going to need it."

When I heard a back door click open, I glanced up and out came Brady with a stupid grin on his face. His blonde hair was flatter than normal and his tee shirt had been ripped across the chest. When he turned and I caught sight of the tattoo on his back, I saw that the entire back section of his shirt was gone too. The fight had gone bad, too bad.

"Deputy Dog!" Brady heralded. "Who do I have to thank for this hospitable visit?"

Deputy Doug stamped harder on a different pile of papers. "You don't have to thank no one, Brady."

Brady lifted his arms, turned back around, and another officer took off the handcuffs. When my best friend caught sight of me, the sparkling blue eyes sobered. "Heya, Rayna."

A tingle shot through my toes from his soft tone, but I clamped down on it. I didn't need to be getting hot and both-ered by him, not tonight. Not ever.

When he took the papers from Deputy Doug, his shoulders tensed. I moved to his side and took the papers.

"Hey!" Brady protested.

I shooed him away. "We all know who can read here."

Brady frowned.

The papers read another court date where Brady would have to appear for assault charges. "You're charging him!" I cried out, but then remembered Deputy Doug's initial frus-tration.

"Well..." Deputy Doug glanced from Brady to me, but shook his head. "I just told you, Rayna. He assaulted Kidrick Stephens. We have witnesses that corroborate this. Mr. Stephens won't let this go away. He's not like the rest."

"It doesn't matter," I breathed out.

"Frank Stephens is an ass. I'll gladly see him in court," Brady growled.

I turned to see the Heat of the Moment Brady, where he'd do anything if it meant he would stand up for his beliefs. Most days that meant fighting, but this time was different. I realized that Brady wanted to see this thing through.

He ripped the papers out of my hands. "I'll see Frank Stephens in court. I have no problem dealing with him." And with that parting statement, he stormed out.

"Brady..." I was still reeling from confusion.

The door slammed shut on his heel.

Deputy Doug raised a hand to scratch his forehead. His fingers moved his comb-over backwards.

"What just happened?"

Deputy Doug leaned forward. He crinkled the papers on the counter. "You need to talk to him, Rayna. Brady messed up. He messed up real good this time. You know me. You know me and everyone else in town. We take kindly to Brady. I mean, we all feel like he's our own boy cause of the way he showed up and how the Forresters took him in. We've all been through his struggles with the shoplifting and the boozing and the fighting —he still does the last two, but you know what I mean. He's become a good man, kind of. I'd hate to think that he's... We all know what happens if you get something on your record when you're an adult. It don't get erased that easy."

He stared at me with weary eyes and I took the papers that Brady had left behind. He had the car running and the passenger door opened for me. As soon as I got inside, he shot around and I fell across the seat into his lap.

"Hey!"

Brady enfolded me against his chest. One of his arms wrapped around my waist and pinned me in place. I was helpless to move...and I didn't know if I wanted to...

"Brady. This is enough. Safety first. Being pissy later." I tried to ignore the pounding heartbeat in my ears. This was not the time for my stupid crush to act up.

Brady's tense jaw didn't agree with me. His shoulder muscles were bunched together and they only moved when his arm jerked to steer the car. I knew he REALLY didn't agree when I saw his jaw clench and his Adam's apple bob, stop midway, and stay there. I couldn't make out his eyes; and I suddenly wanted too. Badly.

An unnerving emotion washed over me.

Brady was fallible, that had never been questioned, but the fact that he might regret his fights—that had never been *considered*. When he fought, there was always a reason behind it. Someone got hurt, insulted, disrespected. He never fought with bad intentions; it was always to protect others. There was something about him that made people believe in him. Brady bulldozed his way through anything and anyone. He'd apologize if he was wrong later, but he never *never* regretted his initial decision.

'*He's scared.*' My hand started to shake slightly. I'd never seen Brady scared. I didn't like it. I didn't like it one bit.

"You can let me go." I felt like it was the right thing to say. Was it?

Brady didn't move. Instead, he slammed on the brakes and cursed. Then he pounded his hand against the steering wheel.

"Brad...d...y," my voice trembled. I hoped he hadn't caught it. So many things were off. The night started out wrong and it was only going to get worse. I opened my mouth—to what, I didn't know. I felt like I needed to apologize to him because I realized that I'd never comforted him. I felt like I needed to bully him how he always bullied me.

I was ashamed in that moment. And then—I watched, mesmerized, as Brady collapsed right before my eyes. His shoulders slumped. His face closed off and he seemed to crumble in front of me.

"Hey," I murmured as I sat up and cupped his face. As I did, I was aware of how close we were...and was it hot in here? I was about to burst into flame. Then I felt Brady turn and cup my face in turn.

Holy.

His thumb started to caress my lips and rub against my bottom lip. He started to play with it. He stretched it out and then dipped between my two lips...and, oh my god, it slipped inside. My heart was going to pound itself out of my chest.

Brady rested his forehead rest against mine. "I don't know what I'm going to do, Ray."

His thumb swept beside my tongue and teased it. It dipped back out and slid against my cheek. I held my breath—I couldn't do anything else—and I was captivated as it slid back over my lips.

"I just..."

That was Brady talking.

It was Brady who was touching me, but it took another second before I pulled myself out of my haze. I realized that Brady didn't even know what he was doing. I caught his hand and pulled back to give us some space.

Then everything was forgotten when his eyes met mine. My hand reached for his face and cupped the side of his cheek. I was starting not to care...

He closed his eyes and moved into my touch. "I don't know what I'm going to do, Ray."

Nothing needed to happen here. Nothing needed to change...and then he dipped his head to the crook of my shoulder and something washed over me. I wrapped my arms around him and closed my eyes to hold him tight. I didn't want to let him go.

"I just want to stay here, like this." His voice was muffled against my neck.

I no longer knew where I ended and Brady began.

"Rayna," he breathed out. He clasped me tighter.

And then he kissed me. He kissed my neck and I groaned in surrender. That was all Brady needed. He tipped his head back, framed my face with his hands, and took one look. Whatever he saw, he groaned right before his lips were on mine. He commanded his entrance.

2

———

"**O**h my God!"

"Oh my God," Brady panted with a rakish grin on his face.

"Get off!" I shoved at his heavy shoulder. A part of me couldn't believe what had just happened. I lost my virginity. I lost it in the backseat of my grandmother's car to my best friend —and he was laughing.

"I just did." Brady tucked a hand around my waist and nuzzled my neck. He yawned a full body yawn—I felt it all the way between my legs. If I would've let him, he would've fallen asleep then and there.

"Brady!"

"Mmmm?" He threw a leg over me and I was again underneath him, sheltered from the world.

It felt nice. Then I remembered that it couldn't last and I twisted my legs out from underneath him, hauled myself backwards into the backseat of the car and collapsed as my hair covered my face. I tried to blow it off my face.

I already knew he was smirking and that he'd be laughing

any moment. Waiting...I heard it start. It wasn't long before the car started to shake.

"Stop it. People are going to think we're having sex."

He laughed harder.

"Oh come on, Ray. How can you—I mean—look at you. Look at me! This is...this is..."

"You and me," I said flatly.

He stopped laughing. "Oh man..."

Exactly.

"Holy shit!" he yelped. "Oh my—I am so so sorry, Ray. Ray....oh God."

I scowled. I knew it wasn't funny, but had I been that bad? He didn't have to act like it was the worst thing in the world.

Brady liked sex. He slept with other girls around town and most of them would hop in any time, but I didn't have sex. I didn't flirt. I didn't even smile hello at guys. I'm not a prickly prude, but the truth was that I hadn't pictured it this way, at least not in my grandmother's car. Viola would kill me.

"Could you find my clothes for me? Please?" My skin was flushed so the cool leather felt refreshing, but it couldn't cover the humiliation, shame, self-disgust...there's too many to name. A moment went by before Brady placed my clothes on my stomach gently. The front seat squeaked and I peeked to see that he had turned his back.

After I wiggled into my pants and fixed my sweater. I noticed Brady had done the same, except he left the ripped shirt off. I had an insane idea to offer him my sweater, but bit back that suggestion. It'd bring another fit of laughter and I couldn't handle that.

After we were done dressing, we sat there until a car turned onto the street and its headlights flashed over for us a second. Brady cursed and bent forward to start the car. I didn't move from the backseat, but when his shoulders drooped, I knew what he was doing and I scrambled up to the front seat.

Brady jolted upright and stared at me.

"What?" I ran my hand over the floor in front my seat.

"What are you doing?"

"This is my car. I don't want you to hotwire it." I cringed when my fingers found something soggy on the floor.

"It's Viola's, but what are you doing? I thought you'd stay in the backseat."

"Why?" Screw it—I didn't know what my hands would touch down there, so I just bent my head underneath the dashboard and squinted in the dark.

"Because..." Brady left the sentence hanging.

Something glinted from the light and I smiled. I snatched the keys and jerked upright.

Brady jumped back.

"I found 'em." I brandished the keys in the air.

Brady glanced at them. "Those are my keys. Thanks. I thought I'd lost 'em."

I muttered a curse and bent down again.

"Rayna," Brady said.

I froze. "What?"

"I have your keys."

I whirled around and barely managed to miss the dashboard. "You have my keys?"

"They were on the floor. You dropped them when you fell in my lap," Brady explained as he watched me with caution.

"Oh."

"Yeah...," He sighed and leaned back against the seat. He watched me instead. I ran a hand through my hair, proud that it didn't tremble at all, but I couldn't stop biting my lip. I always bit my lip. Brady's eyes shifted to my lip and a groan escaped him.

I looked up. Our eyes met and something electrocuted the air. Both of us felt it and my skin tingled. I licked my lips and I never lick my lips, but then Brady's mouth was there. I gasped and arched forward. My hands were twisted in his hair to hold him close. Then, as I felt myself wanting to climb on top of him, another car drove by and honked. Reality clicked in.

I shoved him away. "Stop." I wasn't sure who I meant.

"I can't help it. You just...when you bite your lip like that..." Brady groaned and ran a hand over his head. As I watched, my hand lifted to touch his hair.

"Damn it!" I firmly tucked my hand underneath my leg.

"I'm sorry!"

"No, not you, my..." hand. I bit back that word. "Nevermind."

"Okay."

"Can we just...?" My question trailed off when I looked where we were. Charisteaus and Law Associates were written in white lettering on their glass window. A picture of a hammer that hung over a gavel looked back at me. I could almost see an evil face leering through the windowpane.

"What are we doing here?"

Brady grimaced in embarrassment. "I panicked. Deputy Dog said to find a lawyer so I did."

"No self-respecting lawyer is going to be open at four in the morning." I glanced at the clock. "At five in the morning."

"I know." Brady slid further down in the seat. "What am I going to do, Ray? I screwed up this time."

Brady had beaten up Kid Stephens. And Brady had no father to defend him. He had foster parents who were neither wealthy nor powerful. My grandparents were well known in the community. Neil played bingo at the nursing home and Viola was popular with the Ladies' Aid, especially on the days they put brandy in their coffee. However, I couldn't picture those little ladies going against Frank Stephens, prim and properly drunk or not.

"Why did you beat up Kid? Why is he back in town?"

Brady groaned and then growled. I caught sight of his perfect white teeth. "He's back in town for your graduation."

"Huh?"

"That's what I thought too!"

I straightened in the seat to face him. Brady shifted to meet me, but his eyes traveled over my face: over my rumpled hair, and all the way to where my top had ridden up over my stomach.

"Stop it!" I tried to pull down my shirt.

"Sorry, I just..." Brady gestured to me.

I chose my battle. "If Kid really came into town for my graduation, that doesn't explain why you put him in the hospital."

"It's got nothing to do with you."

"But—"

"Leave it, Rayna."

"But—"

"I mean it."

I tried one more time. "Why—"

"I'll kiss you if you say one more word."

I shut up and crossed my arms.

Brady waited and when I didn't ask again, he started the car. "Nellie's?"

It was our tradition post bail. As we drove through town, my stomach grumbled, but I knew I wasn't hungry and especially not for Nellie's food. Brady liked to go there because it was the only gas station open twenty four hours a day and he loved the owner, Ned. Not me. I couldn't stand the old drunk.

When Brady pulled into the parking lot, I closed my eyes against the glare from the lights. Eight other cars were there with people that lingered around them. I recognized some of them as students from school, but saw others that had graduated in Brady's class a year earlier. Then I saw Clarissa Cumberly break away from a group and saunter towards us.

Brady saw her too and glanced at me. "Are you okay?"

"Are you insane?" I shot him an incredulous look. I loved

that his on-and-off-again ex was going to see us now. We prob-ably reeked of sex.

Brady paused as he had started to unbuckle his seat belt.

"What are we doing here?" My lip trembled a bit.

"We always come here."

"Yeah, but..." Was he that dense?

"I get arrested. We come here." Brady said it like it was simple, two plus two always equaled four.

"I don't feel up to Nellie's."

Clarissa circled around to the driver's seat and knocked on the window.

Brady still watched me as I watched Clarissa bend forward to display her perfect size C breasts in front of Brady. They were displayed in a denim halter top that rode high on her waist. Her matching denim miniskirt rode low on her hips. From the golden tendrils that hung loose over her shoulders, the dangling earrings, and the glossed lips—I knew that every single guy at that gas station was watching our car. Clarissa drew attention. She just breathed and it came to her.

Brady waited until I nodded my permission and then he rolled down his window to grin. "Yo, Claris—what's up?"

Her smart green eyes snapped from Brady's naked chest to my flushed face and then back again. A corner of her mouth curved upwards. She drawled out, "Apparently I'm not that up...heard you got taken to the joint tonight."

Brady stiffened. "I'm out."

Clarissa gave him a full grin. "I can sort of see that, Brady."

Brady flashed a grin and relaxed against his seat. I watched as the old charisma was switched on. "Yeah, well the dude ripped my shirt. I couldn't go around wearing half a shirt, you know? That'd be stupid."

"I'm sure the ladies will enjoy it tonight." Clarissa's amuse-ment dripped like honey, but her eyes trailed past Brady and found me. "Hi, Rayna."

"Hi, Clarissa." In just those two words, I wanted to disappear. I was sure that I'd said more than I wanted. I was okay with most of Brady's conquests and even the ones, like Clarissa, who stuck around to form friendships with him. They all knew about me and about the weird relationship I had with him, but none of them ever took me seriously until they were on the outs with Brady Remington. Then they couldn't understand why someone like me was always on the 'in' with him. Clarissa had hated me in the beginning, but over the years she'd come to show me respect. However, I didn't talk to them unless I was forced to...like now.

Clarissa watched me, but I hugged my sides and jerked my gaze towards the gas station's doors.

Brady laughed. "What's the word out there?"

A mocking grin formed at her mouth before she straightened and took her boobs away. She leaned a slim hip against the door instead. "You mean with Kid? People are excited, Brady. Kid's a legend, but whatever went down between the two of you is between the two of you. We're cool with that."

I heard Brady breathe easier and I didn't think, I just reacted, and I touched his arm to reassure him. He moved quickly and his hand found mine. When Clarissa turned and glanced down into the window Brady moved our hands out of her eyesight.

"I don't throw punches for no reason."

"We know that."

"Do you think you could give us a minute?"

Clarissa waved a perfectly manicured hand. "Don't worry about it. I'll send everyone packing."

"Thanks, Claris."

Clarissa slapped a hand on the door and lowered herself until her boobs were on display again. "If you're still up for some partying tonight, there's a kegger at Barthal's woods. You know the place."

Brady grinned and nodded. "I do."

Her green eyes switched to me. "Hope to see you there, to see you both. It's graduation week, Rayna. It's time to let loose before the real world comes knocking."

With a wink and a chuckle, Clarissa saluted her goodbye and sauntered away. It wasn't long before everyone left the gas station behind her.

Brady's eyes sparked. "Finally."

He was out the door before I could unclasp my own buckle.

3

We were in the back booth, enjoying our food or I was trying when Ned decided to join us. Brady greeted him with a big smile and I dropped my taco. I'd lost my appetite. When a customer came into the station, I picked it back up. Ned had to hurry off, but it wasn't long before we heard him coming back with two beer cans in hand and another surprise. Deputy Doug was behind him.

"What's wrong, Deputy Dog?" Brady grinned as he took one of the cans from Ned.

Deputy Doug slid into the booth by me. "I've got bad news, Brady."

His uniform seemed more wrinkled than it was an hour ago.

Even Ned grew silent. I watched as he pounded his chest and stopped a belch.

How considerate of him.

Then Brady's foot curled into my side on the booth and my hand clutched it. None of us were sure we wanted to hear what Deputy Doug had to say.

"I'm afraid that I have to tell you, Brady, that...the charges have been dropped!" Deputy Doug broke out in a wide smile and pounded a fist down. The beer cans rattled on the table. "Goddamn, boy, I don't know how you do it—but you did it again. The charges are dropped!"

Brady blinked in shock before he said anything. "I don't know...I don't know what I did, Deputy Dog. I didn't do anything..."

"Well, someone did. Frank Stephens doesn't back down from a fight and he just did." Deputy Doug grinned in relief and threw an arm on the booth's back.

Brady shook his head. "I can't believe this."

"Come on, tell me now. You were worried, weren't you?" Deputy Doug pumped his fists in the air, almost gleeful.

Brady laughed shakily, and then shot me a quick plea with his eyes.

I straightened and cleared my throat. "I can't believe that you programmed your cardboard Bigfoot to growl at customers, Ned. It was bad enough that he laughed at us when we walked in, but now he has to growl at us? I was scared to come in here. Do you want to scare customers off? What about all those little kids that come in after school?"

Ned reared his head back as he studied me.

I looked irate, but I really wasn't. Brady looked relieved from the corner of my eye. I even saw how Deputy Doug frowned, scratched his head, and then looked from me to Ned.

"Why, I never...I don't know what you want...," Ned sputtered as his hand clenched around his can of beer.

"That's the problem, Ned. I'm speaking as a constituent of your average customer. I hate the growl. You should get rid of it."

Ned still sputtered. "It's Bob. Bob is greeting people. It's how he greets people."

"'Bob' is not real."

Deputy Doug snorted.

"Yeah, but...Bob's a friendly Bigfoot. Bob the Bigfoot!" Ned looked proud as he scratched his yellow stained shirt.

Brady burst out laughing, but quickly turned away.

"You should give Bob a break. A lot of people love Bob."

"'Bob' is made of cardboard."

"Bob's a lot more than cardboard. His feelings are hurt, missy. You should apologize to Bob," Ned said defiantly, but I caught how he looked from Brady to Deputy Doug.

I pretended to sputter, but the truth was that I didn't care. That's when I snuck a glance at Brady and saw that he was okay again.

"Bob's feelings are hurt," Ned harrumphed.

Bob's feelings weren't the only thing that was going to hurt if I had a say about it.

When Brady and Deputy Doug burst out laughing I realized that I'd spoken aloud. "I am so sorry, I didn't...I mean...I don't—Bob's not real!"

"He's real in spirit." Brady's eyes were laughing. "He's real in spirit."

"You, missy," Ned barked and stood up. "You need to change your attitude. I done have no time to deal with the likes of you." With those parting words, he stomped away from the booth and a little later we heard the cash register ping open.

Deputy Doug laughed softly. "You and Ned always bump heads over things."

Brady laughed his agreement. "You know, Rayna, you don't have to go around and look for things to pick at. You know how Ned feels about that Bigfoot. He's sensitive."

I rolled my eyes. "Well excuse me for being honest. He could have more customers if he'd just get rid of that thing."

Brady chuckled. "And you know what else, Ned's right about your attitude. You really can be negative sometimes."

I was negative? When I was helping him out? My eyes narrowed. "What did you just say?"

Brady straightened in his seat and flashed a grin. "You know what I'm talking about. You need to let loose more, Rayna. Take the stick out of your ass."

Deputy Doug grew quiet.

I saw red. "Well, not all of us are 'cool' enough to get in fights and get thrown in jail every other week. I mean, not all of us are 'cool' enough to go and have a beer the next day with the person you busted up. You're right, Brady."

Brady's smile dimmed—just a bit.

I continued, "Maybe I should do it. Maybe I should let loose and see who I punch. Hell—maybe I should even sleep with someone. That'd be fun."

His smile was nearly extinct.

I kept going. "You're right. I've been meaning to get on that. Everyone else is talking how much fun sex is. I think it's time I have some of that fun. Wouldn't want to miss out, would I?"

Brady glowered at me. "You're talking stupid. Don't talk like that."

"What do you mean? I thought I needed to 'let loose' and 'get the stick out of my ass.' I mean, that's what you said, wasn't it?"

Brady glared.

I glared back.

Deputy Doug had ceased to exist.

It was at that time that Ned chose to make his appearance again. He took one look at us and left again.

Deputy Doug cleared his throat. "Uh...I just wanted to let you know the good news, Brady. And I should be heading back to the station. You, huh, you two have a good rest of the morning, you hear?"

As he left, Brady slumped back in his booth. "See what you just did. You scared 'em both away."

My eyeballs threatened to pop out.

"What?" Brady saw my look. "You did. They like me, Rayna."

"I cannot believe you!" I threw my hands in the air and stormed from the booth, past growling Bob and Ned who'd taken position behind his counter again. Bob's growl roared behind me when I went through the door and I waited in the car, fuming until Brady came out. When the door swung open and I saw him coming, two guys from school stopped to chat. Then Brady stopped mid-sentence and turned my way. I felt the heat of his gaze through the windshield and I gulped, slumping down further in the seat.

The two guys turned to watch me too. One laughed, shook his head, and patted Brady's shoulder before they went inside.

When he got in the car and started the engine, he was quiet for a moment. "You want to loosen up? Tim and Darren just told me the kegger's going strong at Barthal's woods."

I knew Brady and I knew him well. For some reason this was a challenge. The gamut had been thrown and I wasn't going to lose. Brady usually won, but this time I was bound and determined even though my stomach took a steep decline. This wasn't going to end well, but I batted my eyelashes. "Sure. I'll start there."

"Fine."

"Fine."

Brady turned the car towards Barthal's woods. I couldn't slump any further down in the seat.

4

———————

Brady parked in a back cornfield and threw open his door. When his long legs took him across the field, around the maze of cars, and through the first line of trees, I sighed. Then I stuck my hands in my pockets and slowed to a lingering trek. I knew he would already have his drink in hand by the time I got to the party. I was a little hurt that he didn't wait for me, but Brady went at his own pace. I'd accepted that a long time ago and followed behind through the corn stalks.

Barthal's woods were a small section of trees located south of Hank Barthal's cornfields. Hank was the father of one of the football players, another friend of Brady's. They were all friends with Brady. They were not friends with me, which is why I took my sweet time.

As I grew closer, I squared my shoulders and took a breath. I was almost there and then I tripped. I caught my balance before I completely fell and stumbled into the small opening where Brady's friends were.

Sure enough. Brady already stood beside the kegger, cup in one hand and the other in his pocket. He struck a cocky stance while he listened to whatever Clarissa was whispering in his ear. He didn't look at me, but she did. Those smart green eyes of hers seemed to see right through me. Yes, Brady and I were at odds with each other and yes, Clarissa caught onto it. She always saw right through us. I sighed and wrapped my arms around me. It'd grown cold suddenly.

"You're one of those girls, huh?"

A guy with soft features and brown eyes stood to my left. I labelled him as Prettyboy, but wasn't going to let him know that. There was something in his eyes, but then he looked to where I'd been staring and his eyes went flat.

I looked back and saw Brady against a truck with his head bent forward. One of his hands was splayed on the small of Clarissa's back underneath her halter top. A white shirt had been given to him, but he'd only thrown it over his shoulder. He looked too comfortable in his skin.

I almost hated him because of that thought—just for a moment. It seemed unfair that he was so confident while the rest of us just...became comfortable at pretending.

"You like him, don't you?" the boy asked.

"Oh...well...it's Brady." What else could a person say? I shrugged.

He nodded, as if he understood, but I still caught a flash of resentment. "I'm Joshua." He swung a hand to me as he leaned against the tree and I could feel his breath on me. As I shook his hand, I was startled to realize that they were a little rough on the inside.

"How old are you?" I glanced down to hide my blush.

Joshua chuckled and released my hand. "I'm a senior...or I was a senior from Black Ham. I'm here visiting with my cousin." He folded his arms and tucked his hands underneath, which accentuated his lean body. His shirt stretched across his chest and I could see his stomach muscles bunch under his shirt.

"Why'd you ask how old I am?" His eyes seemed to be laughing at me.

"Oh, uh...you just look young."

"So do you. How old are you?"

"I'm a senior here."

"So you're graduating next week." Joshua grinned and leaned closer.

"Uh..." I stepped back, just an inch, but his lips quirked at the movement. "Yeah, I'm graduating next week."

"So you're celebrating this weekend? I heard your classmates are having an all weekend bash."

"I guess, but I don't usually come to these things." A small group had congregated around a truck while a few girls danced to the music, their movements sloppy and drunk.

Joshua scanned the group too. "Is this your entire grade?"

"We come from a small town."

"My cousin's from here. He wanted to come back and see some old friends, but..." He hesitated to finish his statement, but I watched as his eyes darted back to Brady and harden. "Let's just say that I'm more welcome than my cousin."

"Who's your cousin?"

Joshua watched me intently. "Kidrick Stephens."

My eyes widened. "Oh."

"Yeah. Oh," Joshua bit out and glared over my shoulder. "That Brady kid busted up my cousin at a party. I didn't even know what was going on. I was too far away and by the time I heard Kid was taken to the hospital, that kid was already in handcuffs. Now look, he's back here and chatting her up again."

The fact that Brady had been chatting with Clarissa shouldn't have affected me. It wasn't a surprise. They were on friendly terms and sometimes more than friendly terms, but I couldn't ignore the stab of pain. I peeked over my shoulder and swallowed tightly when I caught Brady's glare. He wanted to know what I was doing.

As if he couldn't remember.

I rolled my eyes, this was his idea. He wanted me to loosen up, well I would. Joshua was going to help me.

"Oh, now look at him," Joshua said. "He must've heard that I'm Kid's cousin. Maybe he'll come over and try something with me."

I sent Brady a scathing glare before I turned back to Joshua. "Why'd they get in a fight?"

Joshua just looked at me.

"I mean if it was something Kid said or—"

"What makes you think it was something that Kid said? It was that guy over there. I know my cousin. He doesn't fight. That guy went psycho on him. That's what happened."

Brady got into his fair share of fights and most of them were his fault, but he never started one unless provoked. It was just that he was too easily provoked. "I know Brady and he doesn't react like that unless something's been said."

Joshua sighed in disgust. "I thought you were different. I mean, you look different. You don't look like them and yet, you're defending him—like them."

I WAS different.

Joshua taunted, "You'd probably sleep with the guy if given a chance. Wouldn't you?"

I sucked in my breath and froze. I blinked back tears, but Joshua saw it all and laughed. "See. You would, wouldn't you?"

"You don't know what you're talking about." I still blinked away more tears. "You don't know me or Brady or anyone here. Who are you to judge us?"

Joshua stared. "Sorry. You're right. It's none of my business if you like the guy or not. I don't know you. I don't need to care about you."

"You shouldn't judge, me or him."

Joshua shot me a look. "I wouldn't go that far. He put my cousin in the hospital. I can judge all I want."

"Yeah, but—" I'd been about to argue the same argument,

Brady only fought if and when provoked, but Joshua silenced me when he leaned forward and put his mouth on mine. I gasped and then his lips moved over mine. He drew me against his chest and shifted closer with a hand around my neck. His head tilted for a better angle.

I did nothing. Absolutely nothing.

Joshua's hand slid down my back and pressed my hips against his.

Oh, God...I silently chanted in my head.

As he turned and started to press me against the tree, I wrenched my mouth from his and shoved him. He moved only a few inches, but I was able to breathe again.

"What are you doing?" I hissed.

Joshua gave me a smug look and leaned closer. "I couldn't help it. I've wanted to do that since I saw you. You're cute."

"Yeah, but...you don't just go around and kiss people because they're cute."

"I saw that guy coming over here. I didn't want to be polite to him or get into a fight with him."

"And kissing me was your best idea?"

"Well...yeah."

"Well...don't," I blurted out.

Joshua grinned, looking relaxed as he studied me. "You know," he started, "you're wasting your time if you're waiting for him. You're really cute. I could go for you, but if you're saying no to me because of him—you shouldn't hold your breath. He's into girls like that." He nodded in Clarissa's direction, but Brady was staring at us—at me.

I gulped and ducked underneath Joshua's shoulder to hide.

"And you're even cuter when you blush like that," Joshua whispered. I felt his breath cake my cheeks, but I didn't dare look him in the eyes. I knew he'd kiss me and, truthfully, I didn't know what I wanted. I just knew that Brady was watching. I could feel his gaze on us.

"You shouldn't do that," I finally said.

"Do what?"

Joshua didn't move.

"The leaning thing. You shouldn't do that. Not with me, anyway," I fumbled out my words.

Joshua barked out a laugh, but shook his head. "I like you. You're honest, but you're completely wrong. I think you're the only girl here who I should do that with."

I just shook my head. The guy was wrong.

"I mean it," Joshua insisted. "Most of these people are posers. They just 'pose' for what role they're supposed to be playing. Take a look at your Brady; he knows that he's the king around these parts. He doesn't even have a shirt on. He's too good for a shirt or something. And that girl with him, she's probably his flavour of the week or his recurring flavour of the week. Everyone's predictable. Not you, though. You're just...I don't know who you are. I think I do, but the more I talk to you, the more intrigued I get."

"You don't know anything."

"I think I do," Joshua retorted. "And I think that you're the girl who shouldn't be here. But I'm relieved you are. You don't belong with these people. You're not fake. You're better than them, but you don't think that. You're one of those girls that wants to be popular, but you have no idea how to do it. So you're here, awkward, and hoping that something will change because of your presence. I hate to say it, but no one else has come over to talk to you. There's probably a reason for that."

I didn't know what emotion I was feeling first. Anger. Outrage. Disbelief. So I reacted on instinct and slapped him. Joshua's head was turned to the side from the force of my slap, but the first person to speak wasn't the two of us.

Brady rushed over. "What happened?"

I opened my mouth to explain, but Brady pushed himself in

between us with me behind him. He wasn't listening and he was a breath away from punching Joshua.

I caught his fisted hand. "Don't."

"But—" Brady started, but I shook my head.

"I said no, Brady. It's my problem. I can handle it."

"You just slapped the guy." Brady glared at Joshua.

Joshua rubbed at his jaw, but his eyes darted between us.

"Contrary to what you're thinking, I meant all of that as a compliment." Joshua stood straighter, but he scanned him up and down.

Brady stepped closer. "You got a problem with me?"

Joshua smirked, waited, and then chuckled. "Yeah, I do."

Brady's hand jerked within mine, but I held tight and pulled him back. When he didn't move, I threw my entire body backwards. It hurt, but it worked. Brady jerked with me. I stumbled and was about to fall, but Brady wrapped an arm around my waist and held me against his chest. Then he glared at Joshua again. "You don't need to talk to her again."

"I don't think you have the right to tell me that I can't talk to her. In fact, I don't even know why you're over here. Our conversation had nothing to do with you."

Brady was quiet for a moment. My head fell forward on his bare chest and I watched his taunt stomach muscles breathe in and out, but then I heard, "I have all the right I need. She's my girlfriend."

"What?" I pushed myself away.

Brady ignored me.

His hands reached out to encircle my wrists and I closed my mouth. His fingers slid down and entwined with my own and twirled me around. He wrapped our arms around my front, with my back to his chest, then propped his chin on my shoulder and smiled. "You can leave without a beating. I don't give this opportunity to the other guys who hit on my girlfriend. You're only getting it once."

I bit back a groan, but waited as Joshua took in the sight of us. Brady was the only person who felt comfortable touching me—or I should say that he was the only one I wanted to touch me.

His eyes jerked to mine before he headed towards the cars.

"Can I be the first to congratulate the happy couple?" Clarissa had sauntered up to us.

Brady laughed and kept me in place when I tried to step out of his arms. He moved his chin to my other shoulder and smiled widely. "You could. I don't think that guy was too happy to hear that I was off the market."

Just like that. It was a flip of a switch and broiling Brady had reverted to his old joking self.

I shook my head and sighed.

"What's the matter, Ray?" Brady asked in my ear. His voice tickled me and I couldn't stop a shiver. "Are you cold?" He wrapped our arms tighter, bringing me closer against him. "I was being cool about it, wasn't I?"

Clarissa watched the two of us.

"What do you mean?" I turned my head to the side and tilted my eyes to meet his.

"You know, what I said before—I didn't actually mean it."

Wait—he didn't want me to loosen up and sleep with guys? Really? I rolled my eyes. "What do you expect of me? I'm supposed to read your mind?"

"Yeah." It made perfect sense to him. "That's what best friends do."

I shook my head. "Come off it, Brady. You told me to loosen up. Now you're saying that you didn't mean it."

"Well, I just said that because—" He sputtered to a halt, remembering Clarissa's presence. "We can talk about that later."

"I'm sure we will."

"So..." Clarissa's eyes lingered on our enjoined hands. "It

looked like you were enjoying yourself, Rayna. Until you slapped him, I mean. What's up with that?"

"Nothing," I said primly. "He just said some stuff that I didn't like hearing."

"About what? Or who?" Her eyes sparked at the 'who'. Something told me that Clarissa knew exactly who we had been talking about. And when her eyes snapped to measure Brady for a moment, I knew I was right.

"About me." I WAS different. I didn't fit in with this crowd, but what infuriated me was that he had put Brady in one group and me in another. He said I didn't belong with him. Maybe he was right. Maybe I wasn't experienced or sophisticated like Clarissa, but I had something going for me that Joshua or Clarissa couldn't take away.

Brady was my best friend.

I repeated that statement to myself. It was true. He was my best friend, not Clarissa's. Joshua was wrong. I did belong; at least I belonged with Brady.

Brady might've sensed my inner turmoil, or maybe he did that 'best friend mind reading' thing, because he turned me around and started to move us beyond the trees. "What's wrong, Ray?"

"Nothing." I gritted my teeth and hoped he'd let it go.

He didn't when he turned me in his arms, gripped my shoulders, and forced me against a tree trunk. The bark bit into my skin, but I didn't feel it. My eyes were entranced with his as his bore down on me. "Don't lie to me, Ray. What's wrong?"

"Nothing." I slapped his hands away.

Brady grinned as he caught my wrists with his, but I wrenched them free. When he tried to capture them again, I slapped away his hands—and Brady slapped mine away instead. Before long, his deep laugh came out and I was grinning when I dodged one of his playful slaps. It wasn't long before he wrapped his arms around me, squashed my hands between our chests, and rocked back and forth in a soothing motion.

It felt good. It felt comforting.

I chuckled and rested my head on his shoulder. Then I closed my eyes when Brady soothed a hand down my hair. "I don't know what that guy said, but he was wrong. Whatever he said, he was wrong."

I tightened my hold. Joshua hadn't been wrong about all of it.

"And I'll make sure that he leaves you alone, okay?" Brady whispered.

I looked up. "You're going to beat everyone up if they say something that pisses me off?"

"Depends."

"On what?" I couldn't hide my grin.

Brady smiled back. "On whatever he said to hurt you."

I saw a clear genuineness in his eyes right then. It took my breath away. "It's done with. It don't matter anymore."

Brady tipped his head back, scrutinized me for a moment, and never bothered to point out the incorrect grammar. He just shrugged. "Okay."

"Can you take me home? I'm tired."

"What? You don't want to loosen up some more?" He let me go, but then his hand slid down my arm and found mine. He entwined our fingers and led me to the parking lot.

"Shut up," I groaned.

"You did hit someone. And that make out session, woohee —if that wasn't hot then I don't know what is." Brady squeezed my hand again.

I flushed. "I did not make out with that guy."

"Yes, you did. He even did the leaning thing with you."

"Shut up."

"I can lean for you. You want me to lean for you, Ray?" As

Brady turned to walk backwards he caught both my hands in his. His eyes danced as he waited for my answer.

I held my breath.

Brady just chuckled. "I'm way better at leaning than that prick."

"Could you please shut up?"

Brady tightened his hold and jerked me close for a hug. He whispered, "Next time that guy tries something; remind him who your boyfriend is. That should send him running."

I just shook my head, but a grin tugged at my lips.

5

As Brady pulled into my driveway and parked the car, I couldn't move for a moment.

Bent over the garden gnome was my grandfather in overalls, a John Deere Hat covering his greying hair. His old leather boots still had duct tape around them. The sight of Neil fidgeting with the garden gnome shouldn't have stopped me, but it did. I was my grandpa's little girl. When he found out that I'd had sex...

I swallowed and closed my eyes.

"Ray..." Brady murmured gently.

I knew that he'd read my mind.

"Come on...it's not like you have to tell them."

"I have to."

"Why?"

"Because when they ask why I didn't tell them after it happened—I'm going to have to tell them that I chose to lie."

"It's not lying, it's just...sex is personal and you don't have to tell them everything."

"Of course you'd say that."

"Come on, don't be like that. I know that I can't understand where you're coming from, but it's not like—I was a virgin too once."

"You were a boy! *You are a* boy," I cried out. "It's not the same thing at all, Brady. And you don't even—" I stopped myself, just barely.

The silence was heavy.

"I don't what?" Brady asked quietly, but I heard the savagery beneath the surface. "I don't have parents like you? You don't either, Rayna."

"It's not like that," I murmured softly. "I'm sorry. I'm the good girl. I'm the...I'm the one who makes Viola and Neil go to church. I'm the one who insists on sitting at the table for our meals and not in front of the television. Having sex is not me."

Brady was quiet. I was afraid to look over at him, but I did and what I saw halted my own misery. The sparkle in his eyes was gone.

"What'd I say?"

His shoulder jerked in a shrug.

"Come on, Brady. What'd I say?"

"Nothing," he growled. "Leave it alone."

"What?" I insisted.

"Leave it alone, Ray. You don't want to go there."

I looked down at my lap.

"Look...," Brady started. "...you can just...tell them that you wanted to say something when you knew what to say, but you didn't know what to say for a while. How's that?"

"Thank you and I'm sorry for whatever I said to upset you."

"I'm not upset."

"I know, but..." I knew better. "I'm sorry. Will you tell me later?"

He jerked his head in a nod and I knew an emotion was just simmering underneath the surface. I reached for the door, but Brady's hand stopped me as he squeezed my shoulder. I needed that.

"We'll, um...we'll talk later...okay?" Brady stumbled out.

I nodded my head, thankful, and squeezed his hand in return. "I'm glad Mr. Stephens dropped the charges."

A scowl appeared. "You talk to that asshole, you tell me."

I nodded, but when I straightened and moved away from the car I realized that I didn't know who he meant; Kid, his father, or Joshua. I didn't think Brady would've wanted me to talk to any of them, but that's a confrontation for another day.

When Brady's door slammed shut, I glanced back and watched as he stuffed his hands in his jeans. He had a shirt on now as he strolled to where my grandfather was bent over with a poking stick in hand and a gnome to torment. As the two started to converse I sighed, ducked my head, and reached to open the screen door.

Viola called from the kitchen, "Well, at least you had the nerve to walk through the main door and not crawl back through your window. I'm supposed to thank you?"

My grandmother arched an eyebrow and lifted her potato peeler. "I love Brady. I want that to be said, but you hear me—if I come into your room again and have a heart attack when I find that you're not there—I will use this peeler on his hide."

"Okay."

"And another thing..." Viola skimmed a hand through her greying hair pulled back in a ponytail. "I talked to Sharon and she said that boy did not have supper last night. I know you two have breakfast, but I didn't see it so I don't count it. You call him in here and we're all going to sit down for a good meal."

I nodded promptly and spun on my heel. Brady was on his haunches, studying whatever my grandfather was poking at. Neil would always poke around those weeds by the gnome. I was thankful for a moment that no matter what occurred, some things never changed.

Viola yelled behind me, "And then later tonight, you can explain to me why Kid Stephens called this morning."

"What?" I whirled back around.

She pushed the bowl of half-peeled potatoes away and skimmed a hand down her red pressed shirt. "That boy's nice and all, but I don't want you spending time with him."

"Wait a minute—Kid Stephens called here?"

"Hmm mmm," she harrumphed as she turned to place the bowl in the sink.

"And he wanted to talk to me?"

"Hmmm mmm." She rinsed off the potatoes.

"Why?"

"Why do boys usually call girls?"

I was floored. I was beyond—no, I was just clueless. "I have no idea."

"Rayna." My grandmother turned and rested against the kitchen counter. She assessed me, a variety of expressions flashed across her blue, clear, and wrinkle-free eyes. Viola would never need Botox. Not that she'd use it if she had the thought to, but my grandmother was a beautiful woman. One of those classic beautiful types and she scared the living daylights out of me.

"What?" I shifted uncomfortably.

There it was. All those different expressions again: approval, disapproval, disappointment, and impatience. "One day a boy is going to call this phone and he's going to ask for you. I'll admit that I started to think that day would never come. And now that it has I'm going to tell you a part of me rejoices and a part of me wants to handcuff you inside your room. I *do not* want you spending time with Kid Stephens."

Rejoice? Handcuff?

My grandmother looked pale, more pale than usual, but it could've been the potatoes. She hated peeling potatoes.

Viola waved her hand in the air. "Get Brady in here. Food's ready."

She turned her back before I moved from the doorway. My

grandmother was sixty-three, but she'd live till she was in her hundreds.

"Grandma..." I started.

"What?" She glanced over her shoulder.

Here it was. Do I confess or not? What do I say? I wasn't dumb. I know that she worried Kid Stephens was interested in me in a romantic way, but I also knew the only reason she didn't approve was because of his father. The joke was on her because Kid would never be interested in someone like me. He liked girls like Clarissa. If she was that worried about Kid. I had no idea how she'd react to the idea of Brady.

I bailed. "Nothing."

"You sure?" She studied me again.

"Yeah, I'm sure. I'm just tired."

"Okay. Go get your boy," she shooed.

As I moved back through the living room, I scowled. He wasn't my boy. I wasn't his girl. Nothing had changed. Nothing at all. Then I looked up and my hand halted before it touched the screen door. Brady tipped his head back and laughed at something Neil had said. And then it happened—my grandfather patted his shoulder in approval.

Warmth flooded me and I choked back tears. It didn't mean a thing. It wasn't a secret that my grandparents adored Brady. I was just emotional. That's all it was. I ignored my trembling hand and scratchy throat when I opened the door. "Brady! Breakfast!"

His eyes snapped to mine. I felt my heart pound—it was suddenly so loud that I almost couldn't hear Brady when he called back, "Sweet! I call baby chair."

I rolled my eyes.

The baby chair wasn't a baby chair. It was a wooden chair that had been carved by someone to look like an actual baby. Viola swears that she found it at an auction, but I knew there was a reason why Grandpa constantly tried to burn the thing.

And yet, it always stayed where it had been placed and kept over the years, right at the table. The chair had a head where ours was supposed to rest against. A bib had even been carved into the chair, but Brady only said it warmed his back. The entire thing was wood, but it still looked like a baby.

I had taken the chair against the wall when Brady swooped in and dropped into it. The screen door squeaked again, and then Viola rushed into the living room. Just as my grandfather lifted his foot to step inside, Viola shook her head and closed the door on his face. Neil didn't look shocked as he stared at his wife of forty-three years. He just readjusted his John Deere hat and pushed one of the overall straps back in its rightful place on his shoulder.

Viola placed her hands on her hips. "Oh no. You said you had things to do outside. You do those things outside, I got the inside today."

Neil didn't blink. He turned around and went back outside. It wasn't long before he heard his truck go past.

Brady chuckled. "He didn't want to peel the potatoes, huh?" Then he reached over the table and helped himself to five pancakes.

My grandmother cleared her throat and took her chair. "Now, you two—what happened, Brady?" She looked at him sharply and pointedly.

I would've choked in his place, but Brady finished swallowing his bite of pancakes and smiled. "What do you mean, Viola?"

Her eyes narrowed. "You had my granddaughter scurrying out of here at some ungodly hour this morning. You better tell me why I had a heart attack when I went and found her gone this morning. It had better been worth it."

Brady raised his fork for another mouthful.

Viola cleared her throat and leaned closer. "You come clean

with me or don't you think I won't call Deputy Dog. He'll tell me."

He lowered the pancakes and frowned.

"I think we should pray before we eat."

"Brady. Talk."

"About what?" Brady asked, but Viola had him in her sights and she wouldn't let him out. Slowly, she got up and reached for the phone on the wall.

"Fine. Fine. I got into a fight." He sent me a furtive look that was noticed by all of us.

My grandmother slid her eyes to me, but slowly replaced the phone back in its receiver.

I coughed and raised my linked hands. "Can we please pray before Brady eats some more? We're supposed to pray at meals."

"Fine." Viola folded her hands and resumed her seat.

Brady wiped at a bead of syrup that lingered on the corner of his mouth before he folded his hands and bowed his head.

I prolonged the prayer longer than the normal twelve second chant. It lasted a good minute or two before Viola grew impatient and ended it with a final 'Amen.'

Brady tried to hide a grin as he reached for more of his pancakes, but Viola slapped his hand away. "Brady. Talk."

"I can talk. I can talk about a lot of things, Viola. What would you like to hear about? I can talk about how we went to Ned's. Did you know that Bob growls now?"

Viola grumbled, "I don't know why he named that damn station after his dog in heat. It makes no sense to me. And Bob. Who names a stupid Bigfoot? He wasn't supposed to keep the damn thing after all these years."

I relaxed after that and enjoyed a bowl of oatmeal as Brady dodged more questions. He kept her entertained with comments about Ned, Neil, and even the dog that Ned had named his gas station after. An hour later, I excused myself to my room and shut the door with a long drawn out sigh. I felt like I'd run a marathon. Collapsing on my bed, I curled into a ball.

This was where Brady found me an hour later when he landed on top of me and I shoved him off before I saw the door was shut.

"Thank God," I muttered.

"Thank who?" Brady snuggled underneath my blankets with me. "It's just me."

"Get away." I pathetically shoved at his shoulder.

Brady batted my hand away, wrapped both of his arms around my waist, and threw his leg over mine. I was trapped in place. Then he moved to lay behind me and rested his forehead on the back of my neck.

"You can thank me now, you know," he mumbled.

My skin tickled from his breath. "Thank you for what?"

"I distracted Viola. And she went outside to work in the garden."

We both knew what that meant. She'd be out there for hours.

"You didn't have to do that."

Brady yawned and I felt his chest rise and fall against my back. His arms tightened, but he still mumbled, "Yeah. I did. And you know it."

Tears pricked at my eyes, but I ignored them. He was right. I'd thought about confessing, but then breakfast happened and Brady was being questioned instead of me. That was how it was. My grandmother hadn't even wondered what I might've done that I shouldn't have.

His arm rested heavily on my waist. "Brady?"

His deep breaths answered me. He'd fallen asleep. Here's my confession to myself: sometimes Brady scared me. It wasn't him in particular, but how he affected me. I knew if anyone could coax me into doing things I shouldn't—it was the guy holding me. I felt a yawn coming and as it broke free, I turned in his arms. Instead of slinking out from underneath them—I snuggled into his chest and felt my eyelids close.

I pushed the fear at bay and enjoyed just having Brady close. For now.

6

____

When my phone rang at three thirty in the morning, I croaked, "Brady?"

A husky laugh was on the other end. Not Brady.

"I was calling you, sweetcheeks, to see if he was there."

I sat up and rubbed my eyes. I must've still been asleep because I could've sworn that Clarissa had called me. Clarissa Cumberly had never called me in my life.

"What?" I rested against the headboard behind me. It felt cool to the touch and I looked to my side. My window had been left open and a breeze wafted through the curtains. That's when I realized that I was still in my clothes; I had collapsed in bed after breakfast.

That'd been in the morning. It wasn't morning anymore. Moonlight filtered into my room. It sent a soft glow into my room. I looked in the mirror and my eyes popped out at the nest on top of my head. As I patted at it, my eyes shifted to the left and my bed moved at the same time. Gasping, I dropped the phone and started to lurch out of bed. Before I could, Brady flipped on his stomach and threw an arm to land on my lap...Brady was still in bed with me.

When my heart rate slowed again, I looked at the clock and saw it was four minutes after midnight. I must've assumed it was three in the morning. Which still begged the question—why was Clarissa calling me? More importantly, why was Brady still in bed with me? I poked at him and then jumped when I heard a voice in the covers. I fumbled through the blankets and grabbed my phone again.

"...Rayna!"

"Uh...?" Brady grunted and rolled onto his back. He raked a hand through his hair before he opened his eyes and stared at me. A glaze of drowsiness was evident.

"Rayna...Rayna..." Clarissa's voice was muffled against my hand.

I stared, frozen, as he squinted and then looked at the phone before he took it from me. "Cumberly?"

"Brady!"

She sounded sexy. I had a nest on my head.

Brady pushed up from the bed and scooted next to me.

When I heard him laugh in return, I couldn't take it. I scrambled from the bed, grabbed a robe, and ducked into the hallway. Turning into the bathroom, I saw my grandparent's door was closed and their sounds of snoring blasted through it. Relieved, I stepped underneath the shower spray.

When I got out of the shower, I saw that the bathroom fan hadn't worked well. The mirror was still steamed, so my reflection was fuzzy, but after I wiped a small patch away, I saw that I didn't look *that* ridiculous, not as bad as I had in my room. My hair was normally a blondish brown, but it looked really dark when it was wet. The ends just teased the tops of my shoulders. As I tucked my hair behind my ears, I leaned closer and inspected the rest of my face.

Viola always talked about how pretty my eyes were. They were dark brown, but I knew it was my eyelashes she praised. They were long and naturally curved to frame my eyes. I got my eyelashes from my mother...wherever she was. Then there were my big lips. I got those from my dad. I must've because my mother had thin lips.

Once I overheard Brady talking about a girl's lips. He said they were "come screw me lips." The other guy had laughed, but when I rounded the corner both of them had stared in horror. I never figured out who they'd been talking about, but as I leaned closer I wondered if I had those lips. Maybe. Was that why IT had happened? Or was Brady just hurting and needed comfort? Did he choose me because I was there, convenient?

For whatever his reason was, we had sex. I wasn't a virgin anymore. My reason...I sucked in my breath. I didn't want to think about that.

I touched my throat and wondered...did I look different? Had my grandmother noticed and chosen not to say anything? Did Brady think of me differently?

I didn't really feel different, though a little sore.

KNOCK, KNOCK.

I jumped, but managed to stifle a quick scream. I should've figured that Brady would get impatient, or maybe I woke up my grandparents.

I took one last breath, raked my fingers through my hair, and pulled my robe tight before I opened the door. Brady straightened from the doorframe and whispered, "Are you okay?"

"Yeah. Why?" I whispered back.

He shrugged and went into my bedroom. I followed, but not before I heard two different sets of snores.

"What'd Clarissa want?" When I went in I pretended to look through my closet. I had no idea what I was looking for; I just needed something to do with my back to him. I couldn't look, but I felt his gaze on my back. Then the bed dipped under his weight as he sat down. I peeked over my shoulder and saw he was glaring at me. He had placed his hands back and was resting on his arms, but he was staring right at me.

"What?" I held something against my body, but I had no idea what it was.

"You're freaking out."

"I'm not freaking out."

"You are. You totally are." He nodded again, as if it made perfect sense to him.

"Don't do that! Stop!" But I felt my arms start to shake and then my entire body. I was suddenly cold, really cold.

"This is *the talk*. This is when we talk about it, isn't it?" Brady murmured to himself as he shook his head.

"We're not talking," I managed through chattering teeth.

"Look at you." He lifted a hand to me. "You're totally freaking out."

"I am not!"

"Shh!" He glanced at the door and then turned on the fan. As the sound dulled the air, he crossed to me and grasped my elbow to pull me down on the bed beside him.

I did not lie down. I sat. I only sat, perched on the end.

"Okay..." One of his hands lifted to take mine, but I snatched scurried back. I stopped when I hit the wall and that was how we sat. I was against the wall. Brady was turned towards me with one of his hands in the air.

A confounded look came across his face, but his eyes searched mine for a moment. I wasn't sure what he read in my eyes, maybe panic, but he laid his hand on his leg. I watched, fascinated, as his fingers curled into his leg like he was trying to restrain himself. His other hand was clenched into his other leg. His shoulder muscles were bunched together tightly. I noticed that his hair was wet and a droplet of water slid down the back of his neck, gliding over his muscles.

"Did you take a shower?"

"What?" Brady asked, distracted.

"You took a shower. Did you go downstairs?" Grandpa had his own shower in the basement.

"Uh...yeah. I smelled." Brady stared at something on my floor.

I looked, but couldn't see what it was.

Then my eyes widened in terror when I saw it was a pair of pink underpants that had fallen off the pile of laundry. It caught on a drawer on my desk and hung there, on display. I sucked in my breath and hurled off the bed to snatch it up. When I turned back, Brady's eyes were laughing at me, but he didn't say anything.

That's when I lost it. The fright. The panic. The "freak out" all vanished as one chuckle wracked through my body. Pretty soon, I couldn't stop the giggles. Brady joined in and both of us were laughing until I clamped a hand over my mouth to quiet myself. Tears blinded me for a moment, but they weren't those types of tears. I kept laughing, silent now, and I wiped them clear. I blinked to keep more from appearing. Brady's shoulders shook in laughter.

"Okay..." I murmured when I had resumed enough control to form sentences. I moved and sat beside him again, but this time I knew that I wouldn't scamper off. "I won't do that again. I promise." I patted his knee.

"Thanks." He caught my hand. "I don't like having my best friend scared of me."

Brady lifted his blue eyes to mine and I was startled to see how sombre they were. He'd just been laughing, but...

"You were scared of me, Rayna. Don't do that again."

I couldn't look away. Somehow, my hand found its way to the side of his face and it cupped his cheek. "I won't."

"Promise." His hand rested on top of mine.

"Promise." I could barely talk.

"Okay."

"Is it hot in here?"

He chuckled. "I don't think it's the room, Rayna."

I suddenly missed the nights when I curled up with a book. "So...uh...what did Clarissa want?"

Brady yawned as he ran his fingers through his soft blonde buzz cut.

I loved his hair. My fingers itched to replace his hand and curl his hair around them. Whoa—change the mind topic.

"...her place tonight. I told her that I'd ask you..."

I ripped my gaze from his hair and jumped when I saw a knowing glint in his eyes. Brady smirked.

"What?"

He just shook his head. "You need to get control of yourself. Or else we're going to get in more trouble."

My jaw dropped, but I looked away. We both knew what he meant. "Okay, so what were you saying?"

"I was saying that Clarissa's having a party tonight at her dad's place. I left my cell at the police station or something. She called here because she thought you might know where I was. You want to go?"

"What?" I swung my gaze back to him. He was very close, very, very close. I gulped, itching to move back, but I wouldn't. I could control myself.

"I said..." His lips quirked upwards. "...do you want to go to Clarissa's party?"

"Does Clarissa want me to go?"

"Yeah, actually. She told me to make sure you came. It's graduation week. You need to let loose and celebrate. Plus, you'll keep me out of trouble."

Not at this rate. I almost said it, but I clamped my lips shut and kept them that way. Brady nudged me with his shoulder. "So? What do you think?"

"I don't know." I eyed my door. "You heard Viola. If she comes in and finds me gone again she's going to ground me."

"No, she won't. She'll ground me, but she won't ground you.

She loved that you stayed out all night with me. Your grand-mother is worried about you. She thinks you're never going to loosen up and get married someday."

That was true. She'd hinted enough about it, but I ignored her. A person would have to have sex to get married...and the thought of me *ever* having sex had been like a hot air balloon on a windy day. Something you might look at, but never touch.

I shifted under his gaze.

Brady tightened his lips when he saw that I pulled my robe closer around me, but he didn't say anything. I jerked a shoulder and mumbled, "I don't even know what to wear. I can't wear what I usually do."

"You mean the turtlenecks and baggy sweaters?" Brady nudged my leg this time.

I ducked my head, but couldn't stop a small smile. "You know what I mean. I can't wear that to one of her parties." My wardrobe choices weren't that bad. A baggy sweater, but not a turtleneck. Ever.

"You make it sound like Clarissa is an alien or something." Brady leaned back on his elbows. He kicked his legs in front of him and just like that, the room had transferred from being hot and intimate to being the same as always. Brady was back in charge again. He grinned, cockily, when I stood in front of him.

"You know what I mean," I muttered and scrutinized my closet. I had nothing that would pass as semi-attractive.

"No, I don't, Ray. You've always been weird about Cumberly. Why is that?"

"Why don't you ask her?"

"I have. It bothers her. She doesn't think you like her."

I swung back; eyebrows arched, and stared at him.

Brady liked to use gel in his buzz cut so that his short hairs stuck up a little, but after his shower his hair had already dried and looked soft to the touch. He looked like a little boy, complete with two dimples as he grinned back at me. He was different when he was with me. If we'd been at the party, he would've had the hard edgy look to him. He liked his tattoos to be seen, but I saw that he had pulled a blanket to cover the tribal tattoo on his stomach. The one on his shoulder was hiding in the shadows.

"It's not that I don't like her. It's just that...she's one of them."

"One of what?"

"You know. Your girlfriends."

"My what?"

"Your girlfriends." I didn't think that I needed to spell it out. "She's...I don't know. She's cool and confident and...she's not the type of person that I'm friends with."

"You're friends with me." His voice was quiet.

The air shifted again. Here we were...I knew that I needed to tread lightly, very lightly. I met his gaze, swallowed over a knot in my throat, and felt that we were talking about something different.

"You're different. I mean...we're not normal, Brady."

A scowl formed at his mouth. "What are you talking about? We're not normal?"

"You know—you're...one of them and I'm...not."

"That is the most ridiculous thing I've ever heard." He threw himself off the bed and stalked towards me. "You are just like me. You are no different than me. You are no different from Clarissa."

"Yeah, but..." I was pressed against the doorframe as Brady towered over me. "I'm not one of your girlfriends."

His chest was in front of mine. Another step, just an inch, and we'd be pressed against each other. His gaze was glued to my lips. I kept looking from his eyes to his lips, but then I felt something strange wash over me when he murmured, throatily, "You're more than that."

I sucked in a large breath, I couldn't let it out. I stood there, frozen in place. He skimmed the side of my face with his hand, then tucked my hair back and cupped my cheek. He moved close and slowly, so slowly, rested his forehead against mine. His breath tickled my lips. "You're my best friend, Ray."

My hands had lifted to his arms. I felt his muscles shift underneath my fingers and I clasped harder. I couldn't fall.

"What are you doing?" The words wrangled out of my throat.

Brady didn't answer. He closed his eyes and nuzzled his mouth against my temple. My hands slid from his arms to his shoulders and then behind his neck. One of his hands cupped the back of my neck where he applied pressure and arched my head back. The other hand skimmed the side of my robe. When his fingers spread out, the top of his thumb brushed underneath my breast.

"Brady, I don't..." I couldn't talk anymore, but I knew there was something that I needed to say. I knew it, but...

"Shhh." His lips touched mine. They rested there, but there was no pressure, no demand from him.

Then his lips opened over mine. A surge of need rushed through me and I clasped him tight. Brady pushed me against the doorframe and he urged my leg to wrap around his waist. I couldn't get enough of him. It was like before, but this time it was different. I knew what would happen.

I never thought I'd do this or be like this, but it was Brady.

His thumb slipped inside my robe, touched my breast, and all thought fled my brain.

7

———

"I have to go to church."

I was on my back, entangled with bed sheets as Brady collapsed beside me. I stared at the ceiling, felt the breeze from my open window, and all I could think was—"I have to go to church and pray."

Brady snorted and rolled his head into his elbow. He burrowed into my side, but didn't say a word.

Not me. I continued, but only after I had panted for a few sweat-slicked moments. "And I'm going to sing loud. I'm going to kneel when the pastor says 'bow your heads.' I'm going to do the whole thing. I'm going to kneel, fold my hands how the Catholics do, and I'll bow my head so far that my shoulders are going to hurt. I don't care if Viola looks at me weird. Neil won't care. He'll be proud."

I caught short at those words. He'll be proud. No he wouldn't, not in the slightest.

"And if Pastor Radlinson asks for a volunteer for anything, I'll do it. I'll bake twenty dozen cookies. I'll read stories at church. I'll even..." I gulped. "I'll even sing in the choir."

"You need to shut up," Brady growled with his nose tucked into my shoulder.

His breath tickled me, but I ignored him. "I should go to confession. I should be a Catholic tomorrow—today. I'll go to confession and confess my soul, because...oh God...I have a lot to confess."

Brady lifted his head and glared at me. "Shut up, Ray."

I met his gaze. "I'll pray for you too, Brady. You need prayer more than me."

"Oh, my God." He flipped to his back. I ignored how his thigh slid against mine or how his hand fell on my exposed thigh.

I gulped. "I need to tell my grandmother."

"No, you don't!" Brady sat up. He didn't care that he was naked. He looked relaxed, well—he looked annoyed with me, but he was relaxed too. He was always like that. I blinked as he glowered at me and then my fingers slid through his soft hair.

Brady closed his eyes and moaned.

It was the moaning. My eyes snapped back to reality and my hand retracted itself, like it'd been burned.

I needed to be burned, scalded, something. I couldn't control my hand.

"Why do you do that?" Brady shifted on the bed again, but he moved closer and rested his forehead against mine. As he breathed in and out, I stared straight ahead. I was not affected...

"Ezekiel 33:10 says that our sins weigh us down and we will waste away our lives because of them."

He pulled away and ran his hands through his hair—my hand started to rise of its own volition. Brady slapped it away and grunted when he shifted against the bed's headboard. He folded his arms, which bunched his muscles together.

I swallowed.

"It's just sex. That's all."

"It's a sin. Twice. We sinned twice."

"And you totally took that verse out of context."

"I don't care." I pulled the bed sheets tighter around me and then I looked at the door. I waited until I heard my grandparent's snores. They were like vampires when they slept, completely out of it, but I was still paranoid. It'd be my luck that they'd wake up and decide to check on me the one time I had sex in my room.

"You should care." Brady brought me back to our reality. He added as he yawned, "I think it's a sin to take a Bible verse out of context. It's like you're twisting the message."

"Shut up!"

Brady grinned at me as he skimmed a finger down my back. He swept it up to brush against the side of my breast.

"Stop that." I twisted away from his touch.

He rolled his eyes and collapsed against the headboard.

"Stop that, too."

That got a chuckle from him. I couldn't believe it. While I was mortified, already planning how to repent for my actions, he laughed.

"Look at you." His shoulders shook from laughter. "You're so mad at me right now. Anyone else, Rayna, anyone else, and I wouldn't put up with it, but you—you're mad at me and I just think how hot you look."

I flushed and looked down at my lap. Warmth flared in me, but...anyone else...there'd been lots of other girls, and there'd still be lots of girls, but for now—no! I was *not* going to go there. I tightened my resolve. "You shouldn't say things like that to me. It's not right."

"Why?"

He knew. The bastard knew darn well what I meant.

"You know what I mean."

"No. I don't." He wrapped a hand around a corner of the bed sheet and tugged it backwards. It tightened around me and I was pulled against his chest. He wrapped both of his arms around my waist, held me captive and propped his chin on my shoulder. He pressed a kiss to my neck.

"Don't."

Brady grinned against my skin and then shifted so I ended in his lap. "Brady," I tried to chastise, but his fingers distracted me. They slid underneath the sheet and started to massage my stomach. When they slipped lower, I gasped.

Brady chuckled into my ear. "You only live once, Ray. Even Viola agrees with that."

"That doesn't mean..." I was having a hard time remembering my argument. His fingers now rested on the inside of my thigh. The lower they went, the foggier my thoughts became.

Brady kissed the corner of my jaw and caressed my back with his free hand. His hand was cool against my skin. And I was burning up. I was going to burst into flame, literally.

Then my phone rang. Again.

Brady cursed into my neck, but I collapsed in relief. His fingers left when he answered the phone. When I heard Clarissa's voice on the other end, I jolted upright and grabbed a pile of clothes left on the floor before I ran to the bathroom.

Déjà vu.

I hurled into the shower, blasted the water, and slid to the floor as I wrapped my arms around my knees. Yes, the world wasn't ending, but mine was. Everything *was* different. Me and Brady...we weren't me and Brady anymore. I couldn't deny that anymore. My arms trembled, but I pressed my forehead into my knees. As the water beat down on me, I gasped and took a deep breath. I needed to take a breath, just one. Maybe, just maybe, things wouldn't get so screwed up. Maybe I could go back in there and Brady would be dressed, ready to go party and I could stay home like normal.

When I tiptoed back into the bedroom I saw that Brady hadn't dressed. He sat on the end of the bed with the sheets pooled around his waist. His chest was in shadow while the moonlight beat down on his broad, muscular shoulders.

"I'm not going with you!" I blurted out before I found myself noting how sexy he looked with those broad...shoulders...

"What?" He stared at me, distracted.

"What?" Shoulders.

He shook his head and focused on me now.

"What—you...what?"

"What are you talking about?" Brady clipped out.

"That was Clarissa, right? She called about the party...and I'm telling you that I'm not going."

"Oh." Comprehension flashed across his eyes. "No. I wasn't going to ask about that."

"Oh."

"No, I mean—" Cursing, Brady stood up.

My eyes widened and I squeaked, but the sheets fell to reveal white and blue striped boxers.

"I meant that I'm not going to the party either. So...that's why I wasn't going to ask if you wanted to go."

"Oh...okay." I bit my lip and looked out the window. Brady watched me as I watched the window. Neither of us spoke until I swung my gaze back. His eyes had a gleam in them.

"What are you wearing?"

"What?"

He gestured to my clothes. "You look like a wet clown who's going out clubbing. You look ridiculous."

I didn't think about it, my fist jerked out and I watched in sick fascination as I punched him in the eye. I saw it all in slow motion. His eyes widened when he realized what I was doing and then I saw the jerk of his head as my fist made contact. When he fell back on the bed, it was over so fast that I stood there, shocked.

Not Brady. Brady raised his eyes and saw my shock. He reacted quickly, tucked his shoulder, and rolled off the bed. He picked me up and threw me on the bed and landed on top before I had time to scream. His hand slammed down over my mouth before it ripped from my throat.

"You punched me!" Brady accused me as his eyes danced.

I shoved him back—I tried to shove him back. He held firm and tucked my arms above my head. I was trapped as he stared down at me.

"What?" I huffed, out of breath.

"You punched me. Why'd you punch me?"

"Because."

Brady dissolved in laughter. He tucked his forehead into the crook of my shoulder and stayed there with my hands trapped in his above my head. I was hyper aware of every miniscule of his body that was on top of mine.

He settled so he was more comfortable. "Only you. Only you, Rayray."

"Uh..." My hands were still captive underneath his, but his thumbs softened and caressed my wrists. Then he lifted his head and stared down at me. He was searching for something inside of me, something that I couldn't tell him.

"What?" My voice was husky now.

He shook his head, his eyes were sober.

"What?"

"I..." He held back. He had never held back before.

I gritted my teeth. "What?"

Startled, he released my hands, but he rolled away to sit on the edge of the bed with his elbows braced on his knees. I moved with him and sat with one leg tucked behind him. I wanted to rest my cheek against his back, I wanted so badly, but I held back. I needed to know what was going on inside of him first.

"What is it?"

Brady shrugged his tight shoulders.

That's when I placed a hand on his back and felt his muscles jerk in response. "What is it? Tell me."

Brady shook his head.

"Brady." I needed him and I needed him to tell me what was going on.

"I...—don't know what to do, okay?"

My heart pounded in my chest. My lungs constricted my air, but it didn't matter. There was no going back now. I rested my cheek against his back. "What do you mean?"

Brady stiffened, but he didn't move away. "I—you and me. Sex. I don't know what to do."

I wrapped my arms around him and after a moment, Brady tucked them tighter. He entwined his fingers with mine. "I want to know what to do, but I don't. I just know that I can't lose you."

I closed my eyes. I couldn't lose him either. "You won't."

"Promise?"

I felt a tear at the corner of my eye. "Promise."

Brady relaxed, but we hadn't settled anything. We were best friends. We couldn't replace the other. That was all that'd been settled.

"You know—" Brady cut himself off and stood.

I caught myself before I fell behind him.

"I—" He stopped again, ran a hand through his hair, and paced from my dresser, the bed, the window, and the closet. I moved to sit against the headboard and curled up underneath the blanket. As I watched him pace, restless, I closed my eyes for a moment, just a moment, because I could smell him on my pillowcase.

"I changed my mind." He stopped to stare at me.

My eyes snapped open and I knew that he wasn't even seeing me. He was seeing something else.

"About what?"

"I'm going to Cumberly's. You want to go?" Brady pinned me down with his eyes.

"Uh—" I froze. "I...don't know, Brady."

"Come on." He sat on the edge of my bed and caught one of my hands. His thumb rubbed the inside of my palm. "Please? You'll keep me from getting in trouble."

'Or we'll get in more trouble.'

"Please, please," Brady whispered and bent his forehead to rest against mine.

'Oh no.'

I felt his breath on my cheeks and found myself weakening. "...okay..."

He flashed a smile before he pressed a quick kiss to my cheek and forehead. "Thanks, Ray." His cheek rested on my forehead for a moment, just a quick moment, before he pushed off. "I'm going to sneak home first. Meet me at the car in thirty minutes."

He threw open my window and swept out. I sat down with a thump.

We'd been in our own little conclave and the phone rang. We weren't going to the party. We were safe in our world. Now we were going. What had just happened?

I stared at my closet. I was back at square one. I had no idea what to wear.

8

———

Everyone knew where Dr. Cumberly lived. He was the one and only town's dentist. He owned the mansion that stood elegant and statuesque as it looked over Lake Parley and the Northshire Folk Golf Course. It was a ten minute drive, most of it over gravel roads, but Brady sped twenty over the speed limit. When we got closer, both sides of the road were lined with cars.

He pulled into her driveway and headed toward the opened garage where people stood with cups in their hands. Matt Krone, another football player, waved when he saw Brady at the steering wheel, and jerked his head to the sixth garage door.

Brady nodded. A moment later, the door lifted so he could pull in.

I hadn't realized that I snorted until Brady asked when he turned off the engine, "You got a problem?"

Where did I start? "You have your own parking spot?"

"What?" Brady shrugged a tight shoulder, but a smirk appeared. "Henry Cumberly likes me."

"Yeah, right. Dr. Cumberly."

"I caddied for him in eighth grade."

That's when he started caddying for the dentist's daughter, but in a whole other way.

I had hated Brady that summer. "Maybe I'll get drunk tonight,"

"You don't drink."

He turned toward me and hand could've rested on my shoulder, but he let it hang from the seat. I glanced at his fingers for a moment. They were strong, but the symbol on the inside of Brady's wrist was where my gaze lingered. It was the Hebrew symbol for faith. I hadn't been there when Brady had gotten it, but it always hurt that he wouldn't explain why he'd gotten it. Maybe there was a reason for that.

Maybe it was the same reason why I glared at him and folded my arms across my chest. "Maybe I should start."

Brady lifted an eyebrow. "We both know what happened the first and only time you've drank."

I narrowed my eyes. "That tractor was going anyway. Just because I'd had a few doesn't mean that's why it rolled."

"Rayna," Brady smirked. "...you were three sheets to the wind. And yes, you rolled the tractor all on your own. The tractor didn't roll itself. And let's not forget who took the blame."

I rolled my eyes, but my cheeks got hot.

"Hey!" Matt Krone rapped his knuckles on the window. "You two getting out or what? I've got a brewsky for you, Brady."

Just like that, my best friend flashed his trademark smile and threw open the door. I was slower, but when I came around to the driver's side, he already had two bottles in his hands and three football players surrounded him. Brady was loved. We all knew that. Everyone else saw the flash, but I was the only one who saw his eyes harden with a warning when our gazes locked.

With a sniff, I turned my back and went inside.

Dr. Cumberly had spared no expense when it came to his home. The kitchen too, with a sink made of marble and the keg right beside it, inside a decorated plastic pool. As I caught sight of another cooler in the dining room, I headed in that direction. And just as I bent down and retrieved a vodka drink, a pair of tan golden legs stopped right beside me. A lot of girls had pink frosted toenails, but my guess was on one person and I looked up to Clarissa. She had a smirk on her face that made her look even sexier, sultry even.

"Your boy is in rare form." Unlike my boring camisole and blue jeans, Clarissa wore a pink-frilled tank top over her miniskirt that rode low on her hips. Her hair had been curled and hung down her back from an elegant pony-tail.

I gulped, self-conscious, as my fingers raised and felt my own hair. I had put it up in a braid, but I knew I'd never be as glamorous as Clarissa Cumberly.

"Yeah."

"Look, you're on duty tonight. Do not let him get out of hand. I don't want Deputy Dog coming here." She flicked her eyes over my shoulder. The look switched to a warm welcome when I heard Brady's voice fill the house, followed by a mass of hellos, cheers, and catcalls in the air.

Brady Remington had arrived.

"He looks good," Clarissa murmured underneath her breath.

I turned and had to agree.

The ripped jeans accentuated his bad boy image, but it was the tight black tee shirt and the tattoo covering his left arm that sealed the deal. I wasn't prudish enough not to admit that with his hair gelled into tiny spikes Brady looked adorable on one hand and dangerous on the other.

"Listen..." Clarissa shifted closer. "Kid and his cousin might be coming tonight. If they do, I don't care whose skirt Brady's in, keep him distracted so that the guys can get rid of them, okay?"

I shrugged, but it didn't matter. She'd given the order and I was expected to jump. As I watched her move off to greet him, I knew that I'd do what was best for Brady. As Clarissa arched her head up for a kiss from him, I turned and twisted open my drink.

I had my first taste of alcohol in five years.

I scrunched up my nose in surprise. It tasted like lemonade, but with a slight kick to it. Smiling, I realized that I might enjoy these drinks. Maybe I *would* get drunk...no. I had no intentions of getting drunk. I just wanted a reaction from Brady and it worked, but he looked like he no longer cared, smiling down Clarissa's top as she was pressed against his chest.

I rolled my eyes and took another drink. And I kept sipping on it as I moved around the house. Anything larger than my grandparent's two stories with two and a half bedrooms impressed me. By the time I found the stairs that led to the basement, I was surprised to find my lemonade empty so I passed by the cooler and grabbed another one. Brady was in the kitchen, but I ducked around a group and headed down the stairs.

Silence. No one was down there. It was wonderful.

When I circled around the stairs, I found my heaven. A bookcase travelled the entire length of the wall...and it was filled, overly filled, with books.

I sank down on one of the leather couches, dazed, as I could only stare at the books. Historical textbooks. Encyclopedias. Romance novels. Mystery novels. Cookbooks. There were books on every subject from gardening to astronomy. I shot out from the couch and grabbed as many as I could. Before long, the books were piled all around me. Some were on the couch. Some were on the floor. Some were on the counter beside the couch. Some were even on the other couches. My only regret, as I groaned when I lifted the bottle, was that my lemonade was empty again.

I paused from my reading, glanced upwards and weighed the options. I could sneak up and grab more, but something might happen. I'd get stuck up there. Or I could stay and enjoy reading sans lemonade. The Dinosaurs of Pre-Extinction or a refreshing taste of lemonade?

Call me a blossoming lush. I was going for another lemonade. Just another thing on my list to confess the next day, but He'd forgive me. Let's hope. When my foot touched the stairs I heard muffled laughter behind the door.

I wavered.

The Mussaurus might not be the actual smallest dinosaur in the world, but with the lemonade I wouldn't care. I'd still vote for the mouse lizard.

"Yo, man!"

"Brady—oh my effing God, man!"

My fingers clenched around the wooden stair rail when I heard Brady's muffled laugh through the door. Here we were, best friends, and where was I? Where was he? Not in the same room, that was for sure. Then the door flew open and Matt Krone stumbled above the stairs. He readied himself and squinted down at me. "I win, dude. I found her!" Laughing, he pointed at me and someone pounded him on the shoulder. Three more drunken faces peered over his shoulder and then Brady pushed them out of the way. He crossed his arms. "Whatcha doing, Ray?"

Clarissa poked her head around the door. "My dad's book collection is down there. I bet she was reading."

"My girl wouldn't choose books over me...would she?"

As I passed by him, I replied under my breath, "You tell me."

Brady stopped chuckling and shot me a dark look.

Clarissa laughed. "You should be asking who'd choose books over drinking. That's what you should be asking." The rest of the party agreed as a chorus sounded out with raised cups.

Brady tucked an arm around my waist and pulled me snug against him. Lowering his head, he breathed into my ear, "We're playing a game. Come play with us. It'll be fun."

The tension between us was thick and it had started before the party. I wasn't really sure where it came from, but Brady didn't seem inclined to address it. I knew why I was hurt by him, but I wasn't sure why he seemed angry with me.

Clarissa fell into step beside me. "Yeah, Rayan. We're playing P and A. We've got room for one more."

"It's Rayna," Brady corrected, a bit too fierce for the party cheer.

Clarissa stopped and blinked. She studied him for a second before she shrugged. "I know. I just thought the name was cool."

Without a response, he led the way through the crowd.

"Sorry." Clarissa turned to me.

"For what?"

She tucked a strand of hair behind her ear and bit her lip. "I just—it's like a nickname, you know. It wasn't meant...I wasn't trying to be mean or anything."

"Can I call you Clary?"

She looked horrified. "Hell no!"

It might've been the two lemonades, but I never thought that I'd see Clarissa Cumberly, Princess of Northshire Folk, look sheepish. "I really like the lemonade stuff."

"Huh?"

"Your things in that cooler. I like those."

"Oh." Clarissa looked confused for a moment. "I'll get you some more." As Clarissa darted towards the cooler, I squared my shoulders and headed towards Brady's corner. I'd play P and A with the best of them. I just had to get through a ton of immovable drunks first. When I got there, I wasn't sure who was the most unsure about our situation, me or them. Brady sat to my right and throughout the game, he'd rest his hand on my leg at moments. I jumped every time, which earned me crazy points with the others. He stifled his laughter every time and Clarissa watched with narrowed eyes.

When a seven was laid, I quickly threw my seven on top. "I'm out! I win...right?" I turned to Brady. I hardly won anything.

He choked back his laughter, but patted my head. "You won, Rayray. You did well."

I giggled and reached for my drink.

"Dude, she didn't—" one of the guys started to say, but Brady growled. The guy shut up and I finished my drink.

And then he stood up, ignored the protests, and hauled me with him. "I think it's time we got some fresh air. Don't you think, Rayna?"

I held my empty bottle up. "Empty. Another one, please?"

"Ah no. I don't think so. You've had enough. How many have you had?"

I frowned, tried to count with my fingers and gave up. A dark look flashed in his eyes, but he took my hand and turned towards the back patio door. A path opened for us through the crowd, and just as we stepped through the door, Clarissa called out. She sauntered up with two of my lemonades in her hand and a beer in her other. "Where are you going?"

Brady tucked me behind him. "Going for a walk. Why?"

Her eyes danced between the two of us, but she held her hand out and offered the drinks. "These are for your girl. She likes 'em."

"What? No. I don't think so..." Brady started until I snatched them away. His eyebrows went high.

Clarissa patted him on the chest. "She's a grown girl, Brady. Let her be a grown up."

"Yeah. I'm a grown-up. In fact, you know how grown up I am—"

"We're going to go." Brady rushed out and pulled me down

the path. We went past some trees that blocked us from her view before we heard the door shut again.

"Her place is huge!" I exclaimed as I tripped. He caught me and righted me, but let go with a hand on the small of my back. I'd never admit it, but I loved when he touched me there. I felt safe and protected.

"You weren't kidding, huh?"

"Huh?"

"You said you were going to get drunk. You did."

It took a moment, but I realized that Brady was tense. His jaw was clenched and his shoulders tight. "Are you mad at me?" How could he be? This was his element. He always got drunk.

"No, you just said that...never mind. I didn't think you'd get drunk, Rayna. It's not something you do."

I drew up short. "Are you disappointed in me?" He had no place to be disappointed. He always went out partying. I got drunk once and he was disappointed?

"No. I'm not saying that..." But he was. I saw it in his eyes. His hand fell away.

"Oh no, buddy boy. You do not pull this. I didn't even want to come here, but I did—for you!"

"Well..."

"You're mad at me because I did something that I don't normally do. I don't understand you, Brady. I thought you wanted me to be friends with your friends. That was happening in there, kind of. Even Clarissa's being friendly. How can you—what is wrong with that? You can't have me come to a party and not enjoy myself. I can't be there JUST for you."

"That's not what I'm saying. Not at all." His eyes started to sparkle in anger.

"You wanted me to loosen up. You wanted me to come to the party. You want me...I don't know anymore. I don't know what you want. I can't make you happy. I'm tired of it. I don't fit in with this group. You know it and I wonder if you prefer it. Why'd you even bring me along?"

His fingers wrapped around my arm. "What are you talking about?"

I closed my mouth, but I already started. I might as well finish. "I think sometimes you're embarrassed by me because I'm not 'cool' enough to be your friend."

Brady threw his head back. "You're my best friend. How can you say that?"

"I'm not like Clarissa. I'm not beautiful. I'm not sexy. I can't...I can't be what I'm not, Brady."

He jerked me against him, but gentled immediately. Taking a deep breath, he tucked a strand of hair behind my ear. Then he whispered as he bent to rest his forehead against mine, "You are my family, my best friend. I wouldn't be here without you, Rayray. I'd be in jail. And trust me; you are way hotter than Clarissa."

"Yeah, well...you have to say that. I can sic Viola on you and we both know who'll win."

Brady barked out a laugh and pulled me in for a hug. Relieved from the tension, I brought my hands up to his shoulders and hugged back.

"You're right. Your grandmother would give me an ass whooping. Let's hope it never comes to that."

Well, it would only come to that if Brady did something horrible, like get me pregnant—my eyes popped out and I gasped. Holy...

Brady leaned back. "What's wrong?"

I closed my mouth and shook my head. I didn't even want to think about it. But Brady hadn't used a condom. I overheard some girls talking about "pulling out," but he hadn't done that either. I wasn't stupid enough to think I could go to the doctor without Viola knowing. This was a small town. That meant...Brady might get his ass whooping a lot sooner than he thought. I'd have to tell Viola what happened, this was too serious for me to ignore. Looking down at my stomach, I splayed a hand over it. A baby, a little, little, tiny, tiny baby, might be in there.

I gulped. And I couldn't believe I hadn't thought of that before.

"Hey!" Brady called from down the path. "What are you doing?"

My hand fell away from my stomach. "I'm coming. Hold on."

"There's a playground up here." Brady flashed a grin.

I grinned in response. I couldn't help it and sighed. I couldn't think about a baby, especially one with Brady. We were best friends. Nothing could hurt that. As I turned a last curve in the path, I saw him standing in front of three swings, an old metal merry-go-round, and a tiny rusty slide. I started laughing and was quickly whooshed off my feet. He picked me up and twirled in circles.

"I saw this place a long time ago. We haven't played on a playground forever. And it's all ours tonight."

I patted his hand. As he put me down, I taunted, "We both know who can get the highest."

Brady's smile grew wide at the challenge and he was in the swing next to mine in a flash, pumping his legs hard. Still, he wasn't a natural swinger like I was. It wasn't long before I looked down, high in the air, and stuck my tongue at him.

Brady pushed ahead. "I'm going all the way, Rayray. You're going to have to get the medical kit—" And then his swing flipped over. He fell off the swing, but reached out in time to catch the bar. His fingers wrapped tight and as Brady hung there, I screamed. And then I realized that Brady was alright, just hanging high in the air with no way down.

I went mad.

"You're an idiot! You're a complete moron, Brady Remington! I hope you break your legs when you get off because if you don't, I'm going to put you in the hospital myself. I hate—" I blinked back tears and pressed a hand to my pounding chest. I couldn't breathe...oh, God. A rush of emotions coursed through me and I felt my arms start to shake. My chest felt so tight. My heart was pounding.

"Relax, Rayna," Brady soothed. His grin dimpled again as he let go of the metal bar to fall gracefully on his feet. "I'm fine."

He wrapped both arms around me and drew me against his chest. "And we both know who can go the highest now, don't we?"

He did that to prove a point? My hand fisted...

Brady's eyes widened.

I swung wide, hard, and punched his jaw. His head clipped back and he fell two steps backwards. I pounced on him for another punch, followed with a swift kick underneath his legs. As he fell down, I got another hit to his chest and started to kneel on his groin. I'd been so worried, so scared. Before I could kneel down, I was lifted in the air from behind.

"Oh, God. Thanks, Matt," Brady choked as he looked up with tears in his eyes. "I forgot that I taught her that stuff."

I struggled against the chest behind me. The two arms held me tighter. "Let me go!"

Brady laughed as he stumbled to his feet. "You pack a punch. I should've remembered."

I yelled from Matt's chest, "You don't do stupid crap like that. What if I'd done it? What if I'd been the one hanging up there? What then, Brady? You would've—"

"Okay, okay." He signalled Matt to let me go. I hit the ground running and Brady swept me up in the air. I tried to hit him again, but he entrapped my arms. "I'm sorry. I'm not used to people getting freaked about that stuff. It usually...hell, I don't know."

"You were showing off?"

"I don't know. It doesn't matter. I won't do it again, promise.

Just don't beat me up. If you can do that, I don't want to know what Viola can do." Brady lifted his head. "Thanks, man. I think you saved my life."

"She, huh...okay," Matt only said before he jerked a thumb behind him. "There's a whole bunch coming. Party's not the same without you, man. We brought the party to you. So...I don't think I've ever seen anything like that."

Brady laughed. "She's all prim and proper around you guys, but trust me, she's a spitfire."

"Yeah..." Matt didn't look reassured. He looked alarmed. Then we heard shouts from the path and a whizzing sound was soon in the air. Brady reacted before anyone else. His arms dropped \ and he jumped in the air to catch a flying football. As he fell to the ground, a perfect catch, five guys rushed around Matt and jumped on top, but he was up and running in the opposite direction. They ran after him.

"There's a clearing over there," Matt explained.

I turned back and saw it was just the two of us.

"I'd ask you out if I was pretty sure Brady wouldn't kick my ass."

"What?" My cheeks got warm.

Matt grinned. "That was hot. I didn't...Brady always said you weren't what you look like, but that— Wow. If Brady didn't have dibs on you, I'd be all about you."

I heard a husky, deep throated chuckle from behind us and turned to see Clarissa. Her hands were tucked into her frayed miniskirt, but she shook her head. "You wouldn't have a chance, Matt. Leave her alone before you scare her to death."

"I'm just saying—"

"Don't. You don't have a chance." She shooed him away. "Go play football with the rest of the manly men."

Matt started walking backwards, but argued, "I'll go, Clarissa, but only because you're right. I don't want to scare

Rayna. I'm man enough. I don't need football to prove that. One thing I'm pretty sure you can attest to."

"Get lost before I start speaking the truth about your 'masculinity.'"

Matt tipped his head back and laughed, but then turned and was gone in the trees.

"He's...a handful." Clarissa shook her head and then eyed me up and down. "So what was that about? I didn't think Matt would be your type."

Flushed, I hung my head. I didn't have a type. I wasn't Matt's type and I really wasn't Brady's, but I only shrugged. "He saw me get mad at Brady about something. That's all." I didn't know what Brady was talking about. I wasn't even beautiful, much less "hotter" than Clarissa.

"Cat got your tongue?"

I jerked a shoulder up and still watched the ground. I'd never been chatty with anyone except Brady.

"Ah, hell. Here." She held out a lemonade drink.

I hesitated.

"What's wrong?"

"Oh, nothing. I just—Brady said some stuff."

"Brady can be an idiot sometimes. He's way too protective of you, and if you ask me, you should drink if you want. You're not going to hell. You're not going to become someone like me. You can have fun for one night. Brady needs to lighten up, at least when it comes to you."

I remembered her words from before. "Is that what you meant when you said that stuff about letting me be grown up?"

Clarissa smiled tightly and adjusted her top. "I think Brady needs to stop holding your hand with everything and let you learn a few things."

"What do you mean?"

"You know, it's not my place. Brady would throw me in jail for saying something."

"No, no. I meant..." Did she mean...like, sexual things? Would Brady want me if I knew something more about sex? Would he...no. I couldn't go there.

"I'm just saying that you seem really cool, but I know Brady doesn't bring you around half the time. And when he does, he doesn't let you out of his sight for more than a few minutes. Tonight was the exception, but I think you had more to do with that than him. Am I right? You two have a spat or something?"

"Or something," I muttered. I didn't really know what the "something" was, but there was definitely a "something."

"That's what I thought." Clarissa turned and looked around. "I haven't been down here in a long time. I used to come here to make out with my boyfriends."

"I bet you and Brady used to come here..."

Clarissa looked at me, an odd emotion in her eyes. "No, actually. He knew about this place, but he never wanted to come here. He said it was 'precious childhood stuff'. I never knew what he meant, but it didn't bother me. Brady does what Brady wants to do. I always knew that." She swung her piercing eyes to me. "Just like I always knew I wasn't the girl for him."

I opened my mouth to ask her what she meant when we heard a smattering of giggles and high-pitched whispers. Clarissa cursed under her breath, latched onto my arm, and dragged me behind a clump of trees. I glanced at the road behind us, but she was intent on watching whoever was coming down the path.

"Clari—"

"Sshh!" Clarissa hushed me and elbowed my side. "I hate these girls."

As I looked through the branches, I saw some of the more popular girls laughing together. That was weird. I always assumed Clarissa was friends with them. She was the most popular one.

Nothing about that night was making sense anymore.

9

—————

"Who are they?"

She leaned close and her voice tickled my ear. "Angela and Nicole. They're the ring leaders, but they all hate me. I'm so tired of it."

"I thought you were friends with them."

Clarissa shuddered. "No way. I'm not friends with Angela."

"...a cow, seriously."

"I don't understand what he sees in her, in both of them."

"Totally. Brady has such bad taste in women. I mean both her and Clitty Clary."

Clitty?

Clarissa whispered, "Clitoris."

Oh—OH!

"They're both sluts. They probably just lay on their backs for him. You know that's why he's not dating any of us. We're better than that. We have lives. I mean, if he dated me, I wouldn't be waiting on him hand and foot like they are. Did you see her? She jumped when he told her to play the game. Pathetic."

"She's got no social skills. None at all."

"She's a whore. I bet she spreads her legs three times a day for him. Brady's just so used to getting whatever he wants whenever he wants. I mean, you can't really blame him, but I just wish he'd open his eyes and see that he could do so much better."

"He totally could."

"No doubt."

"Um, yeah!"

"Her name is Rayna. How stupid of a name is that."

"Her and Clarissa. They're both stupid names."

"I wish he had more motivation in life, at least when it comes to girls. He could have me, not that I'm saying I'd date him or anything, but really. He could do a lot better than that girl. She doesn't even have any friends."

"Rayna?"

"Who else do you think I'm talking about? Brady is nice enough to be her only friend. Who'd you think I was talking about?"

"I don't know. I thought maybe...Clarissa?"

"Clarissa Cumberly has friends, she's got all the friends she needs. Male. Hello—her name is Cum-berly for a reason."

They all laughed.

My hand clenched over my stomach. Clarissa patted my arm. And then I heard...

"She really needs not to be a charity case. Brady needs to wake up and see what he's wasting away with. She's not pretty. She's not anything. She's nothing. She's boring. I don't understand why he wastes his time with her. It's gotta be about the sex. She must put out for him whenever he wants. Really. How sad is her life?"

"Totally."

"No doubt."

"Really."

"She doesn't even talk in class. She goes to the library. They're so wrong for each other."

"That's enough," Clarissa growled and surged forward.

I clamped a hand on her arm and shook my head when she looked at me in question. I couldn't...I couldn't do it. Everything they said was right. I had sex with Brady. I wasn't popular. I wasn't the right girl for him. I didn't even understand why we were best friends. I blinked back tears.

"Rayna, no..." Clarissa started.

I didn't want to hear those words spoken to my face, spat at me. I couldn't—they were all true anyway.

"You do not let them win. They're wrong. *They're* the pathetic ones."

But it was true, and I couldn't even tell her how true it was. I *had* slept with Brady, twice. I *did* feel like his charity case for our friendship. "I have to go. I'm sorry...but I...I have to go."

I broke away and started down the road. Clarissa shouted my name, but I ignored her as I wiped away the tears. I might even be pregnant with his child. Then they'd all know how right they were.

I walked back towards the house by the road and tried telling myself that I wasn't my mother's child. I wasn't that girl. I had tried not to be her. Those girls were wrong...and I didn't even want friends, much less friends like them. I wasn't the girl they were talking about, except...I sighed as I faced the truth. I didn't know if I could resist him. If he tried again, I would be the girl they were gossiping about.

Hugging myself, I wiped a tear away. I *was* Brady's charity case. He was too everything, too much for me. Brady belonged in a different world. He was from a different league. Brady could live his life. I'd live mine and not go to parties like this again. We'd be okay. He could be with the Clarissas of the world. And me...who was I kidding? I'd stay with Viola and Neil until they kicked me out. They needed me. Everything would be okay. I'd be okay. Brady would be more than okay so why did I still want to cry? I was being logical.

I hadn't walked far before a car drove past, braked suddenly, and reversed to halt beside me. I tucked my chin down and headed forward. I didn't want another heap of ridicule. I wasn't ready for it to be hurled at my face this time and not behind my back.

"Rayna?"

Shocked, I gasped and saw who I never thought I'd see again. Kid smiled from behind the wheel of some sports car. Beside him sat Joshua, the stupid kissing cousin that I didn't like. It almost dampened my excitement of seeing Kidrick, but I just blocked him out.

"Kid?"

"Hey! What are you doing?" As he bent forward and got a better look, he sobered. "What's wrong?"

I took a moment, just a moment, and drank in the sight of him. I hadn't seen Kidrick for two years. He'd been the best of friends with Brady and now...something shifted inside of me. I hadn't realized how much I'd missed him until he was here and in front of me. I wasn't supposed to talk to him—so said everyone.

"You look...," I started. "You look good."

Dark chocolate eyes. Muscular shoulders. A chin with a little cleft in it. Two lips that showcased two dimples. Not to mention the luscious black locks on his head. Clarissa had said he was a legend and it was true. He'd been the counterpart for Brady in almost every way and now he was back...and causing trouble.

"Hop in. I'll give you a ride." He jerked a thumb in the back-seat. As I moved to the door, I was surprised as Josh scooted backwards.

Kid smiled when I got in. "Are you cold? It's a little chilly out there."

I...I didn't know what to say. I didn't know what I could say so I babbled, "Nice car. Did your dad buy it for you?"

Kid chuckled. "No. I bought it myself, Rayna."

Oh. That must've sounded contrite. I shut my mouth with an audible snap.

Josh groaned in the backseat, but Kid chuckled, "I'm not the spoiled brat that everyone thinks I am. Everything I have, I earned myself. Promise."

I looked anywhere except Kid, but I felt his eyes on me. Then I heard him ask, gently, "You were upset about something?"

"Probably about that douche," Josh grumbled.

Kid snapped, "Shut up."

"What? I'm just saying—"

"You need to shut up. You don't know what you're talking about. You know what—get out. You can walk to the party. It ain't far."

Shocked, I turned wide eyes to Kidrick. I couldn't believe he'd kick his cousin out.

"You serious?" Josh ground out.

Kidrick glared at him. A second later, Josh threw open the door and barged out. He slammed it, but Kid rolled his eyes and kicked the car into gear to shoot forward. He rested an arm on the seat behind me and remarked, "No worries. He'll be fine. I'm just going the rest of the way to the party. That's where you were, right?"

I nodded, feeling ridiculous. I'd been crying. Kidrick had suddenly shown up. I had no idea where Brady was, but it was for the best if Brady and I weren't friends anymore. Maybe...I glanced at Kid, measuring him, and wondered if I could tell him what I felt. Maybe he'd understand, but would he? Brady had punched him. My grandmother had prohibited me from seeing him. What was wrong with Kid? I didn't understand it. He seemed so genuine.

"Okay. That's where I'll take you. I'm sure Brady will be wondering," Kid remarked lightly.

I wondered if he meant how he said it. And then I felt a little bravery kick in from the alcohol. "Do you really care if Brady's looking for me?"

Kid swung his chocolate eyes my way. "I'm not here to mess with you and Brady. He's your best friend, Rayna. I remember that."

"He punched you."

Kid shrugged. His black tee shirt displayed sculpted arms. "He had reason. It's why my father dropped the charges. It's between Brady and me."

Somehow I wasn't so sure. "Why'd you call me then?"

Kid froze for a second and then pulled the car over. After putting it into park, he turned and I gulped underneath the weight of those dark eyes. Nothing stirred in me, not like with Brady, but there was something there, something that I couldn't quite put my finger on.

"I called you because..." He seemed to choose his words with caution. "...You know what? You're graduating next week. That's celebration enough. Everything else can wait."

It wasn't okay. I knew something was going on. So I asked, another testament to how powerful liquor can be, "Why doesn't my grandmother want me talking to you? What is it about you that no one wants me around you?"

Kid opened his mouth, but nothing came out of it. Seeing the stricken look in his eyes infuriated me. He was just another person keeping things from me.

I threw open the door. "I don't need this. I can walk back to the party."

"No, Rayna. Get back in the car. I'll take you."

I hesitated. "Are you going to tell me why my grandmother doesn't want me talking to you?"

He jerked a shoulder.

"Kid." I tried to sound stern.

"I can't tell you the exact reason, but I can guess. That's going to have to be enough."

He was exasperated. I didn't care. It was just like how I was with Brady. I saw a battle and I pounced. We used to be friends too.

"I..." Kid seemed flustered, like he wasn't sure about what he was about to say. "I...my father has some kind of history with your grandmother. I think that's what it's all about, but I don't know for sure. Viola hasn't ever met me so I don't think it's personal. But...I don't know. I just know that my dad doesn't like your grandmother and he's never told me the reason."

I slumped back. I wanted answers and I didn't get anything. "Nothing makes sense anymore."

"You can tell me what happened, you know."

Kid was concerned. He was the complete opposite of everything I'd just overheard and the dam broke. I started sobbing, but this time I wasn't able to brush away the tears. They came fast. They came hard and I looked like a complete idiot.

"Rayna." Kid touched my shoulder. "Whatever's wrong, you can tell me. I'm not Brady's enemy. Trust me. That's the furthest thing here, but what's wrong? I can help."

I shook my head. I considered telling him before, but that'd been insanity. No matter what, I was still loyal to Brady first. Even if it was for the best if he and I weren't friends, I couldn't turn around and befriend Kidrick. That wouldn't look right and it would've hurt Brady even more.

"Hey, I mean it. I can help. Trust me."

I managed to compose myself, though I still sniffled, but I looked deep into Kid's eyes. They looked solid, a little fearful, and kind—this wasn't good. Not good at all. I wrung out, "Take me back to the party. Please."

"Listen...did Brady...?"

"It's nothing. There were these girls and..." I couldn't say anything more. I didn't want to even repeat what they'd said.

Kid leaned. "I can guess what they said. Rayna, don't listen to them. They are shallow meaningless little tarts. Trust me. I've had my fair share of run-ins with girls like them. I don't know what they said, but it's always the same."

I held my breath.

Kid continued, bitter, "They probably said a bunch of crap about how great Brady is and what the hell does he see in you? Am I right? I know I'm right. And you, you're so innocent. Forget what they said because those girls don't even deserve this much attention. They just want a piece of what you have."

"They were right about some things."

"No," Kid cried out. "You are better than them. You are better than everyone, Brady included. He'd agree with me."

I heard what he said. I wanted to believe what he said, but it wasn't true. I wasn't good enough for any of them. I whispered without thinking, "I should've stayed home, like always."

"No, not like always," Kid snapped. "I'm sorry." As he rubbed a tired hand over his jaw, I saw the frustration in him. "Brady should know better. This is because of him."

Huh? "No. Those girls were the ones that—"

"No," Kid cut me off. "I'm not—this isn't you. I'm not mad at you. I know I haven't been around for two years, but you're the same. Nothing has changed. I'm just—Brady knows better. He should've been with you or he should've...we're going to the party, and Brady and I are going to have it out once and for all."

As he started the car and slammed it into gear, I saw the shadows over his face and realized those were the bruises from before. He'd been in the hospital and I hadn't even remembered until now. Brady had put him in the hospital. And I was in Kid's car, upset. Kid was angry at Brady. I knew that Brady would be worried and wondering where I was. Clarissa would've told him I was upset. Suddenly, all my craziness and melodramatics about not being friends with Brady vanished in a heartbeat. I was scared for an entirely different reason now.

10

Kid swerved into Clarissa's driveway and slammed on his brakes, just shy of hitting a group outside the front patio. Their drinks were thrown as a few jumped out of the way, but he didn't care. He threw his door open and stormed out. His jaw was set in stone.

"Kid!" I scrambled out of the car after him. My heart jumped into my throat

Just as he turned the corner that led to the patio, Brady came out of the front door. He stopped. When his eyes snapped to mine, I saw them narrow, linger. I gulped. I knew he saw the tears, but it was too late to brush them away.

Oh dear...

Brady pointed at me. "Did you make her cry?"

"You shouldn't talk! Where were you when I found her on the road crying?" Kid yelled back.

I stopped dead in my tracks and felt the bottom of my stomach drop.

And everything went from bad to worse. A look of hatred passed over Brady's face and with that, he rushed to meet Kid head-on.

No other words were shared and my best friend threw the first punch. Kid dodged and countered with an upper cut, but Brady caught the wrist and slammed his elbow in Kid's face.

From there, it was chaos. People screamed. Some ran. Some froze. And some even cheered.

Kid fell to the ground, was delivered a lethal kick to his face and then some guys rushed to pull Brady off. They got as far as pulling him five feet. When Kid got back on his feet, Brady threw two off and lunged forward to slam him into the garage door.

I jumped at the crashing sound, but couldn't say a thing. I couldn't yell for them to stop. I couldn't run in there. I couldn't plead. I couldn't do a thing. My hand was frozen to my mouth and I just watched. Shocked.

When Brady bent and flipped Kid over a fence, Clarissa joined the group. She braced herself in front of Brady, hands to his chest, and yelled at him to stop. Guys were trying to pull him back, but no one succeeded. Brady ignored Clarissa and shoved the guys off his back. Then she shot me a look and screamed, "Do something!"

Brady forged ahead with Clarissa still pushing against his chest. Her feet dug in, but it didn't matter. He walked forward as her feet slid backwards on the gravel.

"Rayna!" Clarissa screamed again.

This time, I broke out of my paralysis to hurry ahead. I wasn't sure what would work, but I stood beside Clarissa and tried to push him backwards.

"Brady, please. He didn't do anything. It was...Brady, listen to me!"

He was made of cement and my hands were starting to hurt, but when I looked up, none of it mattered. His eyes sparkled from rage and I recognized the cut of his jaw; he was determined. He was beyond anything I could say and then I heard

Matt call out, "Didn't you lay him out before? Do that again. He won't hurt you."

Clarissa looked worried. "I don't know about that..."

I glanced backwards over my shoulders and saw Kid on the ground. He hadn't gotten up and Josh was on the sidelines. He stood there, still, but it wasn't from indecision. He watched Brady and then met my gaze. Then he jerked his gaze and shouldered his way into a crowd until I couldn't see him. I looked at Kid again. He was alone, injured, and not moving.

That's when I decided to grow some balls of steel.

I pushed off from Brady's chest and folded my arms. Clarissa looked at me, dumbfounded, but I ignored her and tilted my chin upwards. I was going for the defiant look and to my surprise, Brady stopped just in front of me. His chest was touching my elbows, but neither of us moved. He was focused over my shoulders, where Kid was now starting to get back to his feet, but I felt the jerking movement of Brady's chest. If he jolted forward, he would've pushed me down. Since he didn't, that meant Brady was listening to reason.

I spoke in a soft voice, "Stop. Now."

He growled.

"He didn't make me cry. He made me feel better. And you have no right to attack him without finding out what he 'did' because he didn't do anything!"

Brady still glared at Kid. "Oh, he did something. He did something and it's not even about that. It's what he's going to do, Rayna. You don't even—"

"So tell me!" I screamed, forgetting who was around us. Right then and there, it was me and Brady and he was keeping a secret from me. "I won't bail you out again if you don't tell me why you're in there. I won't do it. I won't talk to you. I won't do anything."

Brady tore his gaze from Kid's and met mine. When he saw

my seething promise, the hatred stopped and then a wall slammed over him again. "Rayna, don't. Not now. I can't—"

"Oh, yes you can! You will or I'm going home."

Brady measured me.

I lifted my chin up further and tightened my arms over my chest.

"You were crying..."

"Because some really awful girls said some really awful things about me. Kid found me when I was walking on the road and gave me a ride back. That's why I was crying."

He opened his mouth, speechless, and then closed it with a snap. I caught a glimpse of remorse for a second, but it was replaced with another burning emotion. Anger, maybe? I couldn't recognize it and that didn't sit well with me.

"I don't care if he cured cancer. I don't want him around you. I don't want him talking to you, giving you rides, —"

"—comforting me?"

He seethed for a beat and gritted his teeth. "I don't care if he made you feel like Mother Theresa. He's not good news and he's only here to hurt—"

"Hurt who, Brady?" Kid taunted as he wavered on his feet. He sent a bitter smile. "Why do you think I'm here? Who am I going to hurt?"

"You're going to hurt everything! You're going to hurt her."

Kid surged forward, "No. You think I'm going to hurt you, not her. You're scared. This is all about you, about your jeal—"

Brady picked me up with an arm around my waist and moved me to the side. I was deposited on the ground and Brady launched forward. He hit Kid again and again.

"Oh my god—" Clarissa bit off before she rushed around me. Matt and two other guys grabbed Kid from Brady, and shoved him into the house. The door was slammed shut and locked. Brady jumped onto the patio and tried the door handle.

When it didn't budge, he jerked it. When he saw it wasn't going to open, he looked around and rushed around the garage door.

I stood there dazed.

"You can shut your mouth," Clarissa muttered.

I closed it with a snap. "Did you...did you just hear all that?" I pointed towards the house, in Kid's direction.

"He's gotta be pissing blood by now."

"What...?"

"Did you see that beat down? How is he not pissing blood?"

"No." I shook my head. "What do you think Kid meant by all that? Brady's not jealous. Brady doesn't have anything to be jealous about."

Clarissa snorted and rolled her eyes. "Are you this dense in real life or is it the booze?"

"What did Kid mean by that? Brady...why would Brady be jealous? But...I should sit down."

"Wow. You really heard nothing I just said, did you?"

I sat down on the grass. "I should go home. I've been out way too late. Too much these past two days..."

"You're hopeless." Clarissa bent, grabbed my shirt, and yanked me up to press her nose an inch from mine. "Do you have any idea what just happened?"

Fists. Blood. Fighting....Brady.

"Brady drove my car here. I could probably drive it back, but I had five of those lemonades. I probably shouldn't...Brady's going to go to jail again. I don't know if I have enough money for his bail..."

"Okay," Clarissa gritted out. "One, those 'lemonades' are like Kool-Aid. You're going to be fine. Two, Brady just beat the crap out of Kid because of you. That whole fight was because of you. Three, you just laid down the law with Brady. If he doesn't tell you what the fight's about, you can't bail him out so don't start being a pussy about it now."

"That fight wasn't about me."

"And roosters can fly over the moon." Clarissa threw her arms in the air. "You're socially deficient. That's why Brady won't bring you around more often. I always thought he was just keeping you to himself, being selfish and all that crap. Now I know better."

What? Brady kept me for himself? I blinked back to reality. "Oh my god, Brady's going to go to jail again!" Everything rushed at me.

"About damn time you woke up!" Clarissa snapped her fingers in front of my face and gestured to the house. "He's in there or trying. Go get him and cool him the hell down!"

I turned, stopped, and looked over my shoulder. "I don't know what to say to him."

Clarissa looked like she was going to scream. "Is he or is he not your best friend?"

He was. No question about it.

Clarissa saw my response in my eyes. "Then you know exactly what to say to him. Go do it before he puts Kid in the hospital again." As she shoved me, I broke into a run and ignored the garage. Brady wouldn't have gotten in that way. If they were smart inside, they would've locked all the doors. Brady would have figured that out so that meant he'd try for an open window or some other entrance. I rounded the house and found him cracking a window open.

"Stop it."

Brady ignored me.

"I mean it." I reached around and took the wrench from his hands. I didn't even want to think where he'd gotten it.

"Hey!" Brady snarled

"Hey!" I mimicked him and glared. "Stop. Now!" I threw the wrench as far as I could. It landed five feet from us.

"What the hell?" Brady roared.

I blinked back surprised tears, but shook my head. He never roared at me, but I remembered Clarissa. She'd been so strong. I could too. I knew him better than everyone else. "Do not talk to me like that!" I thrust my finger in his face.

Brady quieted. After a beat of silence, he asked, "What?"

I blinked...I hadn't thought it was going to work. I'd never 'talked' Brady out of anything. I was the one to yell at him afterwards, usually as I paid his bail.

"Are you stupid?" This was a good start.

"What?" Brady growled, irritated again, and he turned for the window.

"No!" I grabbed his shoulder and wheeled him back.

He braced himself so he wouldn't fall against me.

I wasn't aware of my own strength. "You don't roar at me."

"I didn't 'roar.'"

"You did."

Brady rolled his eyes. "What do you want, Rayna? I have an ass to kick right now. I'm busy."

"No," I proclaimed.

"No?"

"No!"

"Are you still drunk? Those things are weak."

"I have something very important and wise to say..." Though the lemonades distracted me...I shook my head. I was his best friend, tart girls be damned, and I puffed up my chest. "If you don't back away from that window, leave with me right now, and not punch Kid again—I will rip your pants off."

I held my breath and waited.

Brady froze and blinked, blinked some more, and then threw his head back laughing.

"It's not funny." I was all business here.

"That's not a threat, Rayray. I don't care if you take my boxers. I'll give them to you if you'd like."

I relaxed, a little. "I am being serious, Brady. I'm sure Deputy Doug's already on his way here. He can arrest you for assault and public nudity. You could be prosecuted as a sex offender."

"Not if my pants were taken by force," he argued, smirking.

I muttered, "You could take me serious here. I really don't want you to punch Kid again."

Brady stopped laughing and studied me for a moment. He turned to lean against the house and folded his arms over his chest.

I watched him, now nervous.

"Fine." He surrendered with a dramatic sigh. "But you don't know what's between him and me. You don't know what's at stake."

I lifted my chin. "Me."

He narrowed his eyes. "What do you know?"

"Just what was said. You think he's going to hurt me. He thinks you're jealous. It's obvious to everyone that the fight was about me. You both care about me. You both..." I was hesitant for some reason. "You're both my friends..."

A wall slammed over him. "I'm a little more than your friend."

Did he mean...?

"I'm your best friend. Kid hasn't even been around for two years, and you weren't especially close when he WAS here."

"But you were," I shot back. Brady frowned, but I saw that he was listening. "You were best friends with me and him. Kid and I...it was different. It wasn't what you and I had—have— but I missed him. A lot. I didn't realize it until I just saw him, but he didn't do anything to hurt me. It was those stupid girls. They said things...things about you, about me, about..."

"About what?" He pushed off the wall and grasped my wrists. "What'd they say, Rayna?"

"Just..." I shrugged and grimaced at the same time. I could still hear their voices.

"I want to know. And I want to know who it was."

"They said," I gulped around the knot in my throat. "They said that I just lay on my back for you. You take pity on me. They said my name was stupid and that we shouldn't be friends. You could do better than me." They said a whole lot more, but I didn't want him to know anymore.

Brady cursed underneath his breath and swept me against his chest. He held me tight, tighter than he'd ever held me before, and rocked me back and forth. I felt a soft kiss on my forehead before he whispered, "I am so sorry, Rayna. You are not any of those things. You are my best friend because no one else gets me. I don't need anyone else in my life except you. I know that. I'm sorry if I don't tell you that enough. And I'll deal with those girls."

I shook my head and pulled away. "I know you want to know who they are. And I know you're going to ask Clarissa, but I don't want you to. I need to deal with them on my own. That's why I was upset before. They made me feel like I wasn't good enough for you."

Brady yanked me back into his arms. "Rayna, *I'm* not good enough for you. It's never the other way around, trust me. If anything, that's what Kid makes me feel. I think that's why I want to punch him so bad."

I nodded against his chest and blinked back tears. I could understand the torment even though it wasn't true, on his side. When I wrapped my arms tighter around him, I lifted on the tips of my toes. Brady growled, the good way, and lifted me up so that I could wrap my legs around his waist. He pushed me up against the house's wall and leaned back to look at me. I saw the tenderness and the sincerity and I smiled softly, tracing his cheek with my finger. "Things are changing with us, aren't they?"

Brady nodded.

I didn't know what to say. I wanted to cry, laugh, or run. I wanted to ignore it. "Can we handle it?"

Then I saw the answer in Brady's eyes. He wasn't sure if we could. And my heart dropped.

11

When we rounded the house, Deputy Doug was parked in front of the house with his lights flashing. I couldn't help to wonder if he purposely wanted to make people nervous. Maybe he wanted to sober them up quicker. It worked with me.

"Hey, hey. It'll be fine." Brady squeezed my hand briefly before he sauntered to where Deputy Doug was straightening out of his patrol car. His tan uniform seemed more wrinkled than normal.

As his gaze met mine, I saw what I needed to know. Brady was about to be arrested again. And judging by how tight Brady's shoulders looked, he knew it too. I chose to ignore the carefree note in his voice.

Clarissa materialized at my side with her arms crossed. "Your boyfriend's going back to the tank. Wonder if he'll get charged this time."

I turned and saw that Kid was being helped out of the house with an arm around one of his cousin's shoulders and another guy on the other side. He met my gaze with an apology in his eyes, but his jaw hardened when he caught sight of Brady.

"I bet if you bat those gorgeous eyelashes at Kid, you can get him to drop the charges."

"It was his dad that charged Brady before."

"Kid's got power over his dad. He can pull the neglected child card. Hell, he used to all the time." Clarissa smirked.

I rounded on her. "What are you talking about?"

Clarissa grunted as she watched Brady being talked to by Deputy Doug. She seemed to lap up the drama. Then she focused, "Huh? You're socially neglected. Kid's been on his own for years. His daddy was always around for business functions, but when they were done—off to Affair in Neverland. Kid raised himself. I'm surprised you didn't know. I thought the three of you were tight back then."

"Brady and Kid were best friends. Not me. I wasn't included that much." I wasn't, but I remembered how Kid and I had started to become better friends at the end, before he left.

"Look!"

I'd already known, but I had hoped...then it deflated as I watched Deputy Doug open his back door and cover Brady's head when he climbed inside. When he sat back, he looked for me. I saw a flash of vulnerability in my best friend and blinked back some of my own tears. I rarely saw that side of Brady and only saw it now for a second before his usual cockiness flared back.

No one seemed surprised when Deputy Doug approached me, hand in hat. "I'm sorry for this, Rayna."

"They both fought."

"There are witnesses saying Brady threw the first punch."

"He thought Kid had hurt me."

Deputy Dog scratched his head. "I'm sorry, Rayna. I really am. You know how I feel about that boy, but Brady flares up. We all know this. Kid hasn't had that history. I'd suggest for you to be at the station in the next hour. I'm sure bail will be set. I know that grandmother of yours can be a firecracker, especially with Judge Bailor."

I wasn't quite sure what he meant, but I nodded anyway.

"Again. I'm sorry, Rayna." Then he trudged towards his squad car. As he headed into town, I saw Kid climbing into another squad car. I was pretty sure he wasn't getting arrested.

"Kid's hot," Clarissa declared.

"What?"

"He's hot. I want to jump his bones. Don't tell Brady. He wouldn't like that."

I reeled. "Of course not. Brady and you..."

"Hell no." Clarissa snorted, laughing. "He just doesn't want anyone or anything to do with Kid. Me and BradesKins are buds, but I want to be more than buds with Kid. That's why I'm saying 'don't tell Brady.'" Clarissa caught the mystified expression on my face. "Don't say anything. That's all you gotta do."

I stood there as she sauntered away with a seductive sway to her hips. More than most of the males sent appreciative glances her way. They all looked and they all lingered. I would never be like that. Clarissa was just naturally sexy and me...I was a social deficit or whatever she had called me.

Okay. I swallowed tightly. It didn't matter. Nothing mattered because Brady needed me and I needed him. So I balled up my hands into tight fists and jerked forward. When a group remained in front of the garage, I realized that they didn't see me.

They didn't even notice me.

Brady was gone, therefore; I was gone. If Brady had been there, they would've moved without thinking. He wouldn't have needed to say a thing. But me—I'd have to walk around them, start my car, and honk to get them to move. Sighing, I started to go around when I heard an abrupt bark, "Move, idiots! Rayna's gotta go in and bail Brady out. She can't go anywhere with you blocking her car"

The group looked up. As they started to move to the side, a few apologized, but most just shuffled to the side and continued their same conversation.

I looked over to say thanks to Matt, but he flashed a charming smile and then went back inside, beer in hand. It wasn't long before the door shut behind him and I was left with the idea that I might've made one other friend that night.

I knew the way to the police station like the back of my hand. It wasn't long before I had turned into the parking lot and entered the lobby like before. Except this time, Deputy Doug wasn't at the front desk to greet me. A small lady with greying hair was. She looked like she was from Asian descent, but I wasn't sure. All I saw when she looked at me was blaring disappointment and contempt.

I forced myself forward. "Has bail been set for Brady Remington?"

She sniffed and muttered something unintelligible.

I frowned, unsure, and then said further, "Brady Remington just came in. Do you know if there's bail for him? I'd like to pay."

She glared again, muttered underneath her breath, and stalked away. Her black skirt was so tight it barely moved, but her arms swayed in an angry fashion. When she disappeared around a corner, I scanned the waiting room. Josh sat in the corner. As my eyes landed on him, he glanced up, but remained hunched over in his seat.

"He's coming, you know." He leaned back and looked away. I saw his hands jerk into fists.

"Who?" I had a good guess.

"They brought Kid in and they called his dad right away. He won't be long."

The world fell away in that split second and I couldn't

breathe. Frank Stephens was coming—he might already be there. I didn't want Frank Stephens anywhere near Brady...and I turned, horrified, as I expected the door to open and emit him. But the door didn't move.

"I can't believe you."

I looked back, confounded. "What?"

"Brady. He's an ass and you're....you're here like a puppy dog. What is wrong with you? What's wrong with this entire town?"

"You just don't know him. You don't understand."

"No, I don't. I'm glad that I can say that I haven't been brain-washed by this criminal."

"Brady's not—"

"Yes, he is." Josh stared, long and hard. "He beat up my cousin. He *brutally* beat him up. He could've stopped. Kid was down. He wasn't getting up, but it didn't matter. Brady still went after him and it wasn't just because of you, you know."

I narrowed my eyes. What did that mean?

Josh expelled a ragged breath and ran a hand through his hair. "You're in love with this gorilla. I can't even—when I first saw you I thought, 'Wow. She's amazing. She's gorgeous and not in the normal way. She's gorgeous in that way that she doesn't know how she affects people. That's the best type. I want that.' Kid told me the real story with you and Brady. I know you're not his girlfriend, but it doesn't matter. You're more under his spell than anyone else. It's annoying and it's another reminder that life sucks."

Life did suck. I agreed with that.

"Rayna?"

Deputy Doug stood behind the front desk. When he gestured, I followed him and we went into a back office. He rounded a bare wooden desk and sat down in the chair. It creaked under his seat and I lowered myself to perch on the corner of my own chair. I wrapped my arms around myself, refusing to look anywhere except at Deputy Doug's face. I saw how he was reluctant to say something so I readied myself for what I was about to hear.

"Rayna," Deputy Doug started, exhausted. "I'm here because I need to be real honest with you."

It was worse than I thought. Brady was going to stay in jail forever.

"Frank Stephens is livid," Deputy Doug announced. He leaned forward. "I'm all sorts of torn up here. I love Brady like he was my son. I feel like I've been taking care of him darn near his whole life. He's been in so many scrapes and he can't be blamed. Jumping from foster home to foster home; it's a good thing he had you guys to steady him. That's not why I pulled you in here. I know that Brady ought to get into trouble one of these times, but I hate to think it'll be this one. Frank Stephens is likely to get Brady charged to the fullest extent. I don't feel that's fair."

It was worse than I thought. Then I realized that Deputy Doug was staring at me. "What can I do?"

"Well, I was thinking that grandma of yours can sure be a firecracker. You might not know much about it since it all happened before your time, but—did you call her like I told you to?"

"I was going to call her when I knew how much the bail was."

"I'll give her a call myself and tell her the amount." Deputy Dog nodded. "Good, good. I know she can worm her way around Judge Bailor, but if anyone's going to square against Frank Stephens, I figure it oughta be Viola. She went head to head with him before. She could do it again."

Huh? "What happened before?"

Deputy Dog frowned and pushed his glasses over the wrinkles in his forehead. "It was around the time that your mother was running around these parts. You weren't born yet, but something happened between your mother, Frank Stephens, and another lady that worked in the grocery store. No one really knew what went on, but all the sudden Frank Stephens was divorced and your momma was out of town. After she was gone, Frank tried to run your momma's name through the mud, but Viola wouldn't have it. The two of them tangled on a daily basis. Of course, at that time Frank Stephens was still a young pup. He wasn't much older than his late twenties, but he already owned half the town. But your grandmum, she was smart. She IS smart and she knew most of the town. They banned together and Frank Stephens was forced to shut his trap. I was hoping she'd be willing to do it again. There's a reason why he'd been placed with the Forresters next door to you. We all know how Brady's been taken in by your family."

This was news to me and I wasn't sure how I felt about it. I just heard the words 'your mother', 'Frank Stephens', 'divorced,' and 'out of town.' Leaning back in my chair, I closed my eyes and felt the world swirling around me.

"Rayna?" Deputy Doug looked concerned. "Are you okay?"

"Yeah. It's just...a lot." Not to mention...my mother. She seemed to be involved in so much and yet nothing at the same time. I wished...I didn't know what I wished.

"Have you, uh—have you heard from your mother? How's she doing?"

"She's in Florida. That's all I know." I felt the awkwardness in the room and knew Deputy Dog felt it too. A part of me wanted to say something and cover up the gaping hole that I felt inside, but I couldn't. The necessary energy had been depleted from me.

"I'm sorry to hear that, Rayna. She was...your momma was a good woman."

She wasn't. Everyone knew.

Deputy Doug continued, "I always felt she was misunderstood by a lot of the folks here."

She wasn't misunderstood at all. She'd been exiled.

When someone knocked at the door, I was jolted out of my thoughts. The door opened and someone murmured, "Frank Stephens is here. He's ready for you, Doug."

Deputy Doug cursed and rushed around the desk. As he reached the door, he turned back. "Use my phone. Give Viola a call. We're going to be needing her."

When the door shut, I reached for the phone. Then I remembered that I still didn't know how much the bail was.

12

When Viola swept through the front doors, I jumped from the ferocity of her rush. Then Josh jerked too and I jumped again.

"Holy, who is that?" Josh asked, frowning.

Viola strode towards the front desk and slapped a hand on the desk. "I want to speak to Bailor. Now."

The same grey haired Asian lady scurried away. She didn't frown. She didn't pause. She just moved. Behold the power. It wasn't long until she scanned the waiting room with narrowed eyes. She looked over me, back tracked, and zeroed in as the frown turned into a scowl.

Josh gulped.

My stomach fell to the bottom of my feet. She was dressed in a grey smock, red khaki pants, and yellow clogs on her feet. Her hair stuck up haphazardly with a few curlers that still hung on in desperation. I caught a smattering of blush on her cheeks and saw she'd applied some red lipstick.

I understood Josh's fear.

"Rayna Cassidy Janke. Do you have any idea what time it

is?" She didn't wait for a response. "You call me, wake me up, and tell me that you don't know what Brady's bail is. What am I supposed to think? What am I supposed to think when my own granddaughter calls me and tells me that she's at the police station?"

I gulped this time, just as loudly.

Viola crossed the room, shoulders enraged, arms stiff, and bent forward until her nose was an inch from mine. Then she smiled.

I blinked.

Her smile grew wider as she whispered, "I love it! I was hoping that boy would burst some pizzazz in you. You need some nights like these. You're too good, too uptight at times."

"Wha—huh?" Josh gaped.

Viola glanced over and barked, "You. What's your name and relation?"

I pushed him away. "He—he—he's no one. He's leaving. He's going to sit over there." I pointed across the waiting room.

Josh stood up and sat down in the corner, but at a slow pace.

Viola took his seat. "I know I should be the uppity grand-mother, but I just can't. You've never been involved when he's gotten in trouble and you're involved this time. You were there! I am basking in this moment because I know you'll punish yourself ten times over from what a normal guardian would do. That's why—" She indulged in a sweet smile and patted my head. "—I can't do anything except hug you. I'll make margar-itas when we get home."

Her arms wrapped around me and I stiffened. My face was pushed into her smock and I mumbled to it, "You are completely abnormal."

Viola laughed and then sighed, replete. "God, child. I have been waiting for your rebellious streak to unearth itself. I've been worried that even Brady couldn't get some of that naughtiness out."

"Grandma!" I hissed.

She shook her head and her curlers whipped back and forth. "Rayna, it's not healthy to be as straight laced as you are. This is a good thing. If you get pregnant, that'd be bad." Her hand patted my shoulder. "I know you're too good to be that stupid. And thank god that Brady hasn't impregnated some girl too. Now, talking of Brady—let me at Bailor. Where is he?' She whipped around, fixed the clerk with a determined scowl, and stalked back across the lounge.

Pregnant. That was the only word I'd heard. There was no way I was pregnant...

"That's your grandma?" Josh slipped back into his seat.

I shook my head, lost in my own hazy hell. I could not be pregnant. No way.

"She's scary. I think you saved my life." Josh laughed and shook his head. "Now I get why Uncle Frank always growls when Kid talks about you. I wouldn't want to go up against that either."

I perked up. "Kid talks about me?"

"Constantly. I think he does it because it drives Uncle Frank crazy. Kid gets a kick out of that." He frowned. "I shouldn't have told you that."

I shrugged. "I get it. Brady likes to drive my grandma crazy too."

Josh grunted, annoyed.

Then a back door opened with a harsh bang. Deputy Doug led the way, followed by a stoic Frank Stephens. A bloodied and bruised Kid followed next and his shoulders were tense underneath his shirt. I caught a swooning look from the clerk when she saw the long tear in Kid's shirt, but she felt my gaze. Her eyes snapped to mine and I heard her "harrumph" before she turned back to the desk.

"Dude," Josh greeted as he stood beside me.

Kid grinned and bypassed his dad to thump his cousin on the shoulder. When Josh returned the favour, Kid suppressed a grimace, but Josh wrapped an arm around his shoulder to give him a one armed man-hug.

The clerk still watched him underneath her eyelashes. She reminded me of a hungry cat eyeing up a bowl of cream.

"Are you pressing charges?" Josh questioned just as Kid's eyes met mine.

I jerked in shock at the look of apology and regret. What would Kid would be apologetic for...and towards me? Then I remembered Brady.

He was pressing charges.

"I understand, Mr. Stephens. I can promise that this will be the last altercation between the two boys. The restraining order will come into effect at midnight and this should be the last you see of Mr. Remington," Deputy Dog rasped out. He stood to his fullest height and held a firm hand out to Frank, who ignored it and instead swept cold eyes towards his son. He narrowed them for a brief second and an inaudible look was passed from father to son, but it was gone the next instant as Frank Stephens scanned his nephew and landed on me.

Chills went down my back.

I'd always known about Frank Stephens, how he had terrorized half the town into selling their businesses. Viola had ranted and raved about the injustice of our system when he'd hiked up the prices in every store and gas station that he owned. He would've been banned from having a monopoly over the town if it weren't for a small family-owned gas station. The stories hadn't mattered to me because I had never seen the infamous Frank Stephens in person and now that I had, I wished I hadn't come.

He stood tall with a muscular build underneath a three-piece suit. With sandy brown hair that looked swept carelessly to the side and piercing blue eyes, I could see why the Senior Kidrick was rumoured to go from affair to affair. He exuded a cold disdain that was mixed with strong confidence. None of that mattered to me, but I sucked in my breath at the sight of pure hatred in his eyes when he stared at me.

"Dad," Kid growled in warning.

Deputy Doug cleared his throat.

I couldn't look away from Mr. Stephens. I desperately wanted to, but I couldn't for some reason.

"Let's go, Dad." Kid moved back across the room and stood in the line of fire between his father and me.

I jerked at the sudden loss of...whatever it was. When my hand trembled, I flushed and tucked it in my back pocket. Then a door to the left opened and everyone heard the sound of locks turning in a back room. A police officer led the way and I tensed even more when I heard the familiar sound of my best friend's swagger.

The police officer pointed him towards another desk in the far corner. As Brady bent over the counter and was given a pen to sign some papers, I looked back and noticed that Kid had grasped his father's arm. He pulled him towards the door, but Frank Stephens stared at Brady, riveted. He didn't budge.

"That should be it, Brady," the police officer murmured, amused. He patted his shoulder in approval. "Dougie's pretty adamant, man. You gotta stay away from that other kid or your butt's going to be in a different jail for a lot longer than you've spent here. Trust me. Dougie's serious on this. You can't bust anymore skulls."

Brady laughed huskily and turned around. The amusement vanished as he took in the group behind him. When he straightened in a flash, an ominous feeling swept through the room. I sucked in my breath and glanced at Frank Stephens. Remorse flashed in his eyes before a wall slammed in its place. I saw nothing after that. Puzzled, I looked back and caught

Brady's gaze. He was asking if I was okay and I nodded with a small smile. I didn't dare say anything else. The room was ready to erupt.

"We should go, Dad." Kid tried to pull his father towards the door, but Frank Stephens didn't move. His eyes were still glued on Brady.

Brady took a step towards us, but was halted as the police officer slapped a hand on his arm. "They need to clear the room."

He frowned, but said nothing.

Josh snorted. "Well...this is awkward. If no one's going to start throwing punches, we should go, Uncle Frank."

Then we heard Viola in a backroom. Her voice grew as she approached. "Bailor, if you didn't know how my ass looks in a grass skirt, we'd have to throw down here and now. You let that boy out or I'm going to Veronica about your indiscretion at the CornFestival of 1986. Don't think I don't remember what I saw because I do, even if things were a little fuzzy at the time."

"Jeez, Vi. I was just joshing you. The boy's been released already. No charges were filed in the first place."

She stopped in the doorway as she heard Judge Bailor's sheepish comment and spun around to the assembled group. Unlike Brady, she didn't have a police officer to hold her back as she surged forward. Her finger was drawn in the air with a pinched nerve on her forehead. Rage filled her shoulders. "What did you say to her, Frank? I won't have you berating my granddaughter. You get away from her, you and your son. I don't want either of you in her life!"

Brady jerked forward against the officer's arm. Then Kid stepped in front of his father and stopped Viola in her tracks. "Stop it. He hasn't said a word and he's not pressing charges against Brady. Just...chill, old lady."

Oh no.

Brady cracked a grin and shook his head.

Deputy Doug fought back a snort of laughter. Viola reared her head back, thought for a moment, and then crossed the room to stand toe to toe with Kidrick. She stood an inch shorter and ferocious despite the fifty-year age difference. "You might've sent my daughter away twenty years ago, but you will not speak one word to my granddaughter or I will fulfil my promise, Frank."

Shivers and confusion went down my back.

Kid narrowed his eyes, confused too for a split second before he realized she wasn't talking to him. She wasn't even looking at him. He slowly turned, noticed the locked gazes between his father and Viola, and then stepped out of the way. It was at that moment that I felt someone take hold of my elbow. I jumped, but Brady watched Viola and the elder Kidrick. Disoriented at the sudden cautiousness in him, I touched his chest in wonderment. I didn't know what was going on, but I knew he was fearful for some reason.

"Let's go," Brady murmured in my ear and led me away. No one noticed our departure except for Deputy Doug, who looked relieved. I glanced back a last time before the door shut behind us and my last view was of the silent standoff. My grandmother was brazen and Frank had a blank expression on his face with the promise of danger underneath his surface.

"What was all that about?" And why hadn't he gotten charged?

The usual cockiness was gone as Brady ran a tired hand through his flat hair. "I don't know, not really."

I narrowed my eyes and got inside the car. "What do you mean that you don't know? You know something, don't you? Josh told me that your fight with Kid isn't really about me. Is that true?"

Brady shifted the car in reverse and pulled into traffic. "I don't really know. The thing with Kid and me is stupid and some of it's about you, but some of it's not. I can't...I can't tell you. I'm sorry, but I can't."

"Brady."

"Rayna."

"Tell me."

"No, Rayray. Not this time. At least...not yet."

Hearing the determination in his voice, I leaned back against the seat. "Why weren't charges pressed? That makes no sense. What you did to Kid...you were like a gorilla, Brady."

He snorted and turned into Nellie's parking lot. "Who'd you get that from? That douche who kissed you?"

"How'd you know that?"

The cockiness flared back to his face as he flashed a smile and parked. "No one else would call me a gorilla. They know better."

I followed him out of the car. "You mean they know you think sometimes before you start pounding fists? It sounds like a gorilla to me."

Brady was on the sidewalk, but turned around. I stopped just short of slamming into him, but he caught my elbows and held me in front of me. After a few seconds of uncomfortable silence and a thorough perusal, he asked, "Are you pissed at me?"

Was I? During the party, the fight, and then the police station showdown, I hadn't had time to think about it. Now that I was away, I realized I was pissed. "You're darn right I'm mad. I just spent the night at a party where I got drunk, cried, thought we shouldn't be friends, and then watched you beat Kid up. That's not even adding all the stuff at the police station. You did this. You...you upheaved my night. I wanted to stay in. I wanted to be boring. I like being boring, Brady"

"Okay! Seriously. Stop shouting. Holy cow, Rayray."

I hadn't realized I'd been shouting, but after I thought about it—I had every right to shout. "I feel like I don't know what's going on anymore. Nothing feels normal anymore."

I looked away. I didn't want him to see the tears in my eyes, but Brady caught my chin and pulled me back. With a hand under my chin, he tilted my head up and my eyes met his. He asked in a sombre voice, "You don't think we should be friends? Because I really want to kiss you right now."

<h1 style="text-align:center">13</h1>

I held a hand against his chest. "You can't kiss me."

Brady frowned. "Why?"

"Because I don't know what's going on. I don't know if this means something or not."

"What are you talking about? Of course it means something."

"Does it?" I frowned up at him. He looked beautiful. Shadows graced his cheekbones, giving him a thoughtful look. And the seriousness in his eyes allowed him a haunting presence. I felt my heart skip a beat. "I don't know what anything means right now."

Brady stepped away from me. "What are you talking about?"

Did I know? "I don't know, Brady. I just don't know."

"Well, what are you talking about?"

"Deputy Doug asked me about my mom. Why would he ask me about my mom? Why would Frank Stephens hate me so much? Why wouldn't he press charges against you? Nothing makes sense, Brady. And there are girls who say awful things about me...I don't know what to think. I don't know what to do, but the one thing I do know is that kissing you will make things more confusing. It'll be all sorts of confusing. Do you know what I mean? Am I crazy here?"

Brady sighed as he wrapped his arms around me. I shuddered in them, a good shudder. He tucked his chin in my shoulder and murmured, "Do you know what I thought about in there? You, Rayna."

I lifted my arms, fisted, and pressed them against his shoulders. I wanted to say something, I just couldn't.

"You are my best friend. No matter what's going to be thrown at us, we can overcome it. I'm sure. I promise. I want—hell, I can't say that, but I can say that I want this. I want to kiss you, Rayna."

"Hey you two!" Viola shouted across the street. A moment later we heard her car door slam and I lifted glazed eyes to watch my grandmother dart towards us. She looked giddy.

Brady cursed under his breath, but turned with an arm braced around my shoulders. "Thanks for bailing me out, Vi. I owe you."

Viola swept past us. "You sure do. I need you to keep my grandbaby on the straight and narrow."

I flinched.

Brady stiffened.

Viola laughed and threw her head back. The sound was freeing. "I love it, Brady. You got my girl out for an all-night rager. That's what makes memories. It builds character. I need my baby to have some fun."

I watched as my grandmother bypassed us and went inside of the gas station. "She makes it sound like I'm going to die a nun."

When we heard Bob's welcoming roar inside, Brady hugged me. "Well, we both know you won't die a virgin."

I stopped short, but Brady chuckled and kept going.

Glaring at his back, I retorted, "Not funny."

"That's my job, babe." Brady flashed me a smile as he held open the door.

I wasn't sure which annoyed me the most: Brady's arrogance, my grandmother's expectation that I'd die from boredom, or Bob. At that moment, I picked the Bigfoot. I was going to ask if Ned would get rid of it, but the words died in my throat. He and Viola were involved in a heated discussion or maybe I should say that Ned was proclaiming his love and Viola was ignoring him.

Some things never changed.

"What about Friday night? I will buy a dozen roses. I'll light my humble abode on fire with candles. I'll have a gourmet meal delivered. How about it, Viola Leann?"

My grandmother snorted and reached inside a freezer to pull out a carton of vanilla ice cream. "You mean you'll light the plastic fake-candles that you stole from the church five years ago and you'll order pizza for me?"

"Well, when you put it like that, I could throw in for some cheesy bread. Would that do it for you?" Ned was so hopeful. "Don't forget the red roses. They're expensive."

Viola stopped and tightened her hold on the ice cream. "I have been saying no to you for thirty-nine years, Ned. When's it going to change?"

"I've got red roses, Viola. I know for a fact that Neil's never given you flowers. What kind of man is that?"

Viola turned firm eyes on him. "That man has been by my side for forty-three years. And those were some long and hard years, Ned. You remember some of them. He has not once complained, whined, or made me cry. That is a feat no other man can measure up to. So you ask yourself if you could do better."

Ned opened his mouth, thought for a second, and then closed it.

Brady chuckled beside me and moved forward to follow

them. As they moved further down the aisle, I heard Brady taunt, "You going to back down to that, Ned? There isn't a feat that you can't imagine you'd overcome. Some of your lies sound better than that."

"He ain't made her cry, Brady. I can't do better than that."

Brady dismissed, "Come on. What kind of man doesn't make a woman cry? The best ones make 'em cry."

"Brady Jake Remington. You are not helping one bit with your foolish encouragement."

"Come on, Viola. Ned's just a bleeding heart here. He's a literal standing bleeding heart, right in front of you. How can you turn your back on that?"

I shook my head. Everyone knew Ned would never win over my grandmother, except for maybe Ned, but there was some entertainment in his attempts. I always suspected my grandmother was flattered by his attention, which was why she kept shopping at Nellie's even though she always left with a tenfold promise to never step foot in that store again.

I was proven right as I heard a slight hint of laughter in Viola's false sternness. "If he was literally bleeding, I'd have the decency to hand him a towel. Until then, I don't have the time to even offer him a tourniquet. Now scootch, both of you."

I tuned out Brady's predictable comeback and perused the toiletries. I didn't know if I chose that aisle on purpose or if my wanderings guided me to the right spot, but as I kept moving down, I saw a couple of pregnancy tests resting on the white stand. I caught my breath and stood frozen for a moment. Should I move away, ignore what I already worried about, or should I... I had no idea. This was above my head.

Something kicked in my stomach, perhaps my guilt. Without thinking I reached out and picked up one of the foreign boxes. This box, this tiny, simple box could hold an answer for something that could change my life. I blinked away tears and ignored the sudden pounding in my chest. The box felt too heavy to hold. As my hand started to fall, another caught it and tucked it against his chest.

I looked up and saw Brady. He held me tight against him and transferred the pregnancy test from my numb fingers to his.

"Are you worried about this?" There was a gruff note in his voice, but there was something else.

I shook my head. "We didn't use..."

Brady switched the box to the other hand and squeezed my hand with his free one. "We'll get through it. I promise."

I wanted to believe him. I really did. I wanted to close my eyes and know that whatever Brady said was true. He could do anything. But this, I knew he couldn't stop something that might already be growing inside of me. The time to stop it had already passed.

"Don't make promises that you can't keep," I whispered back.

Looking up, Brady caught his breath at my emotion. I let it shimmer, bright and shining, because I needed him to see how serious I was. I couldn't have him shrug it off and party it away. This was real, could be real.

"Holy. Mother of God. Are you kidding me?"

I whirled around and saw Viola at the end of the aisle. Her eyes were hot and she gripped the ice cream pail until her knuckles became white. Her face lost all the blood flow as she stomped forward. "You had better be joking. This had better be an elaborate pathetic joke, Brady. I won't be laughing if I'm the brunt of this awful, awful trick. Brady? Tell me you're kidding."

A lesser man would've laughed off the false joke. He would've taken the opening and ran for the hills.

Brady tucked me behind him and lifted a sober chin. "We'll handle this. Rayna and me."

"Like hell you will!" Viola whipped out, her eyes storming. She stepped forward with her hand outstretched to grab me, but Brady shuffled me out of her reach. She reared back. "You give her to me now. I can't believe you—I can't believe the two of you—Rayna! What were you thinking?"

"All due respect, Viola, we weren't thinking. We were doing what most kids do. We were living in the moment."

My grandmother's mouth clamped shut, but she flung a finger up and thrust it against his chest. "You know better," she seethed. "Of all kids, of everyone, you know better! You don't give me that crap. Now Rayna, she's sheltered, but you knew better."

"And she doesn't?" Brady firmly planted himself in front of me. "You treat her like she's a two-year old. You act like she's this fragile future spinster who doesn't know how to walk on her own two feet. You're clueless about her."

"You don't tell me about my granddaughter." Viola bristled in her rage. "You don't tell me."

"All due respect, but I know your granddaughter a little better than you do."

"No, you don't."

Brady quieted, but he only lasted a second. "You have always preached to me about making her live a little. You wanted her to have adventures, but still stay the same person. You wanted me to be the person to help her with that. You picked me on purpose. You saw how I was going to be a long time ago and you constantly called me over for lunch and supper. You handpicked me to be friends with Rayna. You knew that I'd take care of her. And now that the friendship has gone to another level, what'd you expect? You know who I am. You've always known who I am. What'd you expect?"

Viola surged forward and gritted out, "I expected you to respect her. I expected you not to treat her like one of your hussies. I *expected* you to not have sex with my granddaughter, who you know doesn't do those things easy. She's not like the rest of them."

"Like the rest of who? The rest of the skanks in this town? Or just the ones I sleep with?" Brady tilted his chin up further.

"I'm inferring that you didn't respect her enough to use a rubber," Viola lashed back.

"Enough!" I cried out.

"Rayna, no..." Brady urged.

I ignored him. "Grandma, we can talk about this later. I think it'd be the smart thing to schedule a doctor appointment for me tomorrow or as soon as possible."

"When?" Viola gutted out.

Brady flashed a triumphant smile, but I inquired, "When what?"

"When'd you do it? It might not even need to be done."

"Oh you mean about the—it was within seventy two hours, but I won't even think about any abortion pill. If it's...," My throat was tight. It was painful to swallow. "If it's supposed to be, it's supposed to be. I do think I could benefit from a check-up and further birth control measures." I finished and then tucked my chin against Brady's shoulder. It took everything I had to muster that maturity.

Viola didn't see my weakness and chuckled to herself as she shook her head. "Which one is the adult here?"

"Welcome to my world," Brady bit out. He swept a hand behind him and held me tight against his back. I felt his fingers flex against the lower muscles of my back, but any reassurance fell to the wayside. I could only hear my grandmother's damning words.

I was a failure.

And I sucked in my breath when Brady massaged my back because a part of me didn't care that I had failed. I wanted his touch. I needed his touch. I knew that if given the opportunity, I'd feel that touch again.

"I cannot believe you two...," Viola grumbled.

I hesitated to ask. "Should we...are you going to tell my mother?"

Viola snorted. "Hell no. Your momma ain't here and your momma ain't a part of your life, not in that way. She don't have no say whatsoever in what we do. Now," she seared us both with her glare. "You two get in your car and you head straight back home. I don't want no stop-over in between. You better be in the house in ten minutes flat. I don't have the time and patience to play games."

As she left the store Brady dispelled a deep breath

"Why didn't she make me go with her?" I wasn't sure if I wanted to guess, but I already knew the reason. She couldn't stand to be alone with me. She couldn't handle having me right next to her.

When Brady hugged me to him, I closed my eyes, just for a moment. I relished the firmness of his chest and the safety of his arms. A tear teased the corner of my eye because I knew he'd pull away in a moment and I'd have to feel the cold alone.

"You okay?"

I burrowed against his chest. I didn't want to answer. I wouldn't lie and I couldn't tell him the truth. My world was ending. I was going with it because I hadn't realized how much I needed him. Now that Viola knew what happened, I knew it'd all end somehow. It'd unravel and I'd be left standing, empty and alone.

"I'm fine," I whispered, raw.

He squeezed my shoulders once more. "You sure?"

I nodded with my eyes closed and pulled away. Then I blinked back more tears. "I can handle it."

Brady frowned.

"I can," I reassured him, but we both knew I was lying.

14

When we got to the house, Neil was sent out to the car to make sure I went in alone. He looked regretful as he explained it'd be best if Brady didn't come inside, but it didn't matter. The damage was done. My grandmother had essentially cast him out of the house. In Brady's world, that meant the family. Of course, a part of me knew this wasn't how it really was, but that's how it felt that moment.

When I got out of the car, I looked at the house. It was large and looming in that moment.

"It'll all be fine. You know that, right?"

I didn't, but I mustered a smile and turned to Brady. "Of course..."

He saw through my lie but didn't dispute it. I sighed in relief.

Brady patted the steering wheel. "I'm going to go. Should I call you later?"

"No. No!"

"What?"

"I mean, it might be best if I talk to you tomorrow."

Brady sighed and nodded. "Fine. I'll—screw it. See you

tomorrow." He jerked the car around and sped down my drive-way. Then he braked and reversed. I watched as he parked underneath the weeping willow, climbed out, and tossed the keys towards me.

He grumbled as he passed by, "Forgot it's not my damn car."

I pocketed the keys as he walked past the house and through the small line of trees that separated our home from the Forresters. When I heard a door slam shut, I knew he was home and couldn't stall any longer.

I still didn't move.

In fact, I stayed for another five minutes. I should've gone inside. I'm a rational near-adult type of person. I had sex with my best friend. Yes, we were stupid and didn't use protection. Yes, we didn't tell our secret, but who does? Yes, I might have to face certain huge, huge circumstances, but Brady was right. We'd handle it. Me and him. But...I'd disappointed someone who looked out for me. There were only three of them.

I wiped a tear away and tried to rationalize that the world really wasn't ending.

"Rayna."

I looked up at Grandpa Neil's soft voice. He stood outside the door with a hand that held it open. One of his coverall straps slipped off his shoulder.

"I'm okay, Grandpa. I just need some time."

"Come on in. She went to bed."

She didn't want to face me.

"Okay." I nodded and slowly climbed off the tire. My throat was thick. "I'm coming in." As I went inside, I felt a chill in the cozy living room. "Did she tell you?"

He nodded and placed a comforting hand on my shoulder. One squeeze and he murmured, "It'll be okay. We've gone through this before. You're not the first to have made a mistake."

A mistake. Was that what Brady and I had done?

"It's late. Morning will be here soon. You should try and get some sleep. We've got church in a few hours."

I nodded and moved upstairs, but my feet dragged as I went past their door. The light flickered underneath it and their fan was whizzing. Instead of turning on my own light, I just curled underneath my covers.

When I woke, I saw the same darkness in my room. Blinking tiredly, I sat up and squinted towards my clock. I stared long and hard before I realized what I was looking at.

Nothing.

My clock always rested on my nightstand, but it wasn't there. When I looked for my phone I saw it wasn't where I usually placed it either. In fact, I looked around my room and realized nothing was the same. Someone had come in and rearranged my room—then I remembered. My clock had been pushed to the floor from when Brady and I had been in there—when my hand had flung upwards. I remembered hitting it, but I hadn't registered what had fallen. And, patting my pockets, I found my phone tucked into my back pocket. When I opened it, it took a couple seconds before I registered that it said 9:03.

I started to climb out of bed, but my phone buzzed in my hand. There were ten text messages from Brady. The last one read, 'Where are you? Are you ignoring me on purpose or is she that pissed off? She wouldn't look at me in church. Call me.'

Church?

That was at nine—oh God. I scrambled out of bed and lunged towards the door. When I opened it, the entire house was dark. No one was home and there was no way that it was nine in the morning.

"Hey!"

I whirled around and screamed when I saw a dark figure crouched in my window.

"Hey! It's me."

Brady. That was Brady. Gasping, I fell against my door and patted my chest. "You scared the crap out of me."

"I think I just peed my pants. Jeez," Brady grumbled.

"That was shut." I pointed towards the window.

"But not locked, babe. I left it open an inch the other night. Figured we might have to climb back inside." He smirked. "That plan went differently, huh?"

"Not funny," I retorted and closed the door behind me. The room was dark, but an intimate feeling swept over me. I shivered, not from fear or excitement, but ignored it as I sat on the bed. "I just woke up."

"I was wondering," Brady murmured as he inspected the pictures on my wall.

I watched his back, noted the muscular build and thin waist. Brady looked good. He always looked good, as he always would, but I saw an extra tension in his shoulders that he normally swept aside.

"What's wrong?" I asked.

Brady shook his head and asked instead, "Have you talked to your grandmother today?"

My 'grandmother.' He asked so formally. I shook my head. "She went to bed this morning before I got inside and I've been sleeping since. I'm kind of relieved. I really don't know if I can handle seeing how she looked at me last night again."

"Yeah," Brady mumbled as he sat beside me on the bed. Leaning forward, he braced his elbows on his knees, cupped his chin with his hands, and watched me steadily. His normally dusty blonde hair was cast in shadow.

A shiver passed through me at the intensity of his eyes. "What?" I tried to ignore the arm muscles that bunched together when he leaned further on his elbows.

"I was just wondering how you're handling this. I mean, you usually freak out. How come you aren't freaking?"

"Thanks for your support." I tugged the bottom of my shirt down.

Brady shrugged. "I'm just saying that you aren't acting normal. I'm concerned."

"You want me to freak out?"

"Oh come on. You're going to freak out sometime. Since you haven't done it yet, it means it's going to be really bad. I'd rather deal with it now, not later."

"Excuse me, but you don't get to pick when I decide to 'freak out.'"

"Don't get all huffy about it. I'm just saying—"

"—I don't care what you're saying. This isn't even about you anymore. This is about...this is about..." I turned away from Brady and wrapped my arms around myself. I started towards the door, needing to get away, but stopped short. I couldn't go out there either.

"Rayna?" Brady asked behind me.

I started to tell him to go away, but I stopped that too. Did I want him to go away? Did I want to be alone? I didn't know what I felt or what I wanted. "Maybe you should go. I don't know what to say right now."

I heard the bed creak in protest as he stood up. "Are you sure? I wanted to make sure you're okay."

"I don't think I am, Brady. I'm sorry," I whispered.

"Rayna...come on..."

He wanted me to say that everything was alright, but I couldn't. I could still see the look on my grandmother's face. She looked at me like I was a stranger. I couldn't get that out of my mind. My throat choked up again. I shook my head and rasped out, "Brady, just go. I'll talk to you later."

He waited another few seconds, which seemed like minutes, before he crawled out of the window. As soon as I felt him go, I breathed in relief. I didn't know why I felt like Brady's presence was so oppressive, but it was. I shook my head and tried to clear my thoughts. I couldn't think like that. It was no good.

"Rayna, are you awake?"

I opened the door to my grandpa dressed in flannel pajamas, ready for bed. He extended a plate of steaming mashed potatoes with grilled chicken toward me. "I heard voices and thought you might be hungry."

"Sorry, Grandpa. I'm not hungry." My stomach growled. "Is she...?"

"She went to bed again, same damn migraine."

I saw the lie and chose to ignore it. "What about you, Grandpa? Are you disappointed in me, too? How come you'll talk to me and she won't?"

"It ain't like that, Rayray. It's not you that she's avoiding."

"Then what is it? Why couldn't she talk to me last night? Why couldn't she wake me up to talk today? Why'd she go to bed early?" My voice hitched on a sobbing note.

I searched his eyes, looking to see some answer that gave me hope, but he gave me a sad smile. "Your situation just sits real close to something else that happened. It ain't even about you, not really."

"But what? What do you mean?"

"You should eat your food and maybe take something to help you sleep. You have a busy week ahead. It's your graduation and you have lots to finish up with school."

As he left, I felt a small balloon of hope had been burst with a sharp needle. I'd been given a brief reprieve that maybe I hadn't disappointed my grandma so much that she couldn't bear the sight of me, but then with his abrupt departure I knew it wasn't so. It really was me that she couldn't see.

When I shut the door and stood there with the steaming plate, I thought over the coming week. I had one paper to finish. It wouldn't keep my attention and it was almost done.

I left the plate of food on my desk and went to the bathroom. I wouldn't need anything to help me sleep. I felt almost numb from lack of energy. When I finished getting ready for bed, I curled under my blanket and closed my eyes to fall asleep again.

When I woke the next time, it wasn't to darkness. I saw the familiar peeking of light through my windows and even heard the birds again. Unlike the last time, I wasn't disoriented at all; I knew immediately what had happened over the last few days. I quickly rolled over and smothered my face with a pillow. After I screamed into it, I didn't feel any cathartic release, only more agitation. I knew the day was not going to be a fun one.

Later, as I got to school and walked through the parking lot doors, I was right. Instead of everyone not noticing me, everyone noticed me. I felt my face get hot and ducked to shove it into the bag that I was clutching.

"If you take one more step, I'm going to flatten you."

Clarissa stood an inch from me holding a huge cake covered in clear plastic. Her eyebrows were arched in a warning.

"Are you getting married?" The cake was covered in white icing with pink flowers around the foundation. A figurine of a kissing couple was on top with a giant pink bow at the bottom.

"Hell no!" Clarissa scoffed and rolled her eyes. "This is the final project in my home economics class."

"I thought we had to sew our own bag. Wasn't that in seventh grade?"

"I'm in the advanced class. I wanted to get a jumpstart for college next year."

My eyebrows shot up. "We have home economics in college?"

"No, but it's going to be my degree. I'm doing a self-declared major. I want to be a wedding coordinator."

"Really?"

"Really." Her eyebrows went flat. "And before you make

some smartass comment, it's not because I want to get married or anything. I just really enjoy weddings. I've never dreamed about my own wedding. I don't even know if I want to get married, but I really like them. I helped plan my sister's and then my other sister's. It stuck for some reason."

"Okay."

"Sorry. I get heated when I think people are making fun of me." Clarissa blew out a breath to cool herself off. Some strands of her hair billowed upwards for a moment before they landed gently and perfectly back into place.

"You'd be great at that job."

Clarissa raked a shrewd eye up and down me, but didn't comment. I thought I heard a slight "huh," but wasn't sure when she turned and went down the hallway. After a while I followed and saw she was at my locker. The cake was gone.

"How'd you know this was my locker?"

She snorted in laughter. "Are you serious? Brady might've been done with school for a year, but he comes around. Trust me. When Brady Remington hangs out around a locker, everyone notices. He liked to wait at your locker."

"Really?" I hadn't realized how much attention we'd drawn.

"Uh huh," she remarked dryly, waiting.

As I exchanged my bag for my books, I watched Clarissa. She pursed her lips in a flirtatious smile at two athletic guys as they walked by. Both of them turned and looked over their shoulders until they were out of eyesight.

"I love boys. I love men. I love anyone with a penis," she declared, laughing to herself as she tucked a strand of hair over her shoulder. It seemed to bring out the golden tan of her shoulders. Of course, her halter-top tank top might've helped since it was black and sexy. Well, it was actually simple, but it seemed sexy and *really* sexy when it was paired with her ripped miniskirt. I sighed in wonderment at Clarissa. She knew how to always look so beautiful whereas myself...I cringed when I looked at my pair of jeans and white tee shirt.

"But you probably knew that, right?" Clarissa distracted me.

"Why are you saying that?"

She narrowed her eyes for a moment, stared at me, and then laughed abruptly. "I'm starting to get why Brady likes you so much. You have no clue what's going on, do you?"

I gulped. Images of a firing squad came to mind.

"Okay. Not that I think you care or are even curious, but I love males, and because I'm in a sharing mood, I want to tell you why I love males."

I waited, unsure if I asked for this or even wanted to know this information.

"Because they're simple. Some girls won't agree with me, but it's because they're stupid. Males or anyone with a penis are very, very simple. They like what they like. They want what they want. And they don't care if other people have an opinion about it. Case in point, if a guy likes you, he doesn't care if other guys either think you're hot as hell or as unattractive as a pig rolling around in mud. Well, most guys. The narcissistic ones care."

I frowned.

Clarissa kept going, "The truth is that they don't want other guys to like you. You're theirs. They've pissed on you. They've marked their territory. The funny thing is that Brady marked his piss on you fifteen years ago. It's not even new to people, not like Kid, who should've known. He should've come back, known what was going on, and stayed away, but he didn't. He talked to you. That's why Kid is not simple and that's why I think I'm so attracted to him."

Wait—what?

Clarissa laughed throatily. "Those two guys that just walked by us, they are simple. They are the most simple of what males can be. They see a girl they like; they want the girl they like.

Girls aren't like that and Kid isn't like that. He cares about you, but he doesn't think you're hot. I know that."

I bit my lip as I frowned even more.

"I think I'm in love, Rayna. Is this what's it like? Does your whole body tingle for his touch? Do you want the entire world to stop moving if it means you could see Brady?"

My mouth dropped open. How was I supposed to know that? Did I...was this love? Was that what I've been feeling for Brady? And I only thought I had my pregnancy to worry about.

"What?" Clarissa barked out.

"Huh?" I blinked at her.

"Are you pregnant?" she hissed.

I clamped a hand on her arm and jerked her into an empty classroom. As soon as the door shut, Clarissa whirled on me. "You guys did it and didn't use protection? Are you stupid? Is Brady stupid?"

"Why does everyone keep saying that?"

"Brady's smart. You're not. Did you guys have sex?"

I swallowed tightly. "Maybe you're Viola's real grand-daughter."

"What?"

"Nothing." I wet my dry lips. "We had sex."

"I knew it!" Clarissa snapped her fingers in the air and grinned in triumph. "Brady didn't use anything, did he? That a-hole. It's like he wants you pregnant or something."

I was fed up. "Why does everyone blame Brady? I was there, too. I was a part of it."

"Yeah, but you're you. Brady knows about this stuff. Hell, he would use two rubbers if he could." Then her eyes went wide again. "But you can't do that—that does the opposite, but if he could, Brady would do it. He is anal, no pun intended, about that stuff. But he's just so freaking blind and selfish when it comes to you. He wants you all to himself. I'm guessing your grandmother blew a fuse, huh?"

"I should've known better. I was there too. It's my fault too."

An unnamed emotion swept through Clarissa's green eyes and she murmured, "You're right. You always protect the one you love."

Wha—huh?

Then she flashed a bright smile and grabbed my arm. "Come on, Rayna. I'm really hoping you aren't pregnant yet because this is the last week of school. We've got too much partying to do."

"What are you talking about?" I wasn't sure if I wanted to know.

"We're going on the senior tubing trip. You're going to get drunk because it might be the last time in two years if you go the whole breast feeding way."

I stumbled when she tugged me behind her. My feet were not a part of my body then and all I could think was...breast-feeding?

15

Two hours later, I found myself self-conscious in a barely-there pink bikini and holding a mug of wine in one hand while I tried to balance a black tube with the other.

Not fun.

"Brady's girl! How are you?"

A sudden surge of water pushed my tube left while I slipped right. Someone jolted their way through the river to my side, but I couldn't look to see who spoke as I scrambled to keep from falling off my tube. Just as I was going in the river, I closed my eyes and gripped the mug tight, but a strong hand steadied me at the last second. When my legs were spread-eagle and my arms held the side, I peeked to see who'd come to my rescue.

Matt Krone stood in the water with his own foaming mug of beer. Instead of holding onto his tube, it looked like it was holding onto him.

"I'm not real good with the water sports stuff."

Matt blinked and then flashed a perfect smile. "Oh right. It was nicely done."

I frowned. "I have no idea what you're talking about." I gripped my mug tighter.

"Nothing," Matt chuckled. "What are you drinking?"

"I'm not drinking," I said quickly.

He looked at my hand.

I'm an idiot. "I mean, it's wine, but I haven't drunk anything. I'm not really a drinker."

"Sure about that?"

I opened my mouth to convince him of my normal boredom when I caught the grin at the corner of his mouth. "Oh. You're joking."

"Yeah," Matt laughed outright. "Trust me, Brady's girl, you've come around once and we all saw what a few drinks could do to you. Wine, not something you should be drinking. That stuff will go straight to your head."

I muttered, "I'm just holding it to fit in." A second passed and then—"I mean, I don't normally drink and Clarissa wanted me to...I'm just holding the mug. I'm not...I might, I don't know. I—"

Matt patted me on the shoulder. "It's okay, but does Brady know you're here? I saw him at Nellie's before school and he seemed worked up about something. You and him aren't my business, I shouldn't be saying anything."

I sat up straighter or tried. The tube started to slip away again. "What do you mean? What are you talking about?"

Matt frowned and glanced to where Clarissa lounged on her tube. She looked like she did it every day as she idly held her own mug of wine and laughed with a guy. I recognized him from the hallway earlier that day.

"What?" I asked again.

"Look, Clarissa's after Kid. She likes challenges especially if they're male. We all saw it at the party, but you're here. Is Brady okay with this?"

"This what? What are you talking about?" I frowned as I remembered Clarissa raving about Kid, but I wasn't too concerned about it at the time. Now I was starting to be.

"Do the math, Brady's girl."

"I have a name. Learn it," I retorted as the feeling of being used was starting to settle in my stomach.

I turned, or the best I could with the tube, and twisted my neck to see Clarissa. She looked the same as she had a few days ago. She liked Kid. I knew this. Kid liked me. I knew this too. Brady really liked me since he was my best friend. I knew that Brady wouldn't want Kid around me...so... I asked, "What are you saying?"

Matt had been staring at me while I pondered between the lines. Now he just laughed and then laughed some more, but then he quieted while his shoulders jerked sporadically. When he hadn't regained control within a few seconds, I got impatient. "I'm not good at this stuff. I know that. Brady's usually around to help me, but he's not here. So don't think I'm dumb, just tell me what you're saying."

Matt's chuckles lessened enough so he leaned forward. "Look, just be careful. Brady might show up later."

"You think Kid will come too? Is that what you're trying to warn me about?" I leaned closer. The tube started to slip, but Matt shot out a hand and held it firm. "That would be disastrous."

He stared down at me.

The feeling that I needed to do something was starting to grow within me, but what? I had no idea. "Brady usually takes care of this stuff."

"He's not here. You gotta do it."

I squinted upwards. "Why not you? You figured it out. Could you do something?"

Matt backed up and shook his head. "Oh, hell no. You're Brady's girl."

"What am I supposed to do?"

"I don't know, but you gotta figure it out."

My mouth fell open.

"Rayna," Clarissa shouted and waved towards me. She grinned, looking a little too happy. "Come here. I want to introduce you to Derek."

The guy next to her grinned as he held a clear John Deere mug filled with green liquid. I wasn't knowledgeable about drinks, but I certain that was hard liquor. I knew I wasn't about to find out because there was no way I was going to ask. With wavy chestnut curls and chocolate eyes, something about Derek was screaming for me not to talk to him...at all.

"Come on," Clarissa called out again.

I looked over my shoulder, one more last ditch effort to see if Matt would help, but he'd already moved to another group of girls. I recognized some of them as the mean ones, Angela and what's her face.

I was on my own.

I moved towards Clarissa and Derek at a slow pace with only one hand in the river and my legs still spread-eagle over the tube. Then I squeaked when I saw Clarissa motion for Derek to help. He stood up and showed off a lean, slightly defined, body as he walked towards me. I breathed out in relief when I saw his reluctance. He had no interest in me. He wanted Clarissa and he was only trying to please her. When he got close enough and reached out to grab my tube, my voice squeaked, "Is there a rest stop on these things?"

He froze and studied me for a second. "Why? You have to pee or something?"

"Maybe." I shifted to switch positions. My legs had cramped up.

"We just pee in the river, most do. Some girls go up on the bank and take a squat. You could do that if you want." He looked revolted as he held onto my tube with one finger.

"Could you hold my mug for me?"

"Why?" So overly suspicious.

"I can't stay like this. I'm uncomfortable."

"Yeah." He motioned. "Your ass had been in the air this whole time. Your back's going to be a bitch by the end of the day."

"You were looking at my butt?" I blushed.

"What?" He looked disgusted. "No! I'm just saying—forget it." Then he took my mug. As I started to wiggle back and forth on the tube to switch positions, he asked, "So are you and Clarissa friends? Good friends?"

"You don't know who I am?" As soon as the words were out of my mouth, I clamped it shut. "Oh gosh. Sorry. That sounded awful."

"Should I? What do you mean? Who are you?"

"Nothing. No one. I might need to leave soon. Do you know how I could do that?"

"Leave? People don't leave the river."

"What if people get bored tubing?"

"Once you're in the tube, you stick it out until your stop comes up. The rides are waiting for us there."

"Oh." I brightened. "So you mean people can't join us once we're in the river?" That would solve a whole bunch of problems.

"Oh, no." Derek was oblivious to my dilemma. "Other people tube too and sometimes they'll join up or people jump in from wherever all the time, especially if they do their own pick-ups. You've never been tubing before?"

Not only was he looking at me like I was an idiot, but he made me feel like one. "No. I'm very studious."

"I figured."

I got hot when I heard his condescending tone. "What does that mean?"

Derek jumped backwards in reflex and let go of my tube.

"Hey!" I tried to scramble to catch him. No avail. My tube caught a torrent in the river and off I swooped.

"Rayna! Where are you going?" Clarissa called out as my tube sped up even more.

I shifted and yelled back, doing my best to hold on, "I don't know what to do!"

"Jump off!" one of the guys yelled out.

"Get off the tube!" Clarissa shouted alongside him.

"Oh man." I heard Matt laugh before he offered, "I'll get her. I'm surprised this girl isn't dead yet."

"Maybe that's why Remy doesn't bring her around."

I gritted my teeth when I heard the snide tones from the number one mean girl.

"Just fall in the water," Matt called as he waded downstream after me.

The river wasn't going that fast and I knew it was shallow, but I was a little relieved my tube had put some distance from the group. Matt's earlier warning concerned me and I wasn't sure what to do if either Kid or Brady showed up. I was almost disappointed when Matt caught up and took hold of my tube.

Then he stopped and studied me, or as much as he could around the glaze of booze in his eyes. "You don't look that scared. You could've just stood up or don't you know how to swim?" A different look in his eyes flared. "Did you do that on purpose?"

Then I heard from above on the bank's cliff, "Rayna? What are you doing here?"

My hope that neither would show shrivelled inside of me. Brady stood in navy blue swim trunks with a rope in his hand. He stood poised at the edge of the bank, frowning down at us.

"Brady! Don't do it, man!" Matt laughed.

The frown vanished and I saw the mischievous Brady come to light. Even though he wasn't dared, he might as well have been. He grabbed the rope tighter and then leapt off the cliff, swung down to us, and scooped an arm around me as we both hurled into the river. Swallowing a mouthful of water, I kicked off Brady's chest, and ignored the sweep of his hand as it grazed my breast. As we popped back up, I pretended to punch him in the chest. Brady dodged my hand and caught my hands. He twisted them so I was held hostage against his chest.

"What were you saying, Matt? Rayna can't swim? That's nonsense." Brady chuckled and hoisted me in the air over his shoulder.

"Don't you dare," I started to warn, but bit down on my words as he launched me in the air. When I slammed into the water, I shot my legs down to shoot back up.

"Rayna's a fish in water. We grew up on the river by her grandparents' farm."

"Really?" Matt asked with an evil grin. "So if I threw her over my shoulder, she'd be fine?"

"Don't you dare! Either of you!" I waved a finger at both of them and then moved towards my tube which had floated near the bank. Just as I caught it, two bodies flew over the cliff and I was drenched again from their splashes. Then three more people repeated the motion and I stared, confused, as I saw the guys go towards Brady. They were all laughing together.

I realized how much of Brady's life I wasn't a part of. I had no idea who all his friends were and I hadn't really cared before. When he looked at me and his eyes darkened in desire, I knew I cared. I had a right to care.

"Hey, guys." He moved towards me. "This is Rayna."

"You're the infamous Rayna," one of the guys sneered, but I caught the amusement in his eyes.

"Don't touch her. Don't look at her. Don't speak to her," Brady casually warned and then picked me up and deposited me on the tube.

"Oh!"

He kicked off down the river and floated with an arm holding my tube. As water dripped down his face and flattened his hair, Brady grinned at me. His eyes sparkled brightly and I found myself almost breathless when he added, "I don't want to punch anyone later."

I melted inside a tiny bit and reached out to trace a water drop from his cheekbone. "I don't think that's a healthy outlook on life."

"Not if you're having my baby," he whispered.

My heart skipped a beat. When he said those words, they sounded like a loving caress.

"Hey, Remy! We're doing shots. You want one?"

With a wink, he shot off the tube and flipped himself backwards in the river. A second later he surfaced and was beside his friends in a flash. Four of the guys lifted a shot in the air, each tanned and muscular, but when Brady tipped his head back for the shot, the others did as well. That was how the rest of the afternoon went. Brady stayed next to me for the most part, but a few times his buddies would call him over for some drinks. I caught curious looks from some of them, but no one approached. They adhered to Brady's not-so-subtle warning.

"I should be annoyed with you right now," I remarked later as my hand dipped into the water and my head rested on the tube, a couple inches from where Brady held on.

"Why?" Brady asked in a monotone as he watched the group behind us. Clarissa and her friends had all waved to Brady when he first joined the group, but seemed content to stay in their own group. It had taken me awhile, but I figured out most of the people weren't students from school. This was their normal partying group. Where they had come from, I had no idea.

"Because you're all protective right now." I lifted my head up and made sure to look him square in the eyes. "You don't have to do that, you know. I don't know if I'm pregnant. Chances are really good that I'm not, and I don't want you being like this just because you feel like you have to be."

He narrowed his piercing eyes and considered me a

moment before he replied, monotone, "Trust me. You having a baby is the last thing on my mind."

"But then...why did you bring it up?"

He shrugged. "I only mention it because I know you're worried about it. I'm not really. I should be, but I'm not."

I opened my mouth, flabbergasted, and then shut it again. He was such a boy; of course he's not worried. He won't be having the nine-month sabbatical.

"And if anything happens, I won't leave you high and dry. You could shoot me and I'd still be knocking on the door with flowers." He stared at me, long and hard. "You're stuck with me, Rayray."

My knees melted and I almost slipped from the tube. Brady shot a hand out and steadied me. Then he leaned closer, an intimate look in his eyes. I held my breath and my eyes widened when he grew even closer till I felt his breath against my cheeks.

Then we heard Clarissa shriek from behind us, "Kid! You made it!"

Brady stiffened before he jerked his head up.

I almost fell forward, but caught myself this time. When I looked Kid was frowning down at a drunken Clarissa. Josh stood behind him and both wore black swim trunks with a whiskey bottle in hand. Neither of them had towels or inner tubes. Josh stood an inch taller, but the familial genes were unmistakable with their dark brown eyes and soft pretty boy features. The only difference was Kid's jet black spiky hair.

"What the...?" Brady stopped short as he caught the look between Kid and Clarissa.

I scooted forward and grasped Brady's arm. Then I jumped on his back. The inner tube be damned. "She likes him. Let them be."

He grasped my arm, but didn't push me off. He just cradled my arm and stared back at them.

"Brady," I urged and clung tighter. "He's not here for me. She wants him."

"He wants you," he wrung out and dipped back down into the river. As the water swirled around my shoulders I wrapped both my legs around Brady's very chiselled waist. Then I placed my mouth near his ear. "I might be carrying your baby so focus on me. Leave them alone."

I felt the air leave Brady as he turned in my arms and legs. We were now face to face and he pulled me forward to tighten my legs around his waist. His hands found my own waist and he squeezed both sides. "Fine," he growled as his eyes lingered on my lips. "But don't expect me to be nice to him."

"He used to be your best friend."

"No, he never was. He's not you."

My eyes clung to his as I held onto him with every bit of strength in my body. When he stood in the air, two things exploded within me. One, I was pretty sure I was in love with Brady. And two...I'd just gotten my period.

It was an awful feeling when something other than water dripped between my legs. I pushed away from him and clasped my legs together. The water erased the feeling and I was tempted to ignore what had just happened.

"Rayna, what are you doing?"

"I—" I couldn't say it, but I had no idea what my plan was. I just needed to get away because I was going to die from embarrassment. If everyone else saw, but could they see? We were in a river.

"Hey, hey." Brady caught up and grabbed my shoulder. He stood closer, intimately close. "What's wrong? What just happened?"

I pressed my forehead to his chest. "I'm not pregnant."

"What?" Brady pulled my forehead away and looked down at me. "What did you just say?"

I couldn't look at him. "I'm not pregnant."

"Wh—huh? But you just said—"

"I got my period, Brady!" I whispered and then groaned as I pressed my forehead to his chest again. I wished to be anywhere except there, anywhere with tampons, no string bikinis, and no water. "I want to die."

When I felt his chest jerk, I thought it was from revulsion. Then when he choked back a snort, I jerked my eyes upwards. He wasn't disgusted. He was hysterical.

"This isn't funny!" I cried out. "Hey, stop it."

He shook his head and covered his mouth. Then he pressed it against my shoulder and tried to muffle his laughter. To no avail. "I'm sorry, Rayna. I am, but you got your period? You shouldn't be embarrassed. You should be relieved. You're not pregnant."

I grumbled, "That really tickles, you know. People are starting to look."

Brady swept me higher for a tighter hug.

"I thought you weren't too concerned about it."

"Are you delusional? Of course I was worried about it. I can't afford a kid. I just said that stuff to relax you. You looked like you could pop a champagne bottle open, you were wound so tight."

"Hey, lovebirds. I don't mean to interrupt the cozy twosome, but we might have something more pressing going on," Matt interrupted. When we looked up, he gestured behind.

Brady cursed when he saw Clarissa between Derek and Josh. She stood with a hand against both of their chests. Each looked fierce, but Josh was taller than Derek by an inch. Both boys were bristling and Kid was behind his cousin. He looked dazed and slightly embarrassed.

Then Clarissa glared at us. "Liddle helb, please?"

"Who the hell is that?"

"That's Kid's cousin." I frowned. "Josh. He was at the police station and he kissed me at that party. He's the one who called you a gorilla."

Brady cursed again. "Not him."

Matt waded beside us. "Derek Stout. He moved here two months ago."

"He's a douche. *That's* why I don't know him."

"What do you want to do?" Matt crossed his arms over his Vikings chest.

"Why are they fighting?" Brady scratched at his jaw. His tribal tattoo seemed to jump out at me as his shoulders bunched in concentration.

"My guess, Clarissa."

"Remy! Brady!" Clarissa called out clearly this time. She fumed, "You're going to let them fight?"

Derek and Josh strained towards each other, but Clarissa seemed to have a firm hold on both.

"She's pretty strong," I noted. Her bicep muscles were showcased. They might've had an inch of fat on them. Barely.

Brady grumbled, "Why should we get in there and duke it out? That poser needs a beat down."

"Derek or Kid's cousin?" Matt asked.

"Both. I don't care."

Matt studied Brady's reserved face for a moment and remarked, "You're awfully upbeat and helpful."

Brady jerked a shrug. "I don't care. Why are you asking me?"

"Because you have beef with Kid and that's Kid's cousin. Plus, it's Clarissa. She's our friend. What do you want us to do? The guys want to wade in, but they don't want to piss you off."

Brady sighed and then yelled, "Clarissa, just let 'em go at it. Get out of the way."

Matt murmured, "its Clarissa."

"That's her problem." Brady gave them a dismissing gesture. "What does she expect when she flirts with every guy around? Some guys don't know her game."

Matt repeated, "its Clarissa."

This time Brady groaned and jerked forward through the water. At his sudden approach, the guys jumped in action. Derek and Josh were quickly held back and Clarissa lost her balance. As she fell in the water Derek yelled at Josh, "What do you care? She ain't yours."

"She ain't yours either!" Josh surged forward, but was held back. I had no idea who held them, but I knew they were Brady's friends as all of them looked at him when he stopped by the group.

Josh strained against his holders, but Derek stopped and watched Brady with a quizzical look. Kid had stepped around Josh so he was beside Clarissa, but while she watched him with a hopeful look, Kid watched Brady. When I saw a sudden jaw clench, I knew that Brady was extremely aware of Kid's focus. He didn't like it.

"Okay. What the hell happened?" Matt asked as he stepped around Brady.

Derek opened his mouth, but Josh cried out, "He's spineless. That's what he is. You don't disrespect women like that."

Derek asked, "Huh? What are you talking about?"

"You swiped her boob, man. You don't do that." Josh strained forward, but I caught the slight relief in his eyes. That's when I harrumphed. The fight was fake. Josh didn't want to fight Derek.

Brady opened his mouth.

The group fell silent.

And he pointed out, "You kissed Rayna at Barthal's. Did you respect her?"

Josh choked and Derek looked even more confused. One of the guys hooted under his breath, "Oh man. He's dead."

"Okay." Clarissa decided to intervene as she stood up. Water glistened down her toned body when she held out her arms again. "Derek did not disrespect me, Josh. He was hitting on me.

I don't need you to come to my rescue especially when it's not even real. You've wanted to fight someone since you came to town, but you're too scared to take on the real person you want to fight."

All eyes went to Brady and the air shifted. It went from entertaining to alarming.

I stood; my period could also be damned.

"Is that what you want?" Brady moved forward a step. "Do you want to fight me?"

Josh held his breath.

Kid froze too, but he waited.

Derek casted dumbfounded looks between the guys.

Clarissa shifted. "Okay, guys. I did not mean for you two to fight. We all know Remy's down for a fight, but since the law can't afford booking him one more time; I'm going to settle this. Brady, I like Kid. You got a problem with that?" As she said this, her eyes skirted towards mine.

"I don't care." Brady moved back a step.

"Wha—huh?"

"Why would I care if you have the hots for him?" Brady further clarified. "I just don't want him to have the hots for Rayna. She's my best friend."

Clarissa twisted her mouth into an ugly smile. "She's a bit more than that, don't you think?"

Brady narrowed his eyes. "Wanna say that again?"

I saw no hesitation when Clarissa narrowed her eyes back, crossed her arms, and stood firmly in her skimpy black bikini. "I know she's a bit more than your best friend. I'm not stupid."

"It doesn't matter what's between her and I. You should be grateful that you're still a friend of mine." Brady was tense as he moved forward again, one slow step. "Now, I'm going to be the friend I need to be for Rayna and I'm going to ask Kid for a ride out of here."

"What?" Clarissa's mouth dropped.

Everyone seemed startled.

I squirmed and clenched my legs tighter.

Brady ignored Kid's incredulous look and asked him, "You drove here, right?"

Kid jerked a nod.

"Can we get a ride? Rayna's place ain't far." Brady was polite and controlled...too much so.

"But...what? What about what I said?" Clarissa cried out.

Brady jerked a shrug. "I could care less. I don't have any idea what that stupid fight was about. I don't care. You have some notion that I'm supposed to care what you do with who. I don't. I don't think I need to spell it out anymore."

"What happened to us before? It's always been you and me on the party scene. I'm your girl those nights and now you start bringing her around?"

"Rayna's always been my best friend. This isn't new, Clarissa. We don't live in a big city. You've gone to school with her since first grade. I don't think I need to explain anything. And right now, she needs a ride out of here. We're leaving."

Clarissa jumped forward and clasped a hand on Kid's rigid arm. "I'm going too."

"What?"

"Hey now..." Derek said and moved forward. "I thought we could hang out? I thought you were into it?"

Josh announced, "She was using you to make my cousin jealous. She was doing *that* to make the King Gorilla jealous and now she's all huffy because it didn't work."

Derek turned towards him. "Why'd you care then?"

"I'm tired of everyone trying to play my cousin! And I'm starting to hate this town," Josh exploded. Then he stepped backwards and grabbed an inner tube. A second later, he sat down and pushed off with the current. "Give 'em a ride, Kid. I came to have fun and that's what I'm going to do from now on."

Kid watched as his cousin sailed away, but moved towards the bank. Resigned.

Brady watched him and stood very still.

I relaxed slightly when I saw the determination in Brady's eyes. I knew he was doing it for me and I hoped that he'd do his best not to start anything in the car. "Are you sure about this?"

Brady jerked a shoulder again. "It'll be fine."

I knew he wasn't sure, but I sighed when I felt another burst between my legs. When Brady touched my arm, I waded where Kid had already climbed up the bank and disappeared in the direction of his car. Clarissa darted ahead of us, but not before shooting a glare over her shoulder.

"I thought she liked me."

"Clary's not real good with girls, but she don't mean everything she just said. I think she actually does like you. She's just hurting right now."

Matt hurried over and asked, "Are you sure about this, Brady?"

Brady asked him, "Do you have a towel or something?"

Matt laughed and held out his bare arms. "I've got my trunks and my booze in that other tube. If you're sure about this, I'm going to catch up with my booze."

"Who's got a towel?" Brady hollered out.

After one was located and handed over, he gave it to me. I knew my face was a deep shade of red, but I stood up and wrapped the towel around my bottom. Everyone else shouted their goodbyes before they took off down the river, eager to catch up with their booze too. The only one left was Derek, who still looked confused.

Brady turned to him. "Don't sweat it. You just got zapped by one of Clarissa's games, but she'll probably be at Barthal's tonight, looking to soothe her hurt ego."

Derek frowned more, but Brady urged me forward. I sighed, my insides all amass. Kid had looked at me once when Brady asked for the ride. I saw the genuine concern and I knew Brady hadn't, but it was going to be unmistakable in the car. He wouldn't like that Kid was worried about me.

When I got into the truck, I had a brief thought that skipping school had not been worth it.

16

The drive to my place consisted of two statements. The first was when Brady instructed beside me in the back seat, "You gotta turn up by Billard's farm. Then left again by the green post."

The second was a tense retort from Kid, "I know where she lives."

I grasped Brady's arm and hoped to prevent any explosion, but was surprised when he clenched his jaw and remained silent.

Clarissa harrumphed once, but was just as silent as the rest of us. And me, I was hoping not to die before we finally arrived. When Kid pulled into the driveway, I didn't stop to think. I shot out of that car and ran through the opened doorway as Grandpa Neil stood there, caught unaware in the doorway. As his foot fell roughly onto the first step, I rushed past and up the stairs to my bathroom. Once I'd taken care of my business, I was in the safe zone. Then I sat there for a moment and went into the red zone—Brady and Kid were both downstairs. Together.

I dressed in a jiffy and ran back downstairs. I burst through the door with my arms up and my elbows flying as I pulled my hair into a ponytail. I knew my cheeks were red from my hurry, but I stopped abruptly at the sight of my grandmother standing in front of Brady, Kid, and Clarissa.

She stood with her hands on hips and a red apron tied over baggy jeans. I cringed when I saw she had pulled out her pepper apron. When she was feeling feisty and hot tempered, she always went for the red peppers. Everyone else rested against the car, but kept wary eyes on her.

When Brady saw I was okay, he turned away. "I'm going to check on Neil. He looked like he needed help in the barn."

Viola snorted and retied the apron's knot behind her back. "Run away, little boy. Run away."

"Grandma," I chastised. When she turned chilly eyes on me, I grimaced and remembered the last time I'd been in the same room with her and Brady. I'd been looking at a pregnancy test and we'd yet to talk about it.

Kid cleared his throat. "Are you okay?" He sent a furtive look towards my grandmother and shuffled awkwardly by his car.

I moved to stand next to Viola. "I'm fine and thank you for the ride."

Clarissa glanced between the two of us, and then turned to watch Brady's retreating back. I watched with a knot in my stomach as her eyebrows furrowed forward like she was figuring something out. She sent a sceptical look towards my grandmother, who was staring with hostility towards Kid and Brady. Then realization hit Clarissa's eyes. I gulped. This wasn't good. She whirled shocked eyes at Brady, but he was already in the barn. When she turned towards me and looked at my grandmother, Viola only stared at Kid like she wanted to eat him up in a carnivorous way.

"What do you mean if she's okay? Why wouldn't she be?" Viola barked out.

I gulped again and dried my sweaty hands on my shorts. I

wanted someone else to speak, but knew no one else would. "Um...I'll tell you later."

Viola narrowed her eyes, looking me up and down. I wasn't sure what she was looking for, but she scoffed, "You have a doctor's appointment in a few hours. Good thing you got home when you did."

"What—oh!" I'd forgotten what my period actually meant. "Uh...um..."

"Rayna?" Kid asked again. "Are you sure you're okay?"

"She's fine!" Clarissa clamped a hand on his arm and forced a smile. "Look at her. She's a shining beacon of health and fertility. Let's go."

"Fertility?" Kid questioned.

"Yep. Like Aphrodite. Let's go."

Viola watched the exchange with narrowed eyes. Then she turned her piercing beacons towards me. When she saw how uncomfortable I was, she looked at Clarissa again. "Now, hold up."

Kid froze. Clarissa sighed in disgust. "We have to go. I'm sorry." She pushed against Kid, but he wasn't budging.

Viola waved a hand towards the barn. "You boy, you go to the barn. You girl, you get inside. I need to feed your skinny behind."

Surprised and then a little offended, Clarissa placed both hands on her hips and brazenly stood in her black bikini. "You don't know me. You don't owe me anything and you can't order me around."

Kid's eyes widened.

Viola threw out her arm. "Give me your keys. Now, you go, Kid."

He threw them over Clarissa's head and tucked tail. They exchanged a glance, hers in mystified anger and his in a silent apology before he darted towards the barn.

"You can stew out here if you'd like, but you heard me. I've got food inside for you. Now, git."

I looked away when Clarissa sent a scorching glare at me. I wasn't going to bend to her will and go against my grandmother. Viola had spoken.

Clarissa snorted in disgust. "Fine. Whatever. It's just a biscuit, right?"

Little did she know.

Viola retied the pepper apron and gestured toward the baby chair. "Girly, you sit there."

"Wha—huh? Are you joking? What is that?"

"It's a chair." I quickly took my normal chair against the wall. I pointed out, "Brady sits there."

"It looks like a baby."

"It is, but it's a chair, too." I felt stupid having this conversation.

Clarissa perched at the edge. "Okay. So what do you have to eat?"

Turning back from the counter, Viola held two glasses and a bottle of bourbon. She placed them on the table. She pushed one towards Clarissa and the other in front of her. Then she poured a small amount in each glass and sat back. Her eyes didn't leave Clarissa's face once, like a hawk.

"What is this? I'm underage. You can't give me alcohol."

Viola smiled. "Something tells me you're already half-doozied up anyways. Besides, if I had a heart to heart with your grandma Bertha, I'm pretty sure you'd be in more trouble than me. She's real tight with Judge Bailor and Deputy Doug."

"You mean Deputy Dog." Clarissa rolled her eyes.

"I call him by his God-given name," my grandmother murmured, deceptively soft, as she leaned forward on her elbows. She nudged the drink closer. "Go ahead. It's just us girls. No one else around."

With a disgusted sigh, Clarissa picked it up and looked

between us. She sniffed the drink, then grimaced and tossed it down her throat.

"There you go." Viola smiled in approval and refilled it.

"What are you doing?" Clarissa's eyes were wide in shock.

"I figure if you can do one, why stop there? Everything's best in doubles. How about it? What's your name?"

"Clarissa."

"Drink up, Clarissa. Let's see who the real partier is."

"What?"

Viola nodded towards the drink and then drank hers slowly, savouring it. She wiped her mouth. "That was good. I'd like another. Your turn, Clarissa."

"Grandma, what are you doing?" This wasn't going to end well.

"Take the drink, Clarissa. Show me how tough you are."

The two stared at each other and I felt a shift in the air.

As I watched, completely baffled, Clarissa reached out with a sturdy hand and took the drink in one gulp. She placed the glass back on the table, jaw firm, and seemed to say 'so there' with her eyes.

Viola poured a third.

Clarissa downed it. Viola took hers and the contest kept going. Each for each until Clarissa started to waver as she reached for her umpteenth drink. She slurred as her eyes began to droop, "Thisss i soo illwegal. Yooou gould go do jawel."

My grandmother straightened in her chair and wiped her mouth. Her voice was clear. "No, honey. I'm not going to jail. I know too much dirt on our town's officials."

"Thenn whiii...?" Clarissa fell back against the chair and winced in pain.

"Why'd I get you drunk?" Viola stood up and put the bottle away. "Because I want you to tell me what you did to my granddaughter. I heard your snide comments out there and I didn't like them. I know your game. You think you're the queen around these parts, but I won't have my grandbaby be a part of your games."

Clarissa hiccupped and squinted at my grandmother. "Whah made you tink awll hurt her? I'm da one gidding hurd. Sthe took Brady away frob me."

"Brady—" Viola started.

Clarissa interrupted with a finger in Viola's face. "Kid likes her, her her more than me, too. I know this, but I hade that. She —Rayna...I don wanna hurd her. I'm hurding too..."

"Don't be one of those girls!" My grandmother pounded the table with both hands. "You don't be one of those girls."

"Huh? Waddya mean?"

My eyebrows bunched together. I had no idea what she meant either.

Viola was passionate. "If Brady and Kid like you then you've got something in you, something more than other girls. I hate to admit it, but Kid's got some backbone." She looked at me. "I still don't want you to have any part of him, but..." She looked at Clarissa again, who was starting to waver back and forth in her chair. "You don't be that girl who plays games. You don't get involved in those bitchy snide comments any longer."

"I'm darry." Clarissa frowned and scratched her head. Her wet hair was now dishevelled, but she still pulled off the sexy look.

"Guys are only going to like you for one thing." Viola pressed as her voice gentled. "They're always going to want sex, but a few will care for you because of you. You keep those around and you listen to me, you have to find yourself some friends of the female sorts."

"I liked Rayna," Clarissa let slip, but gasped and covered her mouth. Her eyes widened in guilt. She whispered, "I'm so darry, Rayna. I wab just...Brady luvs you. I alwayth thought heed come back do me. I'm so darry. I'm tho drunk. I cand believee I'm thaying any of thiss."

"Me neither," I whispered against my own volition.

Viola waved a hand in the air. "You're saying this because I'm making you. Listen to me, whatever beef you have with my granddaughter, you bury it. You make nice with her. You make genuine with her. You do that from now on. You keep away from those girls who are only going to backstab you."

"I don't gibe those bithes the time of day." Clarissa hiccupped again and pressed a hand to her forehead. "How many did I have? I'm tho drunk. I can't beliebe you did this do me."

I could. My grandmother was ruthless at times. Deputy Doug had professed it enough.

Then Clarissa slapped the table and leaned forward. "She had thex. Did you know that? You need do know that. If I'm being right with Rna, I habe to tell you that. She had thex, but I won't tell you wib who. That's for Rayna to thay."

Viola patted Clarissa on the arm. "I know who she had sex with. Honey, there'd only be one boy she'd be foolish about."

"Oh, good. Thaths good. I really think Brady luvs her. I didnna realize it until when he starded bringing her around. She neber came outh before and Brady was always mine, sorta. You can see why I got so jealous, right? I'm jud human. I'm jud...I liked him so much..." She paused and I heard the tear in her throat. When she wiped at her eyes, I felt my own starting to tear up.

Viola cursed and quickly hid the bottle of bourbon. She grasped Clarissa's arm and stood her upright. Clarissa 'wooed' as she stumbled to the side, but grabbed my grandmother's arm for better balance. Then I heard the front door open and slam shut. It opened again to slam shut a second time and then a third time. No voices were heard, but I could hear my grandpa unsnap one of the clips on his coveralls. His boots were shed next. Then Kid and Brady traipsed inside still in their swimming trunks. They had shirts on now and all three males stopped in the doorway to study us.

No one said a word for a moment.

"What are you all looking at?" Viola barked. She shoved Clarissa towards Kid.

"She's drunk." Brady stared. "She wasn't that drunk when we went to the barn."

Kid kept silent.

Grandpa Neil shook his head with a resigned expression and turned for the basement. I was in awe at his smarts.

"We had a little heart to heart," Viola replied curtly and nodded at her. "Get her home. Don't kill each other on the way out. Me and my granddaughter have a doctor's appointment to be getting to."

Brady glanced from the two empty glasses to Clarissa and Viola. He cleared his throat a second later and offered, "I can take her..."

"Like hell you will!" Viola barked, but blanched a second later. "I mean, this is something for the girls to be doing. I'm her grandmother. I should be there for her." She gestured to Kid again. "Go on. Take her out of here. Brady, you go home."

Kid swept intelligent eyes over Viola, me, and Brady. Then he tightened his hold and pulled her after him. Once the door had closed behind them, Brady hesitated for a second, "All due respect, Viola, you've been drinking. I'll take Rayna to the doctor. I'm a part of this anyway."

"You ain't a part of this!" Viola cried out and then paled. "I'm sorry. I'm so sorry, Brady. I know you've got a good heart. I know you care for her. I know you're not like him—maybe I *have* had too much."

My mouth fell open as Viola wiped her eyes and stumbled past Brady up the stairs.

I watched as she left again. A tear pricked at the corner of my eyes and I let out a sob. As I fell to the chair behind me, I tucked my forehead into my knees. Everything was coming down on me. The storm had been held off, but now I couldn't deny what I'd done to my grandmother. She'd gone a little crazy and I couldn't help to wonder if I was the cause of it. Did she push Clarissa because of me? Maybe she was trying to save me a different way? I felt like such a disappointment.

"Hey, hey," Brady soothed as I felt him grasp my knee. He patted it and then combed his fingers through my hair. After a moment, he sat beside me and hugged me against him. "What's wrong?"

I lifted my head and the tears slid down my cheeks. "I think I'm just like my mother. How could I do that? How could I be like her?"

Brady drew back. "Um..."

When I felt another tear come, I sighed and closed my eyes. I'd fought all my life not to be like my mother, but it'd been useless. I was her.

17

We took Brady's car since he'd gotten a ride to the river and my car was still at school. When I checked in at the front desk, I could feel the clerk's disapproval. She was ready to damn me to hell, but I clung to the desk with white knuckles. As she typed in my insurance information, I felt like she could read my plight to the world, like it was branded on my forehead. Devirginized forever.

"You can have a seat and someone will come and get you." Her eyes gave me a bored look, but her voice was cold.

I stiffened and turned to the waiting room. Brady had already taken a seat by the magazines with a pile in the empty chair beside him. When I approached, he gestured to them. "I got all these for you. You know how these doctor places are. We'll probably be here for three hours."

Just as soon as the words left his mouth, the bell rang and we looked over. Frank Stephens walked in with a bleeding Kidrick behind him. As Papa Stephens, stiff in his grey suit, went to the front desk, Kid scanned the lounge and zeroed in on us. Surprise crossed over his face before he made his way towards us.

"You're not going to hit me if I sit within a couple feet of her?"

Brady growled, but ignored him and buried his face inside of a magazine.

"What are you doing here?" I asked Kid when he moved closer.

He glanced over his shoulder. When he saw that his father was still at the front desk, he replied, "Clarissa was so drunk that when I took her home, she fell getting out of the car. I tried to help her and ended up banging my head so hard I was knocked out."

Brady's shoulders jerked. I ignored his muffled laughter. "How is she? Is she okay?"

"Oh, yeah. She's fine. She's zonked to the world. Me, on the other hand, had to stay put because Clarissa's parents wouldn't let me leave until Daddy dearest showed up. They didn't trust me driving. Said I might have a concussion." He cringed again. "I hate this. I feel like an imbecile."

"Because you are." Brady shot him a dark glare, but couldn't contain his smile. "For a tool, you got what you deserved. Drunk Clary knocked you out? Anybody can knock you out."

"Shut up."

"I bet Rayna could knock you out."

"Shut up," Kid growled louder this time. His fist clenched around the wet towel on his forehead.

I flicked the magazine. "Why don't you continue reading? Let the adults talk."

Kid laughed and Brady glared at me briefly, but hunkered back over his magazine. I eyed his father at the counter. "Why are you sitting over here?"

"Because I know he won't come over here. I can't handle too much time with my dad if you hadn't noticed by now."

"He terrifies me." I shuddered.

"He terrifies everyone." Kid grinned from the side of his mouth and then grimaced.

"Not me." Brady looked up and stared at Frank Stephens long and hard. There was no fear, no caution or regret. Nothing.

Watching Brady as he watched Frank Stephens, a shiver passed through my body. This wasn't the comedic or fiery Brady. I was staring at someone who looked like he'd aged thirty years in that moment. He was older, wiser, and stronger. When I glanced at Kid, I was surprised to see a sudden wonderment in his dark eyes. Then he looked at his father and I looked too. Frank Stephens sensed our scrutiny and turned to our direction. I squawked, but he didn't flinch or look away. He stood there, straightened away from the counter, and narrowed his eyes. Cold.

Finally, Brady broke the tension and murmured, thumbing through his magazine, "He doesn't scare me. Not one bit."

"That's not what you said the first night I bailed you out of jail."

Brady shrugged. "I wasn't scared of him."

"You were scared of someone else?"

Brady reflexively looked at Kid, but didn't reply. When I looked over, I knew Kid wasn't going to say anything either. His fierce frown seemed permanently etched into his face and I couldn't handle it anymore. "You guys are driving me crazy! Grow up. You had a fight. Deal with it. You were best friends and then Kid comes back and now you're enemies? Yeah, right."

Brady looked over. "What bee is stinging you in the ass?"

"I am pissed off." I folded my arms and leaned back in my chair.

Brady and Kid both fought off grins, but neither said what I knew they were thinking. I looked like a little kid having a temper tantrum, but I didn't care.

"I'm really mad about this. You guys were so close and now nothing makes sense. It should be a great thing that Kid came back. Instead, you're going gorilla crazy on him and my grand-mother doesn't want me to have anything to do with Kid. I don't know why this is all happening and it's making me go crazy."

"That's the only reason you're crazy?"

It took a second before his statement registered with me and I reacted in the next instant. My fist balled up and I swung wide. My punch was perfectly aimed with my whole body behind it. When I made contact, Brady fell back against the magazine rack, more from shock. Kid gasped and then started laughing so hard he groaned from the pain. As he scrambled for the garbage pail to vomit, Brady reared back and held a hand to his cheek. He watched me cautiously now. "Don't hit me again."

"Don't patronize me again," I retorted. I wasn't stupid. I knew I wouldn't get another punch in. Brady was too fast, but it didn't matter. I didn't want to punch him again. I just wanted to wake him up. This was serious to me and it *was* wreaking havoc in my life.

"Sir, Miss."

We looked up at the approaching nurse dressed in pink scrubs with elephants on them. She was tall, but just as round. However, it was her eyes that caught our attention. She meant business when she added, "There will be no violence in the waiting lobby. There will be no violence at all and if it happens again the police are usually in the emergency room. It won't take long to get them here."

"No, no. We're good. I made her hit me, thought she would hit like a girl and all." Brady saved the day.

The nurse looked from my stormy face to his passive one and arched a waxed eyebrow. "Really?"

"Really."

"Does she hit like a girl?"

"Hell, no." Brady laughed. "It'll be the last time I ask for it again."

"Mmm mmm," she harrumphed. "Don't do it again."

"We won't. Promise." Brady smiled. That was all it took. Sometimes I found it disgusting. The nurse melted, but I caught the awareness in her eyes. She knew he was putting on the charm and she tried to not heed it, but she failed. She plundered. "Well okay, but remember my words."

"We will. No problem there." Brady caught my hand and pulled it into his lap. As he massaged my knuckles, he chuckled again when she left. "Man, Rayray. I can't take you anywhere."

"Says the guy who's been arrested how many times?"

"What are you saying?"

"I've never been arrested. I've never hit anyone except you and you don't count."

Brady nudged me. "There's always a first time, Rayna. You could hit someone someday. I'd enjoy it."

I was about to roll my eyes, but sat up straight when a nurse entered the waiting room. "Rayna Janke?"

"Right here."

"Kidrick Stephens," another nurse called out. She stood right next to mine.

Kid stood hesitantly and wiped one of his hands down the front of his swimming trunks. He glanced from his father to Brady and back to me. Reluctantly he followed me as I led the way with my nurse. Just before we moved into the back area, I turned and looked. So did Kid. We both watched as Frank Stephens slowly sat where Kid had vacated, smack dab across from Brady. Both watched the other. It looked like they wanted to stare each other down.

Kid sighed beside me and touched the back of my arm. "Come on."

"Are you sure...?"

"Yeah. I think they'll be fine." But he didn't sound it.

"Rayna Janke?" My nurse tapped her foot impatiently. She was standing outside a small room.

"Okay. Good luck," I whispered to Kid just as he squeezed my arm in reassurance and then ducked into his own room.

Once inside the nurse took my weight, asked a couple of questions, and ignored my blush when I admitted to being sexually active. "Honey, having sex ain't my business, but let me tell you that it's almost refreshing to see a young girl blushing about it."

I was a little relieved. Then the doctor swooshed in and took a seat underneath me, smack dab in the middle of my legs.

He announced, "So you're here for birth control?"

"Yes," I whispered. Was I being stupid? But I wasn't. Brady and I were best friends, if not...more...and I wasn't going to ignore that we'd had sex twice. We'd probably do it again.

"I see that you are menstruating right now."

I nodded, mute.

He didn't care. "What are you thinking?"

"Uh..."

"A lot of girls your age use a monthly cycle of pills. Would you like that? Any particular brand?"

"One that...works?"

He nodded to himself and made a few notes in his chart. "I see that you were in here for a physical not long ago. Everything checked out then and you've been sexually active since?"

I nodded again.

"Did you want to be checked for sexually transmitted diseases?"

Uh...

"Listen, this is what I'll do. You need to wait a few more weeks before we should check you for STDs. Right now here's a prescription for a birth control pill that I commonly prescribe. It should work out. If you wish to change or have concerns, come back for another visit. Until then, anything else, Rayna?'

I was surprised he didn't need to check the chart for my name.

"Uh..."

He stood, smiled politely, and extended his hand. "Anything else, if your parents or guardians have any questions, just call me. Okay?"

"Okay," I whispered and held onto the prescription paper he'd given me.

When I left, I glanced towards Kid's, but it was still closed. Brady's head was stuffed in some magazine while Frank Stephens watched him. I would've assumed that he'd look at Brady with loathing or hatred, but it wasn't there. I didn't understand it. Instead, the older man watched him with a guarded look.

I bypassed both and went into the pharmacy where no one else waited. When I gave my information and handed over the prescription, the pharmacist barely glanced at me before he started filling it.

"Hey." A hand clamped on my arm.

I screamed.

"It's just me," Kid soothed. He patted my arm again and frowned. "Are you okay?"

"Yeah. Just...I thought I was the only one in here." Brady hadn't heard me so I relaxed. No further fight was to be had. "You scared me, that's all."

"Oh." Kid frowned again, itched his head absentmindedly, and then handed over his own prescription.

"You're okay?" I was embarrassed at how raspy my voice sounded. Why couldn't I be normal once in my lifetime?

"Huh?"

"I mean, you were bleeding. You don't have a concussion or anything? What meds are you getting?"

"Personal much?" Kid mused, half grinning. "I'm just kidding, Rayna. I'm fine. Doc cleaned up some cuts I got from my car and then I was smart enough to ask for a refill of my allergy stuff. You?"

"Same. Allergies."

He nodded easily and then glanced over his shoulder. "That's a little eerie, isn't it? When my dad first found out that I got punched by some kid, he went berserk. And then, I don't get it. He just dropped the charges."

"What about the second time? Deputy Doug told me that your dad was in a tither. He wanted Brady charged to the fullest."

"Nah." Kid shrugged again and scratched his shoulder this time. "My dad's mostly talk. I think he kind of likes Brady, something about how 'he's a man and he stands up for himself'. I don't get it. He hates women and he doesn't seem to like you."

"I've noticed. He hates me." I shivered.

"Which is funny because he loves to...you know...with women, but he loathes them outside of the bedroom."

I marvelled at how careless he sounded. He was talking about his father. Who talked about their dad like that? I didn't even know my dad.

"Um...did your dad ever know my mom?"

Kid snorted and turned to watch the pharmacist. "Probably. My dad seems to know every female around these parts."

"No, I mean...has he ever talked about my mom or anything?" I hated how I couldn't even ask a simple question. Then I did a very Viola-like thing and cursed under my breath.

Kid glanced at me. "Did you just swear?"

"No," I lied, wide eyed.

"It's okay. You can curse, you know. I mean, you're in love with Brady. Do you know who Brady is?"

I froze in place and couldn't look away from Kid's teasing eyes nor could I meet them. "What did you just say?"

I couldn't breathe.

Kid laughed again and threw an arm around my shoulder. He jerked me against his side. "I'm teasing, Rayna, but you ARE best friends with the douche. He swears all the time. Actually, thinking about it, he's not that bad when you're around." His hip bumped mine. "Good job, Janke. What other powers do you have?"

"I don't have powers."

"I'm kidding. I just meant...never mind." He moved slightly away and scratched at his arm.

"You keep itching yourself. Do you have a rash?"

"Oh. No. I just do that sometimes when I'm around my dad. He has that power over me."

I stared, nonplussed, and narrowed my eyes. So your dad's never spoken about my mom?"

"Nah, but who knows. He gets around. He likes to chase skirts, but I don't know why. It's only caused him to become a bitter old man. I don't know about hating you, but he really hates your grandmother. My dad's messed up. Does your mom live around here? Isn't she in Florida or something?"

I swallowed painfully. "She moved to Florida before I was born."

"Oh. So you were born down there? I thought you lived up here all your life."

"I have. My mom thought my grandparents would do a better job raising me so they took me in when I was a baby."

"Oh." Kid shifted on his feet, uncomfortable. Then he relinquished, "My dad did the same thing. Or, well...I guess he didn't give me up, but he let my mom raise me. He didn't fight her about it. They divorced when she found out she was pregnant with me. My mom told me that she didn't want me to be raised with my dad as a role model. He was always having affairs, but after they got divorced, he went nuts. Or so I've heard. Some woman in the grocery store told me how he had an affair with a new woman every week when my mom divorced him."

I did the math and realized, "That must've been when my mom left for Florida. She'd been down there six months before I was conceived."

"Really?"

"My grandma told me that when I asked who my dad was. She said it isn't anyone around here because, 'Your momma'd been gone half a year before you were put in her belly'. I was little back then. I didn't understand that my dad was someone I'll never know. My grandma still gets weird when I ask about him."

Kid turned and stared at me directly. "So you don't know who your dad is? Your mom never said anything?"

"I've spoken to my mother six times in my life and they're always awkward phone conversations. She came once for Christmas, but Grandma wouldn't let her stay at the house so the dinner was really uncomfortable. She left an hour later."

"Why'd your mom give you up?"

I shrugged. "I don't know. That's something else my grandma won't talk to me about, but I've always felt it's because my mom has problems with men. Like she sleeps with them all the time. My mom caused problems for this town. She didn't want me being raised around that environment."

"Huh," Kid grunted, still perplexed. "At least your mom did the right thing and let your grandparents raise you. Sounds like she was trying to do what was best for you. My dad is never at the house when I've been around. He's either traveling for business or off with 'some secretary.' I think my mom had enough of it and just moved away."

"Yeah. That was when..." ...when we'd started to get close. I remembered those days. Kid had been Brady's best friend and I'd always been left behind. Then something changed and Kid started teasing me. He asked me to hang out with them. We'd even gone to the movies once without Brady. I'd felt guilty at the time and felt even more now.

Kid coughed. "That was back then. Things are sure different now."

Yeah...

"Rayna Janke?" The pharmacist waved from the cash register.

After I paid, it felt weird knowing that I had birth control in my pocket. When I looked towards the waiting lounge, I saw Brady with his head still in a magazine. Viola should've been there. I would've gone through that moment in my life holding my grandmother's hand. Then I looked at Frank Stephens, who sat stiffly and regally in his chair. His hands seemed to be resting on the sides of his chair with his fingers curled inwards towards the wood. He didn't fool anyone. He didn't want to be there and he looked down his nose at everyone around him. Even the clerk noticed it.

Kid's name was called next.

I didn't know what to feel, not with Kid. He went away and things were fine, but now he was back and everything seemed up in the air. I'd never really talked about my mom like that to anyone.

When Kid turned around with his allergy medication in hand, he stopped and stared at me. "So..."

I bolstered up my courage. "Does your dad go to Florida for business?"

"Oh yeah. All the time," Kid replied, distracted. He started scratching again.

I felt my stomach drop and then Brady appeared at the door. "Rayna? You got what you need?"

I couldn't look away from Kid, who seemed jumpy now. "Uh...yeah..."

18
———

Was Frank Stephens my father? Was he the reason why my mother left town? Did he banish her? Did he go down there and make love to her? Did my grandmother know? And Brady...what would Brady say? He hated Frank Stephens. Would he hate me, too?

I rested my head against the school bus window and looked out on the way to school. I didn't want to think anymore. All bad, it was all bad.

As I walked into school, I saw another bad situation waiting by my locker dressed in tight blue jeans. I was surprised that Clarissa only wore a loose white tee shirt over it. With her hair pulled into two braids that hung on each side of her head, I knew she was still every boy's fantasy, much more than me as I was dressed in jean shorts, blue tank top, and my damp hair grazed my shoulders. I always felt so dowdy compared to Clarissa, but this time she was the one who looked self-conscious as I approached.

"Hey." She looked at me and hesitated.

"Hey." I didn't move to open my locker. This wouldn't take long anyway.

"So..." She took a deep breath. "Um...I feel really stupid about yesterday. I mean with the river and how I acted really, really stupid with your grandmother later. I shouldn't have done what I did. I apologize."

"For using me to get Kid to the river? Or for using me to try to use Kid to make Brady jealous? Or for how you still love Brady?"

"Okay. I got it. I did a lot of stupid things yesterday," Clarissa rushed out. She kept glancing up and down the hallway.

"Are you embarrassed to be seen with me now? You invited me to skip school with you yesterday."

"Because you're ripping into my ass!" She blew a deep breath out and shook her head. "I officially apologize for using you, for being jealous of you, and for being a crappy friend. I feel bad about it all. Trust me. I *really* felt bad at three in the morning when I was vomiting. Your grandma is a fierce lady."

She didn't know the half of it.

"If it's any consolation, she stayed in bed the rest of the day too. I don't think it was from the booze, but I know she didn't feel good." She'd stayed in bed when Brady dropped me off after the hospital and she hadn't emerged by the time I left for school this morning.

Clarissa pursed her lips and scanned the hallways again. "So are you staying here today? It's going to be boring."

I shrugged and opened my locker. Our classes weren't even being taught anymore so I didn't need any books, but I still felt bereft without one. "I guess. I feel weird skipping again. Look at what happened yesterday." I wanted her to go away. She reminded me of bad things.

"Yeah, but yesterday was an aberration. It won't happen again. We're not going tubing today—"

I couldn't hold it in anymore. "What do you want, Clarissa? I've learned that you usually have an agenda."

Score one for me.

Clarissa stood taller and then flashed a wolfish grin. "Look at you. You've grown fangs. Little bunny fangs, but fangs none-theless. I'm sure they'll draw blood on someone. Maybe someone with dementia, but still."

I flushed. "You don't have to make fun of me."

"Sorry, sorry, sorry," Clarissa immediately apologized and actually looked it. "I went into automatic defense. I'm used to it when I deal with the other girls here. Sometimes I forget that you're not like everyone else. It's refreshing. It's why I really AM sorry because I really do like you. I didn't think I would, not for years. Brady always talked about you even when he and I used to hook up, but I just thought you were some stupid novelty to him. Then you finally came around and I saw it. I saw why he likes you so much. You're...I don't know how to explain it. You're not like anyone else."

That was...I grabbed a book and hugged it to my chest. "Okay...well, I'm going to go."

"Where are you going? I'm in your first period and our teacher closed the class last week. We don't have class."

"I'll go to the library then." Libraries were safe, lots of corners to hide in.

Clarissa nodded with a knowing look in her eyes. "Listen, I'm heading out to the Corner Diner. Everyone should be hanging there most of the day so if you want, you could come any time. It don't matter. I'll probably be there all day wasting time."

She started to walk backwards, towards the parking lot.

"I'm still staying in school today."

"Okay. See you...sometime then..." Then she was gone with a small wave. And why did I feel like I should've gone with her? Clarissa had proved I couldn't trust her. She still had feelings for Brady. For that reason alone, I shouldn't be friends with her. Then why did I feel like I was missing out on something?

"I'll have fun today. I don't need classes to have fun..." And I didn't so I went to the library and found a corner to hunker down. A part of me did feel foolish because seniors didn't have to be in school for the last week, but the truth was that I didn't know where else to go. Brady worked during the day and I went to school. I suppose I could've stayed home, but I shuddered at that situation.

Later when the last bell of the day rang, I lifted my head and yawned. I'd read most of the day, fallen asleep a couple times, and emerged only once to find something to eat. After that I had stayed put and eventually curled back into a ball on the floor.

Now, as I was headed home, I passed the Corner Diner and glanced over. Sure enough, Clarissa was right. The parking lot was overflowing with cars and a few trucks filled with water tanks. Some guys held water balloons behind their backs and I sighed in slight amusement. At least I wasn't there where I would've gotten drenched. Brady was probably there. Brady was probably the one who had the idea.

When I got home, I was surprised to see the front door propped open by a potted plant. The screen door flapped open briefly every now and then, but as I stepped inside, I was met with siesta music and the smell of baked jalapenos. My grand-mother sashayed around the kitchen with the pepper apron on and her hair swept up in a high ponytail. She looked showered and refreshed.

"Hey." I was cautious. I never knew what I was going to get now.

"Hi!" Viola turned with a bright smile on and a forced twinkle in her eyes.

My heart fell. It was all a show. "How are you?"

My grandmother chuckled heartily as she produced a pan of muffins from the oven. "I'm good. I'm good. Why wouldn't I be good?"

I let my bag drop from my fingers. "Are you okay?"

"What—huh?"

I'd never seen my grandmother like this. She was the kind to tackle whatever demon or obstacle lay in front of her and hoot and holler as she did. This Viola looked like the type that I knew she detested. She was faking. And she was bad at it.

"You're singing and you're dancing and you're baking?"

Viola deadpanned, "Yeah. Why?" Her pan of muffins didn't waver in her jalapeno potholders.

"I had sex with Brady." I took a deep breath. Let's get this started.

My grandmother took a breath and then another one. The muffins started to waver now.

I pressed, "Ever since you found out, you've been avoiding me. You haven't wanted to talk to me. How is that normal when a parent-like figure is avoiding the teenager? I'm supposed to be the one avoiding you. Not the other way around. Now you're dancing around and acting like everything is hunky dory? It's not."

As Viola swallowed visibly, I watched how the muffins almost dropped.

I cried out, "I am sorry that I have shamed you SO much that you can't even talk to me. I am sorry that you can't bear to be in the same room as me except when Clarissa was here. I am sorry that I turned out just like my mother and you've had to deal with all this past stuff again. I am so sorry that...I don't even know what anymore. I'm sorry for disappointing you and for not being the perfect daughter that my mother never was!"

The muffins dropped.

I brushed away some tears. "And you don't even know what's been going on in my life. Brady and I had sex. Then Clarissa acted like my friend only to not really be my friend. There are these other girls who hate me. Kid—what do I even say about him? Brady hates him. You hate him, but I don't. Then he tells me all this stuff about his dad. Is Frank Stephens my father? And if he is, then why does he hate me so much?"

I gulped for a breath and wiped away more tears before I looked at my grandmother. She stood there frozen with the pan still in her hands. Her eyes were glazed over like she was seeing a stranger.

I took another shuddering breath.

Viola choked out, "Are you saying—are you in love with Brady?"

My eyes went wide. "That's all I get?"

She took another deep breath and slowly placed the muffin pan on the table. "So...you two had sex."

"Yes."

She nodded with her lips pursed and a look of concentration on her face. "Okay. So...have you had sex again?"

I nodded. Then I rushed out, "But I have my period so I know I'm not pregnant. I went to the doctor and I have birth control now. Just in case, you know."

"So..." She looked in pain. "Are you two a couple?"

"I..." I had no idea what to say. Were we? We hadn't talked about it. I loved him. I knew that, but that was about it. I hung my head and whispered, "We haven't really talked about it except that Brady once said he couldn't handle the changes."

My grandmother always knew what to say, but this was the one time I saw that she had no clue. A myriad of emotions flickered over her face. "So...I am sorry, Rayna. I know that I'm supposed to be the perfect and wise grandma who knows what to say to you, but I don't. Do I like the idea of you and Brady? No. Am I torn because I know that you're my granddaughter and you've finally given yourself to a boy? Yes. I want to hug you, soothe you, and tell you that everything is going to be okay. But I can't. Do I love you? Of course I do. Do I know what to do to make everything alright? If I did, things wouldn't be this screwed up. I would've known what to say the first time I found out."

My eyes were brimming in tears as I looked at her. I saw the torment on her face and my heart matched it. It tore at my insides when I whispered, "So you don't hate me?"

"Why would I ever hate you?"

"Because I'm just like her." A sob ripped out of me.

"What? You are *not* like your mother. Well, you kind of are, but not in the way you think."

Tears fell freely down my cheeks, but I paid them no attention. "Did she sleep around? Was she really empty inside or really lonely or what? I've been trying to wrap my mind around it and I can't figure it out. I can't figure out why she would do that. I have no urge to do that. Brady was just because..." I couldn't say it.

Viola finished, "Because you love him?"

I looked away. Could I tell her that?

My grandmother stepped forward. "So you think that because you slept with Brady you're like your mother?"

For some reason I couldn't speak anymore. I nodded instead.

She hung her head. "You are like your mother in only two ways." She looked up and pierced me with those eyes now. "You look like her and you fell in love with the wrong man."

What—huh?

"I know the rumours. I know what everyone says about your mother, but I'm telling you that those rumours are just rumours. They are complete lies."

It was my turn to again—"What?"

"Your mother never slept around. I know you think she did. Everyone talks about it, but it's not true. She was keeping herself, much like you, for the one man she loved. It just didn't happen the way we all wanted it to be. But she didn't sleep around, Rayna. She wasn't like that."

Again—wha....huh?

19

"**B**ut you said..." I realized that my grandmother had never said anything about my mother sleeping around. She just said that she had caused enough problems around town.

I'd assumed.

Viola clamped her mouth shut and grabbed the wall. I shot to her side, but she shook her head with her eyes closed and pushed me away. "I can stand on my own."

A second later, her face cleared of all expression.

I stood back in awe.

Then my grandmother stood firm once again. "Your momma wasn't a slut or whore. She wasn't like that and neither are you. You both just fell for the wrong men. I stand by what I said. And you need to stay away from Brady. He's not good for you."

I couldn't believe what I was seeing or what I was hearing. Everything I believed was a lie. I thought my mom was a certain way and now I found out that she wasn't? Then the room started to spin and I reached out for the wall too. I found a chest instead. From a distance I realized it was Grandpa when I heard his muffled voice, "You didn't need to say it like that, Vi."

"Look at her. She can't handle it."

Grandpa curled an arm around my shoulders and held me against him. "She's in shock. She'll need to hear the rest."

"She can't handle it all," my grandmother replied from a distance. She sounded regretful.

I tried to focus, but found everything starting to get blurry. A moment later, Grandpa Neil lifted me in the air and took me upstairs. When he laid me on my bed, I barely noticed anything. My eyes were open, but the only thing I saw was a picture. It was of Brady and me. Our arms were wrapped around each other. We'd been wrestling that day. Viola took out a camera and yelled at us to stop. We'd frozen in place, smiled, the camera flashed, and Brady flipped me over his back.

A tear slipped down my cheek as I stared at that picture. It had been taken last summer. Brady had graduated that morning and told me that he was going to stick around for another year. I'd been so happy because I wasn't going to lose him.

He'd been my rock. He had steadied me for so long, but everything was different now. I had a gut feeling it was only the beginning. It would get worse, much worse.

Then I heard his voice. "Hey."

I didn't react. My eyes were glued to the picture, but I felt him approach from the door. He sat on the side of my bed and took my hand. "I saw you drive by the café and came to get you, but what's going on? Viola's crying downstairs and baking at the same time. That can't be good. Your grandpa didn't even look at me. He's just sitting on the couch and staring at the television. There's some soap on. And now you..."

I rolled on my back and stared at Brady. He loomed above me. His tribal tattoo stood out on his arm underneath his sleeveless black shirt. I felt like it was shouting its existence at me. When I touched it, I grazed it with my nail.

"Why did you get this?"

He retrieved my hand. "Come on."

"You never told me."

He looked away. "There's a lot I don't tell you, Rayna."

"You told me once that you tell me everything."

"I lied." He hung his head.

"Everyone lies."

"Hey, come on." He twisted to look at me again, but I looked at that frame instead.

I mumbled, "I felt safe that day."

"What day?"

"I've never really felt safe, Brady, but I did that day because I knew you'd still be here. I'm not safe, though. I thought I could handle my last year, but things are so complicated. I never knew how complicated it could get, but it is. Everything is a lie. We all lie. I lie to you even."

Brady sat there for a couple of seconds in silence. Then he asked, "What do you lie to me about?"

"About how I feel about you. I lied to myself about how I've always felt about you." There. I'd let the cat out of the bag. He'd have to bite, but....I waited as my heart pounded.

Nothing.

Brady cleared his throat. "Is this all because of your mom?"

When I heard his answer, I closed my eyes and felt something tear inside of me. I rolled away from him until there was a foot between us.

"Viola told me that you're the wrong guy. I can't be around you anymore."

"What? Oh come on. What are you talking about? It's Kid that she doesn't want you around."

Frank Stephens could be my father. "I don't think Kid's a problem anymore."

"Rayna." Brady scooted close to me, but his legs didn't touch mine. He made sure. He didn't want to be too close. "What's going on with you? I feel like I'm losing you or something."

I looked at him finally and then sat up when I saw the nervousness in him. His blonde hair had been wetted down so it was a sharp contrast between dark and light, but his eyes were the best liars. He looked concerned, genuinely concerned, but I saw that he was hiding. When I looked closer and inspected him as he always seemed to inspect me, I saw that there was a lot there.

"What are you keeping from me?"

"Noth—," he started to lie, but stopped. "I keep some of my past from you. I don't tell anyone that stuff, Rayna. It doesn't mean anything about our friendship."

"Friendship," I said the word. It felt bitter in my mouth. "We are not just friends and I told you that I've been lying about my feelings. Why didn't you ask about my feelings?"

A wall fell over his eyes. "I've been thinking about this, and I don't think...ah, hell. I don't know. I just think that with Clarissa going after you and those other girls who made you cry—"

"You are not taking it back! You can't. We had sex, Brady. I gave myself to you, and I did it because it was you. You have been the one pushing it. You're the one so protective of me with Kid. You're the one hanging all over my inner tube. You're the one that calls me in the morning when you get arrested. You're the one who doesn't want other guys to look at me. You're the one who wants to kiss me after you get out of jail. You're the one who takes me to the doctor so that I can get birth control pills. *You're* the one, not me! So don't you dare change things now because if you do, I will lose it. I can't have one more thing change on me."

Whoo. I fanned myself, but kept glaring at Brady.

Suddenly my door was thrown open and my grandmother stood there. Her chest was heaving and her eyes were wild. Her greying hair was frayed with strands flailing in the air. She took two hurried steps inside before she stopped abruptly and stuck her jalapeno potholders on her hips.

Brady and I looked at each other, but neither said a word. I didn't dare. I was still heaving from my speech to Brady and my grandmother looked like she would let loose in a second.

"Brady," Viola spoke in a shrill voice. "You need to leave."

"Oh. Okay. Rayna, I'll call you later?"

Brady started to get up from the bed, but stopped when my grandmother spoke further, "No, Brady. I mean, if the two of you are having intercourse, then you can't come over here anymore. You can't be in Rayna's life."

My mouth fell open. So did Brady's, but then his eyes narrowed. "You got a reason for this decision? You can't keep us apart. She's an adult."

"It's obvious that you two plan on continuing to have sex and I can't have that. I have to look out for Rayna. You can't be in her life. I can't trust that it won't happen again even if you promise me that."

Slowly, I stood up. "He is my best friend."

Viola stared at me. "Brady is wrong for you. You can't be around him."

"He's my only friend."

"Wrong? What the hell?" Brady stood and clipped out, "I haven't hurt her. Yes, I shouldn't have pushed for sex, but you don't know what I was feeling then. You don't know how scared —" He stopped suddenly and looked down as his fists clenched and then unclenched.

I watched, fascinated. They kept clenching and unclenching. Then I looked at his face. His eyes were tightly closed. His jaw mirrored his hand movements, clenching and then clenching again. He was so tightly strained. I was afraid when the control would leave him...

"I can't explain it. I'm sorry, Brady. I....," her voice faltered on a sob. "I am so sorry it has to be this way. I wanted you two to be close. I wanted you to grow up with each other and lean on each other. I just never thought..." She took a shuddering breath. "I never thought it'd end like this. I never thought in a million years...I mean...Brady's so different than my baby."

I should've been falling apart. I should've been wailing, pleading, or threatening. I wasn't doing any of it. I stood there and stared at the two people who I loved most. They were both falling apart and it was because of me. It was then that I realized that I had checked out. I was watching a show play out in front of me. I was the audience, but I had no bearing on the show's content. Or...maybe I was starting to figure things out, maybe for the first time.

"I can see Rayna if I want," Brady argued though he wouldn't look up.

My grandmother shook her head. Her hair strands flew around with the jalapeno potholders in the air. She choked out, "I can't. I can't risk it. I'm sorry, Brady. I love you like my own grandson. I do, but I have to think of Rayna first. This is detrimental to her."

"What? The sex? Are you for real?" The fury was right there, just swimming under his control. He took a step closer. "Rayna's going to be with another guy then. She's going to have sex, but he won't care for her like me. He won't be the guy for her that I can be!"

Everything seemed to slam against me. I felt myself hurled back into reality and it hurt. I whispered out, "How dare you stand there and say those things."

Viola cried out, "I'm sorry, baby. I am, but I can't..."

My eyes were glued on Brady. "You just sat on my bed and talked about our 'friendship.' You just tried to hide from me, hide from what we've become, and now when you're faced with losing it, you do this? Look at you. What are you going to do? Punch my grandmother? Because she said we couldn't be together when you're the one who was going to tell me the same thing?"

"Oh." Viola hustled back a step.

Brady faced me squarely. A storm of emotions flew across his face, but I saw the last one. Regret.

"Tell me you weren't going to say that. Tell me I'm wrong. You're not fighting against something that you were going to do anyway."

"Rayna," he started.

"Tell me!"

He broke, "I can't. I just..."

"You are such a hypocrite!" I screamed and then I grabbed the first thing I saw. I threw my pillow at him. When it bounced off him and he didn't deflect it, I threw the other one. Then I threw my blankets, a book, and I caught the frame in my hand. I reared back, ready to throw it, but stopped myself. I stopped with my chest heaving and stared at it in my hand.

He allowed me to breathe that day and now it was all gone.

When I looked up, I didn't care what Brady saw in my eyes. My heart was broken. "Get out. Get out. Get out!"

"Rayna, come on..."

"Out!" I screamed again and this time I chucked the picture frame at him. He ducked and it shattered against the door.

I fell on the bed. The pain was so strong. I didn't notice when Brady left until I finally looked up and only saw my grandmother. She held a hand to her chest and watched me in concern. I could barely stomach her concern, not now, not after everything she'd lied to me about.

It was then that I asked, "So is Frank Stephens my father...or Brady's?"

I sat there for a full minute; of course it was probably only a few seconds, but it felt like an hour. My grandmother stared aghast while I sat there, tear drenched. I felt like I was facing death. The idea of Brady and me being kin...or more...I shuddered and clamped my hands closed.

It was the only thing that made sense.

"Whose father is he because with the way you're acting, he's got to be one of our dads. So who is it?" I sounded firm, but my insides were turning inside and out. When I felt vomit come up my throat, I closed my eyes tightly and forced it back down. I couldn't go there...I couldn't deal with that....not knowing...

Finally I heard, "He's Brady's."

She whimpered like she was ashamed. I was disgusted and I turned away.

I took a breath.

"And me? Who's my father?" I'd never been told. I barely even knew my mother and I'd never asked. I wanted to know, but if it meant what I feared it meant I knew no amount of vomiting could empty my insides. I loved Brady. I loved him so much and if those words that she might utter passed through her lips.... I sat there paralysed. They were the hardest words I've ever had to wait for.

Viola whispered, "I don't know who your father is."

"Explain." I didn't blink. I didn't ponder. I needed to know.

"Your mother was one of the most devout girls I've ever known. I was almost ashamed."

I shot to my feet and exclaimed, "I don't want to hear this! I want to hear who my father is!"

"I'm trying to tell you. I have to explain, Rayna. I've got to explain it all or it won't make any sense."

The need sat on me as if it was a separate entity.

Viola kept going, painfully, "You know I'm not no religion nut. Neither is your granddad, but he believes. I don't know what I did right, or maybe what I did wrong, but your momma grew up going to church. She wanted it. She asked every Sunday to go there. We went, but when she could drive, she drove herself. That was how it was."

She took a breath.

"I have never claimed to be the best mother. Ever. But with your mother...she was a lot like you. I felt like she raised me. I don't know what genes you girls got, but what's done is done.

She ain't anything like me. She grew up going to church. She planned for the future. Leann liked bake sales. I have no idea why and then..." She drew in a quaking breath. "He came along. He was young. He was good looking. He was rich. He was on the rise."

"Frank Stephens?" There was nothing in me when I said his name, my possible father. I almost loathed him.

Viola nodded. "When Frank first hit the scene, he was dashing. I'll admit. He had a charisma about him. And he was funny. He could charm anyone. I was a bit taken with him myself, but that's all an old lady does. She looks at what might've been without a few years attached, but it don't matter. It all changed when he met Leann. Of course, he was married by then. Newly married, but he wasn't the marrying sorts. Everyone knew it."

My fingers pressed into my hands. Blood seeped from them.

My grandmother continued, "He took one look at her and thought he had the granddaddy of all challenges. Truthfully, I don't know who won that battle. Leann had stopped talking to me by then. She wanted to grow up in the church. I wasn't having none of it. I wanted her to live. I wanted her to have babies. I wanted her to laugh, to cry, to get her heart broken. I wanted her not to have any regrets when she reached my age, but it didn't matter. She was so stubborn and the two of us didn't see eye to eye."

"Is he my father or not?"

Viola surrendered, "I don't know. Maybe. Hell, no. I don't know. I just know that he wanted your mother so badly and things got bad. Frank was pressuring Leann to have an affair with him. He said he loved her, he wanted to be with her, he'd leave his wife, etc., etc., etc. They all say the same things. It don't matter because in the end, if she gave in or not, Leann decided to go to Florida for some reason. She said something about maybe finding salvation down there. I don't know what that meant. I just know that Frank Stephens was heartbroken, if he could be heartbroken."

"What then?" I knew it didn't end there.

Viola seemed to crumble before my eyes. She'd been standing near the door and now she looked like the world conquered her. As she folded to the floor, she choked on a sob. "I have no idea."

"You must!" It couldn't end like that.

"I don't!" she cried in return and held her hands in front of her. She looked at them like she didn't know what to do with them. "I wish I knew. I wish I understood it all, but I don't. All I know is that she brought you up here about a year and half later. She asked us to raise you because it wasn't safe for you. Your momma and I don't have the kind of relationship where we tell each other things. We don't say nothing to each other. You don't think it eats at me? It does! I have a daughter who I don't know nothing about, but I got one thing from her. I got you! I got you, Rayna!"

I sat there and watched my grandmother. She'd been the fiercest woman I'd known all my life. She could've stared a bull down most days, but not today. As she sat on my floor, I knew my grandmother was crying for more than not knowing my father. My mother was in the room with us. Her presence was so strong, so powerful, that I looked towards my window and wondered if I'd see her.

"I don't know who your father is. I'm sorry, Rayna. I know it's so awful. Only your mother knows that and we haven't heard from her in six years."

I didn't know what to say. I'd been so terrified and then nothing. I got no answers. "What do I say to Brady?"

Viola shook her head.

I couldn't not tell him. I couldn't let him go on with his life not knowing why we couldn't be in each other's lives, much less knowing that I loved him.

"How do you know that Frank Stephens is his father?"

Viola looked me straight in the eye and spoke in a clear voice, "Because he brought him to me. He showed up here one night and said the mom didn't want him. He was his, but he wanted us to give Brady to Leann. He wanted her to raise his son. He didn't know where she was. He didn't know anything at that time except that she'd left. He kept asking us where she was, but we never told." Viola nodded with tears on her cheeks. She repeated, "Brady came from an affair that he'd had when he was chasing Leann. At that time, Frank was still with his wife. He hadn't divorced her yet, but it didn't matter. Everyone knew Frank Stephens was a skirt-chasing bastard, but on paper he was squeaky clean. It was always rumours. A kid would've been proof that he was the bastard everyone said. I went..." She took a deep breath and composed herself. "I went crazy when he offered Brady to us. I lost it. I'd been patient with him, but when he said that about a child—I didn't care if he'd been the devil, I would've taken a pitchfork to him."

I watched as she remembered that night. Her hands curled slowly into fists. Her voice raised, stronger and angrier.

She seethed, "I snatched that baby out of his arms and I ordered him to get the hell away from us. I told him to stay away from Leann and stay out of this child's life. He had no right to act like God. He had no right to pass along a child like the child had no soul. No right!" She waited until she had calmed a bit. "He didn't give one damn about Brady. Not one care for him. I told him that Leann never wanted to see him, and if he ever tried to claim Brady as his son, I would go to the police."

I could almost see that night enfold. A younger looking and trimmer Frank Stephens stood at the door with a baby in his arms. My grandmother was on the other side, hearing what he had to say with horror.

Viola finished, "Frank Stephens didn't like anything I said.

Something snapped in him too. After that night, he went crazy. I think he might've realized it really was over with Leann. I don't know. I didn't care, but he went through a host of women after that. Eventually his wife found out and they got divorced. By that time, she'd already had Kidrick, but it didn't matter. The damage was done."

"What about all those things about Mom? If she only slept with him, why does everyone say she's a whore?"

"He wanted to hurt us...me really. He knew how your momma really was, so he said the opposite. He knew it'd hurt us if people thought Leann was a loose woman. It did at first, but then I got mad. I got all my friends to freeze Frank Stephens out of anything and everything. Those women knew your mother. She'd gone to church with them. She'd baked beside them. They knew what really happened and I'll tell you that damage can be planned at a monthly Ladies Aid meeting."

She laughed to herself. "We knew what to do. Each of them went to their husbands and Frank Stephens was frozen out of every business venture he hoped to have. Any banking loans he wanted were cancelled. He was denied membership at the two country clubs he wanted into. Pretty soon he stopped saying those things about your momma, but it didn't matter. People talked. They gossip, they'll always gossip. But Frank Stephens was put in his place."

There was so much history in that room. It swirled around me and it hurt. It hurt Brady. It hurt my grandmother. For the first time, I wondered how it hurt my mother.

"I threatened Frank that I'd go to the police if he ever tried anything with Brady. I knew if he was willing to give the child away, he couldn't be trusted to raise him. I ended up going to the station anyway. Deputy Doug was working as the dispatcher that night. I told him what had happened. I had Brady with me and the two of us figured to keep it quiet. He had proof to bring against Frank if he ever did anything, but that's when Brady went into foster care. He stayed with us for a little while until Doug found a family to place him with. I'm afraid to say that Brady bounced around to a few homes, but Doug worked closely with the social worker. They finally found the Forresters right by us. I wanted him close. I wasn't stupid. By that time, I knew about you and I knew that Frank had been going down to Florida. I never asked, but I always wondered if you and Brady were siblings. I wanted the two of you to grow up together. I thought he could be the big brother to look out for his little sister. I just never..."

I whispered, "I love him."

She looked at me and nodded. "I know."

"I wouldn't have..."

"I know, Rayray. It's why you did what you did. I know."

I glanced at my hands and saw they were white. They were trembling. It was like no blood flowed through me. For a moment, I wondered if I should be concerned and then I looked at Viola and saw the same paleness in her.

When a door shut downstairs, Viola sighed, exhausted. "I should make some supper. I think your granddad must be getting hungry. I'm sorry about you and Brady. I'm sorry that I can't give you the answers you need. Your momma might've been the Godly woman, but I'm a believer too. Things always seem to work out."

When she stood, I felt my grandmother touch my shoulder. She pulled me close for a hug and whispered into my neck, "Things always seem to work out. Good comes out. It always does. It always wins."

I was numb in my grandmother's arms. I didn't know if good would win this time. I didn't feel it.

20

____

When I woke up the next morning, I sat on the edge of my bed and stared at the wall. My world had been turned upside and given another shake to make sure nothing was hidden away. I was a waste of space.

Brady might've been my brother. I had sex with him twice. I might even have sex with him again. When I acknowledged that shameful secret, I closed my eyes tightly and felt the sobs store up inside. It was worse than a forbidden love. Those people were kept away by feuding families, maybe even physical space. Their barriers could be torn down. But this...sharing blood...nothing could tear that down. It was the surest way to drive my best friend away from me.

But I drew in a shuddering breath and opened my eyes. I needed to focus so I took inventory from the mirror. My eyes were swollen from tears. My cheeks were splotchy. My hair was a mess, half of it held up in a ponytail. My skin was pale, the same shade of my shirt I'd thrown on the night before.

I hadn't cared about sleeping. I hadn't really slept. I knew I wasn't alone. Viola paced the floorboards. I hadn't heard any snoring so I figured my grandpa had been awake too. I wondered if he'd just watched Viola throughout the night.

There was a soft knock on my door and Neil spoke through it, "If you're ready, I can give you a ride to school."

It was my last day. I croaked back, "Okay. Be down in a few."

When he walked away, I closed my eyes and bent forward. My forehead rested on my knees and I needed one more of those deep breaths. How was I going to get through the day? How was I going to get through anything anymore?

"Rayna." Viola knocked next. When I didn't respond, she poked her head in and sighed. "I have breakfast ready..."

"Not hungry."

"Coffee?"

"Sure."

"Okay." She attempted a smile, but it came out looking painful. "I'll get that ready for you."

When she closed the door, I stood. I needed to start somewhere. My body ached so I focused on one thing at a time. Everything else buzzed around in my head. I didn't know what I chose to wear that day. I didn't care, but I must've passed the "you don't look crazy" test when Viola didn't blink an eye as she handed my coffee over. My grandfather didn't comment either. In fact, he didn't comment about anything until we got to school. "Have a good day. If you want to...go out or something, that'd be alright with your grandmother and me."

I looked at him in surprise.

"I mean it's your last day, Rayna. You should have some fun today. Forget everything else and make some memories today. That's what your grandmother always said, still says. She likes to make memories. Says they're good to tell around a night of family."

"What family?" I couldn't help asking.

"Rayna."

"Sorry." With my coffee in hand, I bid farewell before heading inside with an empty bag to my chest and the determination to ignore all the peering eyes. What did they care? Did they know? It was like they knew my secret. Brady didn't even know.

As I shouldered around a group of giggling freshmen, I swallowed painfully. I didn't know if I wanted him to know or not. How would he react? Probably with violence, but I wasn't sure beyond that.

Then I looked up as I neared my locker and my throat closed off. Brady was lounging against my locker. I froze in the hallway. I didn't care that students grumbled as they bumped into me. When I didn't move, they flowed around me. I couldn't look away. Brady was at my locker, just a few feet away from me, but he was talking to Matt Krone and Clarissa. All three of them were laughing, looking like the gods and goddess that could've reigned over us all.

Dressed in faded blue jeans and a white shirt, Brady looked confident and dangerous. His blonde hair was gelled slightly and the tribal tattoo peaked out from underneath his sleeve. Clarissa was his twin with her own simple white tank top and a blue jean miniskirt. Her hair had been pulled back into a high French braid that as she laughed, she twisted around and the braid smacked Matt Krone in the face. The golden giant grimaced and caught the hair. Clarissa laughed harder and leaned into him. Her hand fell on his chest for balance.

Brady watched it looking sombre. And I watched him. Instead of jealousy or even annoyance, I was surprised to see a slight flash of regret. But what did he regret? Choosing me over her? Was he rethinking all of it? Is that what he wanted to tell me when he came over?

Then I realized how crazy I was becoming. It didn't matter. Nothing mattered because at that moment, I didn't even know if I could handle being his friend. I caught my breath when Brady started to turn his head. His eyes started to sweep the hallway and it was a matter of seconds before he saw me. I couldn't talk to him so I took the coward's way out and ducked behind the group of giggling freshmen to sneak away.

The library was within reach. But when I reached for the door handle, Brady spoke behind me, "Hi, Rayna."

Everything stopped in that moment. My heart. My breath. My mind. It all stopped until he added, "Can you turn around? It's humiliating enough to have to come to my old school to talk to my best friend because I know she'll avoid me if I don't."

I looked down. "We shouldn't talk here."

"You threw me out last night. I...listen, I know you think that I was taking back things, but it wasn't the case. I was just—"

I couldn't hear how he felt about me, not when he didn't know. It wasn't fair to him or to me. "Stop! Please. Please stop."

"Look at me," Brady demanded.

I did, but I looked past his shoulder. Clarissa stood in the hallway beside her locker now. She stood still as she watched us. When she saw I was looking at her, she tried to smile at me, but I couldn't take it. Who was she to give me sympathy? She wanted Brady until yesterday. People don't change, not really. She wasn't really my friend.

I knew what I had to do. So I closed my eyes and braced myself. "You should be with Clarissa. You should be with someone who can be there for you."

"Come on. Don't be dramatic," Brady tried to soothe, but I stopped him again when I stepped backwards. That's when something snapped in him. I saw it in his eyes. He looked even more determined, almost fierce, as he grabbed my arm. "I was going to tell you last night that I was worried about how people might handle us. I was worried about how YOU'D handle it if we were together. Last night I was just rethinking things, worrying about you not me. Do I want to be with you? Haven't I already proven that? Then last night you go crazy. You start yelling. Your grandma is almost pushing me out the door. What are you doing to me? I know that I should be calmer, but I can't take this anymore. I feel like I'm going crazy, Rayna."

I couldn't hear what else he had to say. I'd already almost convinced myself that he didn't care and now he was saying he did. I felt tears on my face. "Stop. Please. Stop."

"What? What? Why do you want me to stop? Decide what you want! Do you want me or not?"

Clarissa dropped her book and I jumped. Brady cursed. "Rayna!"

He ran an irate hand through his hair and I saw the anger in him. The problem was that I couldn't figure out what he was angry about. There was a time not many days ago where I would've spent hours agonizing and thinking about why Brady was angry. But this time I could barely handle my own emotions, much less figure out his.

I looked away. "I don't want you."

I clasped my bag to my chest and my lip trembled. Every nerve was stretched thin.

"If you don't want me, then I'm gone. Screw this." His voice was quiet, but rage came off him in waves.

I gasped for breath and looked now.

As Brady marched away, he brushed past Clarissa and I wondered if he even knew she was there. He shoved open the doors a second later and they slammed shut a second later.

My heart was ripped out. He'd dragged it behind him in the hallway.

"Hey....Rayna...hey."

It took another prodding before I realized Clarissa was in front of me. "Huh?"

"What was that about?"

I couldn't focus. I couldn't...Brady just left me.

"Are you okay?"

"I...I don't know."

Brady wasn't going to change his mind now.

Slowly, I turned and pushed open the library doors. They closed behind me with a soft swoosh, but I didn't hear them. I didn't hear anyone or notice anything. I slid numbly into a seat and sat there for the next hour, staring straight ahead.

When I heard the bell ring, I got up and went somewhere else. I sat there until the next bell rang. Sometime later I found myself in the hallway with books clutched against my chest. I stared blankly into an empty hallway. Some part of my brain knew the bell had rung again, but I wasn't sure how long ago it was. I didn't know what time it was.

"Rayna?"

Kid stood there in a black polo shirt over trendy sport shorts. He raked a hand through his brown locks. "Are you okay?"

"Yeah. Why?" I tried for normal. Maybe he'd buy it.

He frowned and scratched at his jaw. "Because you're standing in the middle of the hallway and school's done."

"Oh."

"Everyone's gone." He tilted his head to the side and studied me further. "And I mean everyone, like...I even think the janitor is gone. What's up with you?"

What was up with me? Wasn't that the question of my life? I lied with forced cheerfulness, "It's the last day of school. Can you believe it, Kid? I'm done here. I'm done..." with so much more.

Kid cursed and jerked me towards the parking lot. "What is wrong with you? You look like a zombie, like you're in a coma or something. What happened?"

I mumbled, "I don't remember you being so bossy."

After he pushed me into his car, Kid grumbled when he got in on his own side, "You're right. Brady's the a-hole of us. I'm the nice guy, but you're driving me crazy. You're both driving me crazy. I can't take this anymore!"

That's when I started crying.

"Oh god...," Kid groaned. "I don't know what to say now. Come on, Ray. Stop. Don't cry."

I cried harder and folded my head into my hands.

"Seriously." Kid cursed. "I'm screwing this up right now. I don't know what to say to you anymore. Is this about Brady? The school?"

"Not helping," I hiccupped between sobs.

Kid swore again as he fell back against his seat. "You're too much Brady's. I just...you were still Rayna from before. I knew you, but now there's too much Brady over you. I don't know what to say to you anymore. I used to know. What would he say?"

What would Brady say? He'd say screw whoever was the problem.

"Hell," Kid sighed as he held onto the steering wheel. "Brady would say something like 'forget them' or worse. I can't do that, Rayna. I don't know what the problem is. Should I call Brady?"

I started sobbing again.

"Stop crying! Please!"

I hiccupped and wiped the snot from my nose. Then I looked at Kid probably for the first real time since he brought me to his car. I saw some sort of struggle within him. And I was tired of the lies. I'd just started lying, but I was already done with it. So I asked, "If you knew you had a brother, what would you do?"

I listened with every part of my soul.

He drew a breath in. "I would...I don't know. Maybe that's my problem."

From the fear in his voice, I saw a Kid that I'd never seen before. He'd always been so larger than life before. Confident. Charming. Good looking. Smart. He'd been smooth when

Brady had been rough. Kid had known what to say when Brady chose to fight, but then things changed. Brady became smart. He started to know what to say while Kid had started to flounder. Still, Kid always had his composure, but not now. This time I saw a little boy sitting beside me, uncertain.

Then I risked it. "I know that Brady is your brother."

21

Kid stared at me and then his body slumped down. "Finally."

"Finally?" I croaked.

"Finally someone else knows."

"You knew?" Now so much made sense. I sat up straight. "Is that why you came back? Is this what you two were fighting about before?" And much more importantly, did Brady already know?

Dazed, Kid shook his head. "No. I mean, yes. I came back because I found out Brady was my brother, but no, Brady doesn't know. I don't know what he'd do if he did."

"I'm confused."

Kid faced me. "Brady thinks I came back to be with you. It's why we fought that first time. It's mostly my fault. I always knew he was in love with you. I meant to come back here to tell him about our dad, but when I saw him that night, I got so angry. He's like my father in some ways and I wanted to hurt him."

"Why would you do that? It's not Brady's fault that your dad is a whore," I snapped.

Kid commented, "I am aware of that. Thank you, Rayna. I went to that party, but I didn't know if I'd see Brady or not. I had every intention of finding him the next day, but there he was. When he saw me, I knew he was pissed. He was threatened because the last time he saw me, I told him that I wanted to take you out on a date. Brady doesn't forget anything. He's like a woman that way. I wanted to hurt my father, but my dad wasn't in front of me. Brady was. So..." He took a deep breath. "I might have said some things to push him over the edge."

"What did you say?" I was on the edge of my seat. Literally.

"I'm stupid."

"Kid!"

"I asked him if you were still single because you were pretty easy on the eyes before. Then I might've said something about how easy you could be in bed."

My hand flew up and I slapped him. Then I thought about it some more and slapped him again.

Kid cupped his cheek. "I deserved that and I realize Brady would've pounded me even if he wasn't in love with you."

"You're the asshole. Not Brady," I seethed and folded my arms over my chest. "I thought you were the good guy. I thought you were always so nice. You disappointed me. You just reminded me that you're male."

Kid chuckled. "You make that sound like an insult."

"It is," I snapped. "I cannot believe you. You were always the smart one. You were the one who did the right thing even when you didn't want to. Then you said those awful things about me? I don't even care that they're not true. I don't care that you said them about me because they don't hurt me. They hurt Brady. They hurt him."

"That's what I wanted."

"Congratulations. Your father hurt you, so you hurt someone else. Way to think only about yourself. I am so tired of everyone thinking about themselves. No one thinks about the rest of us, the ones who are the secrets. Don't you think that our lives are going to be affected too? That we're going to be hurt just as much, probably more so? NO. No one thinks of us."

He relented, "I didn't think about Brady. You're right. My dad kept this other kid a secret from me. Do you know what that's like? To find out that you have a brother? Or that your own father had been lying to you all your life?"

"No," I replied dryly. "I have no idea what that's like."

He continued without pausing, "I knew my dad was a liar and a cheat, but I didn't think he treated me like them. I was his son. I thought he loved me. And he's probably got more kids out there."

"Newsflash: your dad isn't nice."

He stiffened next to me. "I get you're mad, but back off a little. He's still my father. And he hasn't had it so easy lately. He just got back from a funeral."

"So you can gripe and complain about him, but I can't? Another newsflash: his other son is my best friend. I can say whatever I want. I don't know who died. He seems to only care about himself and be damned with everyone else, including his children..." My heart was thundering so loud, it was deafening. I knew I had to calm down. Kid had no idea about my situation. Then I realized that I was doing what he had done. I was hurting so I wanted to hurt someone else. "I am so sorry, Kid. You're right. I can't say anything. Your father is still your father. I apologize."

Kid scooted over a little. "Sometimes, you're odd. This is one of those days. And it was my dad's old business partner died. It sounds weird, but he respected the guy."

It had been an odd day, an odd week. And I was suddenly exhausted. As I wiped a tear away, I asked, "Can you give me a ride home? My grandfather gave me a ride in today."

Kid nodded. "Is this really about me hurting Brady? Is that

why you're kind of off today or is there something else wrong? You're not you, not completely."

"It's the last day of school. I didn't get much sleep last night." I knew I was becoming a good liar when Kid didn't question me anymore. He patted my hand this time.

Then a different thought came to me. "Why are you here, Kid? You don't go to this school. You don't even go to school."

A guilty look flashed over his face, but the back door opened at that moment. Clarissa hopped inside. From the determined look in her eye and the apology in Kid's, I knew I'd been set up.

"Oh no. You both did not just manipulate me."

She rolled her eyes. "Get over it. I called him to talk to you. Something was seriously wrong with you and Brady today. Kid's the only one I thought you might talk to about it." She folded her arms over her chest and leaned back. "I was being a good friend."

"A good friend? You know what those are?"

"Yes!" She flicked her braid over her shoulder. "What's going on with you? What's going on with Brady?"

"Leave it alone, Clarissa. Please, leave it alone. It's complicated."

"Does this have to do with your mom being in town?"

The world fell away underneath me. I was starting to hyper-ventilate...

Clarissa continued from a distance, "I saw her at the Stephens' house when I went over to tell Kid that something was wrong with you. Does this have to do with her? Because if it does, that's horrible. She's a bitch. Does she not want you and Brady to be together? That's the only thing that'd make sense to me."

I reached around the seat and grabbed her braids to yank her close. "Why was my mother there?" I glared at Kid, "Why was my mother with your dad?"

Kid's eyes were wide and he leaned all the way back against his window. "She came back with him from the funeral."

"What funeral?" I ground out.

"The one my dad was at."

"Where?" My heart was racing. I couldn't catch my breath. Everything was rushing at me so fast now.

And then Kid answered quietly, "Florida."

My mom. His dad. Florida. She was back. At that moment, I was barely aware of anything. Then a door slammed and someone pounded on my window. Everything was spinning around me now.

It couldn't be. There was no way. She was back...

I blinked back the darkness. I was about to faint and I didn't want that. I couldn't go away when so much was within my grasp. Then my door opened and I started to fall backwards.

"Rayna!"

I was caught by someone.

"What the hell, Kid? Clary?"

"We didn't do it. She freaked out on her own."

"What'd you say to her?"

Kid's voice was far away. "Nothing. She just found out her mom's at my house."

"Are you kidding me?"

"Brady?" There he was. He was holding me and then he looked down. I felt him brush my hair back from my forehead. "Rayna, it's okay. Whatever's wrong, it's okay."

Was it? I had no idea, but I stayed there for a moment and relished the feel of his arms. It felt so right to be in them again. When I looked up again and saw the concern there, I knew he loved me. I saw it for real for the first time. It was there, underneath the surface he always shows to everyone. I saw how he loved me and I choked up. How could we have wasted so much time? Then again, we still didn't know...I took one more breath, closed my eyes as Brady swept a hand down the side of my face and then pushed away.

I reeled for a second. Everything felt right when I was in his arms.

"My mother is here."

Brady pulled me out of the car. As the others followed he wrapped his arms around my waist.

Clarissa explained, "I thought maybe that was why you and Rayna fought today."

"You saw her mother?"

"Brady." I didn't want him to say anything more. I didn't fully trust Clarissa.

"She hasn't seen her mother in six years, Clarissa! Goddamn it. Think sometimes," Brady snapped while he cradled me against his chest.

"I didn't know. I just wanted to help her."

"Brady, that's not fair. She doesn't know Rayna's history. No one really knows it."

"I do and you should've come to me before you cornered her." Then he turned his back to them and whispered in my ear, "You want to go there?"

My body had grown numb, but I needed to see her. I needed to know.

"Okay. Okay, we'll go there." With his hands on my hips, he steered me to his passenger door. I huddled against the door until he got in on the other side. Then he scooped an arm around my waist and pulled me over the divider, pressed against his side. He kissed my forehead. "I told 'em not to follow us. You need your time alone with her."

I rested my forehead against his shoulder as he pulled onto the highway.

"It'll be okay." Brady found my hand with his.

"I hope so." I hoped so much.

"I know that you haven't really talked much about your

mom. You've said before that you didn't want to have a relationship with her, but she's here. That's something. If my mom was in town, even for a day, I'd be happy to get any time I could with her."

Brady had never talked about his parents. He'd always said he was happy with foster parents that didn't kick him out. But now, I heard something else.

"Do you think about your mom?"

"What kid doesn't?" He jerked a shoulder up.

"Do you think of her a lot?"

He shrugged again. "I mean...yeah. Obviously, you do. Your mom's in town. You can talk to her; maybe learn some things from her. I don't know. Yeah. I think about my mom."

"What do you think about? Do you like her? Do you want to like her?"

Brady studied me before he replied, "She's a part of me. She gave birth to me. I..." He hesitated.

Why was he hesitating? Why was he choosing his words so carefully?

"I know my mother's name, but I don't know her. I've talked to her only a few times and most of those was when she asked for Viola on the phone. She's never come around except once for Christmas." I felt something wet on my cheeks. Why was I always crying? "Do you ever feel like you're watching life and you're not actually in it?"

Brady laughed. "Only when some guy rushes me. I check out for a second and then I'm right in. I'm all in."

"No, I mean, I don't know what I mean."

He slowed the car and replied, "That just tells me that you can't feel what you're feeling because it's painful. Like it's almost too painful for you to handle right now, but it'll click off when you can handle it. I know it. And," he took a deep breath. "We're here."

I saw Kid's old house. It looked like the same mansion from

when we were kids, but smaller. The two pillars in front of the door weren't as large, but still grand. They looked like massive guards, there to intimidate trespassers.

"You ready?" Brady asked.

No.

I nodded.

He got out first and then the front door opened to emit a business man. He was dressed in a three-piece suit with a brief-case. When he looked at us, I knew his blue eyes reeled in most women, but they weren't close to how beautiful Brady's were. No one's were.

"That's a lawyer," Brady said.

"How do you know?"

"I recognize him. Deputy Dog told me who Frank Stephens' lawyer was when I got arrested the first time. It's some big hotshot from the city. That's him."

"Why is my mother meeting with a lawyer?" Or maybe she had nothing to do with it?

I had a weird sensation Brady knew something more, but he wasn't sharing. "I don't think your mother is. I think Frank Stephens just met with his lawyer. We're at his house, remember?"

"Oh...right..." A flashback came to me when Kid, Brady, and I were little kids. We must've been in seventh grade and all three of us raced inside those doors. The last one inside was the loser. We were laughing, so carefree back then.

"You ready?" Brady asked softly.

"No." I started walking forward anyway.

While Brady rang the doorbell I felt my heartbeat through my toes. The silent wait was long and tense. I was going to explode in one second and completely calm the next instant. Then I was back to being numb until the door opened. I braced myself, but some stranger in another dark blue suit stood there.

"Is Leann Janke here?" Brady asked as he held my hand and rubbed his thumb over mine.

"Ms. Janke?" The guy gestured inside. "Please come in while I fetch her."

My heartbeat exploded. Sweat poured down my back. This was it. This was going to be it. He showed us to a waiting room that had two beige couches, a desk, and a fireplace in the center. Everything about it was formal, cold. Even the drapes seemed to tell us not to get comfortable; we were only there for a short while.

"You okay?"

I shook my head. "Before..." I wet my lips. "Before she comes in here, you need to know something."

Brady looked at me strangely, almost amused as he held both of my hands in between us. "Yes?"

"I..." He was so beautiful.

He spoke, "Look, Rayna. I did some thinking this afternoon and I want you to know..."

This was my moment. I was supposed to be able to stare at how beautiful and wondrous he was. How he could never be mine...

"I know you said before that you didn't want me, but I think it's a load of crap. I mean, obviously you do. You had sex with me. You don't do that unless there are feelings and I know you have them. I don't think you should freak about your mom knowing. It's not like she has a say about who you're with."

My mouth fell open. "What?"

"You're all nervous. Usually I can handle it, but I hate that it's because of me."

"What in the world are you talking about?"

He gestured between us. "You and me. It's why your mom's here, right? Viola got all pressed. I don't get her freak out, but she must've called your mom and told her. Why else would she be here?"

"My mother is not here about us. She has no say whatsoever in my life. She doesn't know about us and if she did, she wouldn't be here. She'd be at my house with my family, not at Frank Stephens' house."

"I didn't think about that." Brady slid his hands into his front pockets, leaned against the wall, and transitioned back into the confident bad boy. At least, he looked like it. Whatever had been troubling him was gone.

"Stop it. I don't need my badass best friend. I need my actual best friend. Stop the charade."

Brady straightened abruptly. A second later, he asked, "Your best friend?"

"You gave me a ride here to see my mom. I need my best friend beside me right now."

Brady hesitated.

I felt my heart stop once more. "You brought me here because you're my best friend, right?"

He opened his mouth, but nothing came out.

"Or did I lose my best friend the second we had sex?" It was the million dollar question. Maybe he didn't love me how I had thought. He'd never told me...

Brady answered, "I think that things are very confusing right now."

"Did you do this to be my best friend or because you want something more with me?" Why did this matter now anyway? Everything depended on what she was going to say.

He gauged my expression. "I did it because I care for you." A myriad of emotions flashed over his face. "Deep down, beneath everything, I am here because I am your best friend. I love you in that best friend way. I saw that you were upset about your mom and I wanted to help you. This is where you need to be."

My heart melted, all the way down past my knees. "Thanks."

Brady narrowed his eyes. "Thanks?"

"Thanks." I couldn't tell him how I really felt.

"Have I done something wrong?" He frowned and then his eyes shifted to look out the window.

On the contrary, he did everything right. "NO, no. You say the right words when I shouldn't hear them."

Brady cursed underneath his breath. "Kid and Clarissa just pulled up outside. I don't want them interfering with this."

Nothing made sense, but my heart was breaking in that moment. I wanted to spill everything. He should know, but I nodded my head. "You should stop them."

As soon as he left, I collapsed on a couch and caught my face with my hands. I bent over my knees and dry heaved. I knew I was being dramatic, but it was so hard, so seriously hard. I didn't know how much more I could take, but I knew more was coming. We were just stepping into the storm.

"You have some nerve coming here."

When I expected my mother, I looked up in surprise to see Frank Stephens instead. He wore a custom tailored black suit. His hands were clenched into fists and he jerked forward two steps, but stopped abruptly. As his jaw tightened, I saw the rage in his eyes and jumped to my feet, then wavered a second. The room spun around me, but I remembered Brady's voice. *'I'm your best friend.'*

Everything calmed in me. I opened my eyes then. "She's not here, is she?"

I was ready for the storm to come.

F rank Stephens looked like he could commit murder as he stared me down, but I wasn't a coward. I would not run away. But as his rage seemed to grow, I was tempted to tuck tail and scram.

"You are every bit the whore that your mother is. You spread 'em for any guy that comes along."

I reeled from his words, but he continued, "I loved your mother so goddamn much. I would've done anything for her, just like my son would do for you, but you're like her. She destroyed me, just like you're going to destroy Brady."

Did he just say...?

Frank jerked forward and crossed the room to a bar hidden behind a counter. As he filled a glass, he grunted. "When I first met your mother, I thought she was special. I thought she was a goddamn angel sent to save me. Can you believe it? I couldn't." He laughed harshly and finished the drink to pour another. "I loved my wife, or I thought I loved Teresa, and then I met Leann. I realized what love really was. Everything was upside down, and I thought I could do right. I thought I could be the guy that I knew she'd need for her. All she'd do is look at me and smile and I wanted to be a better man. I tried. I really tried, but it wasn't enough. Your mother humiliated me. She tortured me. When that wasn't enough...you know what she did? She screwed the one guy that I respected in this world. That's what she did. She did everything to hurt me. She succeeded. My marriage fell apart. I fathered another bastard child. I could've lost everything. My business could've gone done the drain and it's your mother's fault. She stomped on me. And you're just like her."

I should've left, but I wanted information. I wanted whatever he was giving out. I didn't care if it was hateful words. It was something.

He finished another drink. "I should toss you out. I should call the cops, but I already know they're on their way. It doesn't matter. Domitri was snowed by her, just like I was. I never knew how bad it was, how much she got under his skin. I never knew about you. Never even considered it, to be honest. If I had, trust me, I would've destroyed you and your mother. I would've taken Domitri down and sent him to hell myself. And Theona. She would've known everything. She would've died knowing how her life was just as much a lie as mine. The business would've burned and I would've set the match myself. I'm not going to see my life's work in your mother's hands."

I heard a car door slam outside the window. Voices were heard a second later and then dulled. After Frank finished a third drink, he moved to fill a fourth. I looked down at my hands. They were sturdy. I thought they'd be sweating or trembling. Nothing. For some reason, his demented hatred didn't touch me.

"All of its gone. All of it. I have the majority shareholder, but she's got the rest besides the board. It doesn't matter. I can't get around her. She's a damn woman. I hate women. They belong in the bedroom and that's it. I thought I loved her, I did love her. And now, goddamn...I knew she was smart, but I didn't realize. She's a goddamn witch. All those should be strung up and killed. I can't stand the lot of them. That's how she got Domitri in bed. She got her hooks in him. Theona wouldn't have allowed it if she wasn't dying." He swallowed painfully and slammed his glass on the counter. As it shattered, he didn't blink. He didn't notice blood was starting to pool underneath his hand. He stared at me, beyond me. He might've been seeing me, but it was her that he wanted to murder.

Something kindled in my spine and I stood slowly. "I don't know my mother..." When he jerked, I jumped. "I don't know...k-k-k-now about anything what you're telling me. I don't know my mom. I really don't. I came here because I wanted to ask her questions, but I can see that she's not here—"

"Your mother took off two hours ago. She's probably already on the plane. The car was going to the airport," he coldly delivered. "She's smart, so smart that she might walk away with twenty million for you. Little does she know you're here in my living room, within my reach. I could do anything to you and she couldn't stop it. She couldn't save you, much as she might think she did. She hasn't saved you at all. You walked into the lion's den. You're mine for all intents and purposes. You're mine."

I heard the threat and stared back. Something told me he was looking for weakness and I couldn't give him that. "I am anything but yours. I am Brady's and you've already told me you know he's your son. You know what he can do, so I wouldn't push it. Because you're right. Brady does love me and I love him. What do you think he'd do if he knew you were speaking to me like this?"

Frank looked at me with contempt. "I own this town. The only reason your boyfriend isn't in prison is because a part of him is from me. He's my son and his mother was one of the sweetest pieces of ass I've ever had. Call me weak, but I couldn't bring myself to charge my own flesh and blood. He's a part of my legacy. Hell, for all I know he might be my only legacy. Kidrick's a disgrace. He can't even bag the town's whore."

Cold tears fell down my cheeks. "You are less than me. You are less than Brady. You are less than Kid and you know it. You loved my mother because she made you want to be a better man. You loved her because—"

Frank wiped a hand over his mouth and interrupted, "You have no idea what you're talking about. You're just a kid. You're a girl, that's worse. And, sweetheart, my boy is not in love with you. He's just obsessed with you, but obsession ain't love. He wants your ass, probably has since growing up. Oh, yes. I've watched. I know everything about Brady. You think I'd really let my own flesh and blood go? He's an asset of mine. He belongs to me. It's a good thing that Viola took him in. She wanted him to be hers because she was disappointed with you. I can't blame her. I let her have him. Far be it from me to take an old woman's only saving grace in her life. She's got nothing else. Her own daughter abandoned her and stuck her with her kid. I've always wondered who your father was, if he was drifter or some poor schmuck who wouldn't pay child support."

I'd grown numb again as he said all the words that I'd held inside, too scared to say out loud. I'd always felt like a burden. I always wondered if my mother had sent me away because she didn't want me. Maybe my father HAD been so awful that the very sight of me revolted her. Did Viola wish Brady had been her grandchild instead of me? It would've made more sense.

I would've believed everything except one part.

Brady wasn't just obsessed with me. It was more. He'd never told me, but I knew it as sure as I breathed. He cared about me and if Frank Stephens lied about that one thing, I knew all the others were lies.

He couldn't hurt me.

As he spewed more abuse, I glanced out the window and

saw Deputy Doug's car parked outside. When the door opened, voices filled the hall.

Idly, I crossed the room to grab a poker by the fireplace and held it tight. As I moved back, I placed myself where Frank Stephens would have his back to the hallway. As he continued to spew those hurtful words to me, I knew he wouldn't stop. He was drunk. He was angry. He was evil—he was just that kind of guy. I also knew that Brady would hear him and Brady would react how he always did.

Looking back over the years, Brady always had a hot temper. He was an "all in" type of guy and that meant protecting the ones he loved. He protected them all the way. Brady had worked on his temper. He was a lot better than a few years ago, but he still fought over one factor. Me.

I heard their footsteps grow closer.

"Mr. Stephens, I feel it's my duty to forewarn you about certain events." When he stopped, I continued, "That son of yours doesn't take kindly to people saying hurtful words to me. I might not stop him from hurting you, but since the law is present right now, I figure Brady shouldn't chance another arrest. He's going to want to hurt you and I figure the only way to stop him is if you're already hurt. So...."

I tightened my hold on the poker and looked beyond Frank Stephens' shoulder to see Brady turn into the room with Deputy Doug beside him. They stopped and Frank Stephens cursed out, "You think I'm afraid of your threats. You're nothing, but a little whore that was born a mistake and you'll die—"

Brady jerked forward with his hands already in fists. That's when I swung the poker with all my weight behind it. The poker slammed into Frank Stevens' face and he fell to the ground. It was so quick and it was done just as quick. Silence filled the room as Frank Stephens lay there, shocked, until he started to get back up with more threats.

Brady started forward, but I turned again and hit Frank

Stephens over his back once, twice, and then again. He wouldn't shut up. I was surprised he didn't back, but the liquor might've helped me.

Then I was jerked from behind and pulled backwards. As my arms were pulled behind, I looked up and met Brady's eyes. His were shocked when mine were calm. "I didn't want you to hurt him. I didn't want you to go to jail again."

Deputy Doug spoke from behind me, "I need to arrest you, Rayna....I'm sorry."

I started to cry, but I nodded. "Brady has to come with us. He can't stay here."

"I'll make sure of it."

As I was led outside and placed in the back seat of the squad car, I watched what was happening. Brady followed and lingered on the front steps of the house. Kid's car pulled back into the driveway. An instant later, he and Clarissa both got out with shocked looks on their faces when they saw where I was. When they went to Brady, an ambulance arrived, and paramedics went inside. After that, I closed my eyes. I didn't care what else happened because Brady wasn't alone. The front door of the police car opened.

Brady crawled inside. "What happened in there?"

My voice was hoarse. "He was angry and saying a bunch of bad stuff to me. He wouldn't stop, Brady. I knew you were coming in. I didn't want you to hurt him because you'd get hurt worse."

"He can't hurt me, Rayna."

But, he could. And I knew it. Frank Stephens had kept quiet for so many years about Brady being his son, but he'd done it because he was scared of losing his business. He didn't have much to lose now. I might not be all-knowing and worldly about men like Clarissa, but I saw a quality in Frank Stephens that I knew very well. It was in Brady too. He felt his world crumbling and he was going to take as many down with him as possible. If Brady had physically attacked Frank Stephens, all bets were off. Everything would be told and I wasn't sure if I wanted Brady to learn about his parentage that way. It didn't matter now because I was the one who'd hurt Frank, not Brady. Brady would be okay. I was sure of it now.

"You really did him one. I'm surprised he didn't swing back at you. Viola is going to be so proud."

I laughed and then whimpered as pain shot down my arms. "What's wrong?"

"My arms hurt." I tried to lift them, but they were too weak.

Brady nodded. "You really walloped him. I'm sure you pulled a muscle doing that. You're nothing but a hundred plus? A pint-size girl took down Frank Stephens. Even Kid's impressed. I think Clarissa has a newfound lesbian crush on you."

I laughed weakly as I felt tears slide down my cheeks. "I'm a mess, Brady."

He slipped two fingers through the bars and caught my hand. "I'll clean you up."

"Promise?"

"Promise."

My heart skipped a beat when I looked in his eyes.

23

———————

"Why did you assault Frank Stephens?" Deputy Doug interrogated me with one leg propped by his phone and his chair tipped backwards.

Deputy Doug should've handcuffed me. As I rubbed where they could've been, I was thankful he hadn't. "Because I didn't want Brady to get into any more trouble."

He slammed a hand on his desk. "You can't say that, Rayna. Any second now, Frank Stephens' hotshot lawyer is going to sweep through those doors. I can't help you after that. It'll go over my head. I've already been lenient bringing you in here and not cuffing you. I might get my rear-end handed to me for the likes of you."

"Did you get a hold of my grandmother?"

"Already told you. She ain't answering the phone. It don't matter none. Judge Bailor's coming in to discuss the situation. You're eighteen. Brady can post your bail if you need it." As he eyed me, he added, "Besides, we both know you ain't in any trouble with your grandmomma. She's going to have a parade when she hears what you've done."

"Grandpa did tell me to make memories today."

Deputy Doug smothered a chuckle as peeked through the blinds. "No lawyer's showed up yet. I'm in a pickle of what to do with you."

"I thought you were going to arrest me."

He scoffed, "I should throw you in jail, but I can't arrest Viola Janke's granddaughter. When it comes down to it, I'm more scared of her than Frank Stephens. We all know a poker can take him down, but your grandmomma...I don't think a buckshot would graze her."

"Then why am I here?"

"Because I want Judge Bailor to sweat bullets with me. He's more scared of Viola than me. I don't want just my head on the chopping block."

"When is he getting here?"

Deputy Dog sat down and sighed, "Hells if I know. He went golfing. It might take him hours to sober up."

"Can I talk to Brady? Can't he come back here if you're not arresting me?"

Deputy Doug scratched his head and nodded jerkily. "Sure. What's it to me to keep you two apart?" He moved around the desk and opened his office door. "Brady. Get your bee-hinder back here."

A moment later, Brady sauntered through the door and flashed a grin. "Couldn't bear to be apart from me, Dougie?"

He got a snort in response. "Just don't get all hanky panky on the desk. Viola or not, I will arrest you both."

"Deputy Dog, you know how I feel about challenges," Brady taunted. When he sat the chair next to me, his thigh brushed against mine. "I'd say put the handcuffs on her, but you did say no hanky panky. I wouldn't want to be tempted."

"You're funny, Brady. You're a funny guy." Deputy Doug rolled his eyes before he gave us a stern glare as he exited the office.

When the door was closed, Brady turned to assess me. All

laughter faded. He sighed instead and took my hand in his. "It'll be fine, Rayray. Trust me. How many times have I been where you're sitting?"

"I'm not you." I entwined our fingers and held on tight.

"No, you're prettier."

"I mean it." I wasn't smooth or sophisticated. I wasn't what Brady could be at his choosing. He got people to listen to him, strangers even. They followed him, did what he said to do. I didn't have those qualities. I was plain, boring, and sheltered. "I've never done something like this, Brady. I don't know what to do. I don't know what's going to happen to me. I don't know if this'll hurt my future. I don't know what to feel right now except that I'm scared and a little...content."

His eyebrows shot up. "You're content? To be a criminal?"

"No, not that. I'm scared about that, but I'm content about...I don't know, maybe like I was standing up for myself."

"Because you were being hurt by him?"

I wiped a tear away. I was sick of crying.

"What was he saying that was hurting you?"

Could I tell him? He already knew the rumours about my mother, but he didn't know the truth so I shook my head. "I can't explain it. He just said a bunch of stuff about my mom. And he said stuff about how she never wanted me, that I'm a burden to Viola and Neil."

Brady hissed and flexed his knuckles. "It's a good thing you laid him out. You're right, if you hadn't, I would've. No one should say that stuff to anyone, even if it's true. No one should hear that."

I heard an inflection in his voice. Had someone spoken those same words to him? I was about to ask when he suddenly exclaimed, "Wait a minute. Why was your mom at Frank Stephens' house? How does your mom even know him?"

Um.

I had not foreseen this.

"She was there because of my grandmother. You know Frank Stephens hates her." My soul was going to hell.

Disgust flared across Brady's face for a second. It was gone just as quickly, but he stared at me. Then he stared some more at me. No word was spoken from him.

I heard the clock ticking behind us. It was loud, too loud. And I couldn't take the silence anymore, especially from him. "Say something."

"You just lied to me. Why did you lie to me?"

"I..." I had nothing. I wasn't quick on my feet.

"Don't lie to me again, Rayna. Why was your mother there?"

I couldn't look away from his eyes. They were so clear and demanding. It was almost as if this moment was a make-or-break moment. I didn't know what to say so I opened my mouth and uttered, faltering, "I...I...I don't know. He wouldn't tell me."

Brady's eyes snapped shut for a second and then he cursed underneath his breath. At the same time, he shoved his chair back and stood up.

"Where are you going?"

"I'm going to find out some answers once and for all."

"Wait! Where are you going?" My heart was beating so loudly, I almost didn't hear his response.

As the door closed behind him, I heard him say, "I'm going to see my father."

It took a moment before I realized what he'd just said. Panic slammed inside of me and then I shot to the door. The doorknob was locked so I tried to unlock it from my side. When it wouldn't budge, I pounded on the door. "Hey! Hey! Hey!"

Brady knew.

Brady knew who his father was. And he was going to find out why my mother was there. This was not good. This was not good at all. And Brady was not stupid, not at all.

"Hey, hey, HEY!" I pounded on the door until the same irritated clerk came back, even more irritated. She called through the door, "What you want?"

"I have an emergency. I need a phone." And boy, was it an emergency.

She crossed her arms and pointed behind me. "You have a phone in there."

"No, I need..." I gulped for breath and felt everything starting to sway around me. Everything was just too much...and he knew. I couldn't wrap my mind around it. Brady knew...what did this mean? "I need to get out. I can't...he knows..."

She shook her head. "I can't hear you. I'll get Doug. Sit. Sit. Sit."

I stumbled to my chair and bent forward to cradle my head in my hands. Deep breath, one, two, three. Exhale, one, two, three. I kept up my breaths and hoped my heartbeat would slow a little.

Brady knew.

He already knew.

Holy crap.

Then Deputy Doug came back and I shot up from my chair. "Please. I need to go. I have to go. Brady—I have to go."

"We still need to wait for Judge Bailor."

"Please, Doug! Please! I have to go. Brady—" I couldn't tell him what Brady knew. I couldn't tell him because I didn't even know what it meant.

Deputy Doug narrowed his eyes and sat slowly. His hands curled into his desk's edge as he sat forward. "What do you mean? What about Brady?"

"Nothing. Never mind. I just really need to go."

"Rayna, tell me what's going on," he commanded.

"I can't—" But wait, could I tell him? I remembered my grandmother saying, 'Deputy Doug was working as the dispatcher that night...figured to keep it quiet...Doug had found a family to place him with...' My mouth fell open as I gasped, "You know!"

He frowned. "Wha—huh?"

I was lost in my thoughts. "All I heard that night was that Brady is Frank's son. Grandmother told me that she brought him to you. You helped her. You got Brady with the Forresters so he'd move next door to us. You've helped all along."

"Oh. Rayna. Oh..."

"You've known all along," I whispered out and wondered how much else I hadn't heard that night. "But every time you arrest Brady, you..." He always tried to help him. "You told me that you thought of him as your own son."

Deputy Doug's voice was soft. "I'm old, Rayna. I knew back then that I'd never have kids. Got something wrong with me, medically speaking. I might act dumb sometimes, but I ain't stupid. I know people call me Deputy Dog. They say it to my face half the time, but it didn't start out as a good nickname. People called me that because they thought they could, I was less than them. I wasn't. I needed to help however I could. I've always helped your grandmother, and I've always looked after Brady like he was my own. I love that kid, more than he knows. If your grandmamma brought me another one of him, I'd do the same thing again."

My eyes closed and I took a deep breath. There was so much going on, so much that had always been going on. I didn't know what was real anymore, but the one thing I did know was real was Brady. Renewed strength flowed through me from some unknown place and I opened my eyes. They were clear and strong. "Brady knows that Frank Stephens is his father. And he's gone to confront him about it."

I braced myself for the shock to flash over the Deputy's face, but I was the one surprised. A calm acceptance was there instead and he stood to scratch his jaw. He spoke as he went to the door, "Always knew this day would come. Frank Stephens has some inspiring qualities in him, but the one that makes him dangerous is his lack of caring. He don't care about no one.

When he fathered a child like Brady, who has all those same qualities plus a few he don't, I'd known this day would be one for the books."

His hand went to the door handle and I could tell that was all he was going to say. I shot to my feet. "That's IT? That's all you're going to say? Aren't you going to go after him or something? Do you know what Brady might do?"

"That boy turned into a man quite a while ago. I don't think he's going to go off the deep end finding out who his daddy is. The only thing that'll push him over is you—"

"Brady thinks Frank Stephens and my mother had an affair." I didn't realize I had thought it until I blurted it out, but it made sense.

He snapped his mouth shut, stunned. Comprehension and horror all flashed across his face. Then he stated, "Then you best be getting over there, Miss Rayna."

He swung the door open a second later and stood back.

As I started to go past him, I held his gaze for another second. Everything felt surreal now. No words were shared between us, but I knew what we both thought. Only I could stop something from happening. It rested on my shoulders. With that realization, I was again taken aback. Any other day I would've hid, but this time there was no fear. There was only a feeling of purpose. And strength. I felt strong.

I was starting to like this feeling.

"You're not going to put me in jail?" I questioned.

"Nah. You don't deserve jail for hitting the likes of Frank Stephens. You deserve a medal."

I looked down when I felt tears in my eyes and tried to blink them away. Then Deputy Doug roughly squeezed my arm in reassurance and they fell free. These tears were different. I couldn't explain them, but they were different.

I wasn't hiding anymore.

"Go on, Miss Rayna."

As I made my way out of the station, I felt foolish and oddly brave. I knew people in the waiting lounge were probably watching me, wondering what kind of a freak I was, but I didn't care. I just didn't care anymore. I felt the sunshine hit my face in a new light when I pushed through the door and embraced it. I wanted to see the sun and the sky in my newly acquired confidence.

"Rayna!" Clarissa screamed at me.

I jumped back and the glass door hit me forwards. As I stumbled forward, I tried to brace myself so I wouldn't fall onto the sidewalk. My hand flattened on the pavement and a sharp pain flared in my wrist, but I caught my balance.

Clarissa watched from her car. "Hurry, hurry. We have to go. Now!"

"What? Why? What's happened?"

"Get in the car!" she ordered.

I complied. "What's happened?"

We shot down the street. "I was at the hospital with Kid when Brady showed up. It is not good, so not good, Rayna. Kid shoved me out the door, but they were all yelling and then something crashed into the wall. I tried to get inside, but the door wouldn't budge. Someone hit someone and I took off to get you. You gotta stop 'em."

As she continued to ramble on, I wasn't scared. It was time the secrets were told.

24

Brady burst through the hospital doors. It didn't take a detective to figure out which room his father would be in. It'd be the best room in the corner. The hospital officials wouldn't want to be sued so they'd give him their top service, including two nurses on hand and a doctor close to his door. So when he saw a group of hospital workers outside a room, he headed there and pushed through the doors.

Clarissa had been standing behind it with a carton of coffees. The door knocked them from her hands and she gasped, but Brady stalked to the bed where Frank sat up in a nightgown. He paled at the sight of him. Kid remained on the other side of the bed. He froze in place.

"Did you sleep with Leann Janke?" Brady ground out.

Kid jumped forward. "Clarissa, maybe you should head outside."

"What? No, I—"

He grabbed her elbow and led her through the door. "Thanks for all your help. I'll call you later."

"But—" The door closed and Kid stood in front to block anyone else.

"Did. You. Sleep. With. Her?"

Frank blinked, but that was his only reaction. He stared in Brady's eyes. Kid saw all of this and jerked forward a step. "Brady, what's this about?"

Brady reached for Frank's collar and Kid lunged for him. He threw an arm around his neck and jerked back. Both of them crashed into the window, but Brady rounded with a fist formed. He punched Kid across the face and then reared back with an elbow.

"Stop!" Frank yelled and hit his call button.

Brady shook his head and shoved Kid backwards into a chair in the far corner. "Stay out of this, Kid. You've done enough since you've been here."

"I've done enough?" Kid laughed on an empty note. His face twisted into an ugly frown. "Are you kidding me? I've done nothing but help you."

"Help me? How?"

Kid stood and shook his head. "Do you know how frustrating it is to leave a place I loved? I loved this place. I loved being friends with you and Rayna and then I come back. My whole word has been turned upside down and I come back to see that yours are all fine. They're all the same. Nothing's changed. Nothing!"

"Is that what you wanted? Your life's destroyed so you wanted to destroy mine?"

"No." Kid let out a growl. "No, but I hated it. I hated seeing you being this stupid drunk party guy. You're better than that. You're smarter than that. You're not a frat guy, but that's how you act around here. Yeah—it pissed me off to see everything going so great for you."

"What are you talking about? Nothing's going good for me."

"Rayna was."

"Rayna is!" Brady snapped. "She's the best goddamn thing I've got going and that was something you wanted to screw up.

You came here and you were all talk about getting with her. Don't try and act like you did that for my good or hers."

Kid reared back. "*No*. Okay? No. I wasn't thinking that through. I wanted to hurt you. I wanted to make you sweat a little. My only problem is that I was stupid enough to say it to your face. Of course you would do something about it before I could."

A corner of Brady's lip curled upwards in an ugly smirk. "The difference between you and me is that I'll punch someone in their face. You go behind their back. Someone comes at me square and fair, I'll respect that person. You, you're pathetic."

Kid's eyes narrowed. "I wasn't going to do anything with her."

"You called her."

"Yeah, I did, but that was it. When I saw her, I knew it was pointless. The girl is so stupidly in love with you, it makes me sick. Do you know how lucky you are? Girls aren't made like that. I haven't found anyone as nice as Rayna or as pure as her."

"You two make me sick," Frank's voice interrupted. Disdain dripped from his words. "She's a whore. She's nothing, but another weak-minded slut who will get on her knees for any guy who shows her attention."

Kid and Brady turned as one.

Frank continued from his bed, "I never slept with Leann Janke, but I wish I had. I wish I had used her, screwed her so hard she wouldn't walk for a week. I wished I had cu-"

"Shut up, dad!" Kid shouted and lunged for him. Before his hands could take hold of his father, he reared back and threw himself sideways into the wall. His chest heaved as he couldn't speak for a moment.

Brady had grown still, eerily still. He looked at his father and smirked before he took a step towards the bed.

"Brady, what are you doing?" Kid gasped as he tried to contain himself.

Frank turned his head and watched his older son in a similar fashion how a wolf might study a panther.

"I don't know Rayna's mom, but for the fact alone that she rejected you makes me think she's the exact opposite of everything you think Rayna is. And you're wrong about her. You're wrong about Rayna, so much that it makes *you* look like the weak-minded pussy. You're old. You're losing your power in town. Everybody hates you. And the money you got, we both know someone who has more."

Frank paled and his eyes widened a fraction.

"I know that you're my biological father."

"What?" Kid jerked from the wall.

Brady never looked away from him. "My mother came looking for me a few years ago. When she asked you where I was and didn't get a response, she came herself. She told me that you raped her."

"She was nothing. The girl had the mind to demand money from me to take care of you. When I didn't, she deserted you. I found you in the trash can outside my house. What kind of a mother does that to her son? Don't believe her lies. Kristina was always good at lying. She came onto me that night. I was drinking and upset about Leann. I missed her so much that night and your mother came in. She knew exactly what she was doing. She wanted a rich baby daddy, but this baby daddy never paid. Who looked the fool then?"

Kid watched his half-brother across the bed, tense.

Brady waited. He wanted Frank to think that he considered his words, but then he laughed shortly. Frank's small grin vanished and Brady leaned forward. "She went to her home and had me. She brought me back because her family disowned her. She couldn't raise me on her own. You said you'd take care of me. You said that you had a plan for me. She trusted you."

Frank's eyelid twitched.

"I grew up in foster care. Was that the plan?"

"I never wanted that," Frank objected, but clamped his mouth shut. A beat later, he was more controlled. "It doesn't matter. That's where you ended, but I've watched you the whole time. I would've stepped in if anything had happened to you."

"No." Brady's voice had grown sombre. "I wouldn't have wanted you to. I don't want anything to do with you. I found out a long time ago. I've had time to adjust and the only thing I have a hard time taking is that a part of me is from you. I believe her when she said you raped her. I'm surprised you didn't rape Leann, but maybe that's why she left. Maybe that's why she couldn't come back."

Kid had been quiet, but he spoke now, "I came back because I found out about you. I found the letter your mom sent to him." He glanced at his father. "It was on your desk underneath your phone. My cell wasn't working and the house' land line was tied up. I tried using your business line, but I hit the phone. It moved a little and I saw the piece of paper underneath it. You had it taped in place for all those years." He looked back to Brady. "He had a hard plastic thing over it to protect it, but he never threw the paper away. I read it. She knew your name."

He jerked his head in a nod. "She gave me the name. It's how she found me when she came to town."

"Well this is all nice and sweet. We should have tea." The sarcasm was rich in Frank's voice. He looked down his nose at them. "I can't believe you. You're bonding over this? You're both a disappointment. Kidrick, he's everything you should've been. Brady—"

"Don't talk to me." His eyes were cold. "You have no goddamn place to speak to me. I disowned you in my own way. I want nothing from you, nothing at all. I don't give a shit what place you might think you have in my life. Your seed helped with my D.N.A. That's it. You're nothing else. You told her to abort me then when she didn't, your plans changed, but I don't care. I came here to find out one thing and I know it now. Thank you for that. If you ever come near me or Rayna, I will destroy you. You're not the only one who watches. I've been studying you this whole time too, but I'm better than you. You have no idea." Then he turned for the door.

"She knew."

Frank's voice stopped him in his tracks.

Brady looked back and Frank gave him an evil grin. "Rayna knows I'm your father. If she's so wonderful, why didn't she go to you first?"

He stared at him, long and hard as Brady grew pale. Then he jerked forward again.

"Brady." Kid started after him.

"Don't." He threw a hand up to stop him.

"Where are you going?" He followed down the hallway.

"I'm going for a drink. That's where I'm going."

"Where?"

Brady shoved through the last doors. "To Highpoint Bridge."

THE HOSPITAL WAS busy with people rushing back and forth. I walked inside, but stepped back as two policemen rushed past with a guy in handcuffs.

"You don't see that every day." Clarissa stood behind me with wide eyes.

I didn't care. I was on a mission. "What room?"

She gestured straight ahead. "The best in the hospital."

I zeroed in and walked past a group of hospital staff. No one dared stop me as I moved ahead, but I stopped in my tracks. Frank Stephens seemed empty as he stared at me. His eyes didn't blink. His body didn't move. There was no reaction at all.

Then he murmured, "I lost. How did I lose?"

"You lost Brady?"

He nodded, but his eyes watched something that wasn't there.

"What happened?" I clenched my hands together. A part of me didn't want to know what else he knew, what else I should've told him I knew.

"He..." Frank Stephens shook his head.

I watched as his hand jerked beside his leg. It was like he was coming to a decision, but what that was—I had no idea. I just knew he'd made it when he choked out, "He knew everything." Then he blinked at me. "What are you doing here?"

"Where's Brady?"

Frank Stephens closed his mouth.

"What did he say when he was here?"

He shook his head and a wall came over him. "Why the hell would I tell you anything? You're nothing. My son can do better, will do better—"

I stepped forward. "You might not have a great opinion of me, but that's your problem. You think you're above everyone else, but you're wrong. No one cares about you. No one likes you. No one wants you. No one thinks about you, least of all him."

He jerked with every statement I said.

"I don't know what your thing with my mother is or what you thought your thing with Brady was, but I know its wrong. You're wrong."

His eyes darkened and he opened his mouth, but the door opened behind me. "Rayna, its Brady."

Every tentacle was stretched inside of me. Then those words flipped everything on its head. I whirled around to Kid. "What happened?"

His face looked like a mask as he looked from his father to me. "He's at Highpoint Bridge. He's been drinking."

No one said a thing. No one had to. Highpoint Bridge overlooked a fall of more than a hundred yards. It was a dam twenty minutes away. "I thought he just left..."

Kid clipped out, "He did, but he was driving fast."

I already knew what could happen. My insides wanted to hurl. "I have to go there."

"I'll take you." Clarissa shouldered through the door. "You're in no condition to drive."

I moved to follow her, but Kid grasped my elbow and pulled me tight. "He's dangerous right now, Rayna. He's not who you think he is."

"I've known him almost my whole life, you're right. I don't know who he is at all."

"Sarcasm doesn't fit you."

I shrugged off his hold and glared. "This is how I am. I don't know what happened between you and him, but I'm tired of people getting between Brady and me. Even if we're not together, he's still my best friend. Look up the word loyalty."

Then I followed behind. Clarissa was quiet as we got in the car and turned into traffic. All I could hear was the sound of my heartbeat.

"Did Brady say anything? Do you know what happened back there?" I wanted to know if there was more.

Clarissa's hands were clenched around the steering wheel. "He went in and I heard yelling. I know someone got hit. I didn't hear what they were saying, but it didn't sound good."

"Why would they fight? Kid told me he knew. If Brady knew and Kid knew and Frank knew, why is everyone fighting?"

"I have no idea what any of this is about so you're in the dark with me," Clarissa snapped.

"Huh?" Why was *she* pissed?

"I'm pissed because it's the three of you in your little circle of secret trusts and I'm on the outside. I'm tired of it."

My mouth fell open. "Uh—?"

She continued her rant with her arms in the air, "I just, forget it. Forget it. I'm done. I'm done, okay?"

"Okay."

"*Okay*? You think its okay?" Clarissa exploded and jerked forward in her seat to slam back against it. "It's not okay! This is not okay. I want to know what's going on."

When she pinned her beady eyes on me, I shrugged. "I have nothing. I'm worried about Brady."

"AHHHH!" Clarissa screamed and then started to mutter under her breath.

I didn't speak until we got closer to Highpoint Bridge. With Clarissa, I never knew what I was going to get. Her eyes took on a crazy look the closer we got, but I only focused on Brady. I didn't know what had happened back there or if Frank was my father, but it didn't matter.

"There he is," Clarissa muttered. She peered straight ahead.

He was on the fence that separated the road from the steep incline. The dam was ahead. The sound of falling water was overwhelming when we got out of the car.

"Straight whiskey. Just what he likes when he's in a mood," Clarissa noted.

Brady glanced over his shoulder before he took a long drink from the bottle. "You better have a damn good reason for bringing her."

We stopped, frozen for a second. Then I opened my mouth. "Brady—"

"Not you," he interrupted. "Why'd you bring her, Clarissa? I don't want her here. I don't want either of you."

His rejection slammed me. My mouth closed with a snap.

Clarissa stumbled out, "Uh, she's, what's going on, Brady?"

"None of your business." He was so cold. "Just leave. There ain't anything here for either of you."

A third swallow.

Clarissa looked at me. I knew she wanted me to say something, do something, but I didn't know what. He was furious with me and I wasn't sure why. I'd never really seen him like this. I'd seen him livid, but never at me. It wasn't a good feeling. The fetal position in bed was starting to look tempting.

"Brady, I—" Clarissa stammered out.

"LEAVE!" he roared. Then he turned and threw his bottle at us.

Clarissa jumped and ducked out of the way and that's when my nervousness left. I knew that bottle wasn't going to hit us and it didn't. It sailed clear over our heads and shattered into pieces across the road. Brady would never hurt us, not physically.

A calm came over me. "I already know."

He flinched. That was enough for me. I stepped even further. "What happened at the hospital? Why'd you leave me at the jail?"

Clarissa said, "I just wanted, I came up here because I was worried. I brought her because you two are—"

"We are not anything!" he roared again and jumped off the fence to land in front of us. He moved like a cat, lean and fluid.

Clarissa stumbled backwards. "I was trying to help. I was worried and I wanted to help and she's usually the ticket. What's wrong with you?"

He wasn't going to listen to her. I moved between them. "What happened?"

Brady jerked as his hand tightened into a fist. Then he grabbed another bottle from his car.

"Brady," I murmured. "Please tell me. What happened?"

He shook his head and turned back to take a long drink. "Did you think I was going to jump? Is that why you guys came up here? I wanted to be alone."

"Kid was worried. I'm worried. Rayna's worried." Clarissa glanced at me.

"Rayna can't be worried!" Brady exploded. "She's the reason

for all of this." Then he seethed at me, "You didn't think I wouldn't find out? How long did you know? Or a better question, how long did you know and not tell me? Has it been since we were together? The first time or the second? Obviously your grandmother knew. Did you think it was funny? Were you both laughing at me?"

"Ooh." Clarissa stepped back even further, almost to the other side of the road. "I should go. This is between you two. I should, yeah. I'm going to go."

Brady whipped his glare at her and taunted, "What, Clary? You don't want the gossip? You don't want all the sordid details? Can't handle the aftermath of what you do?"

She sent me a pleading look.

"You're just as bad. You've used me all my life. You like screwing the guy at the top. You like the power it gives you."

"Brady." Clarissa made soothing motions with her hands. "We're friends. We've been friends forever."

"Friends don't fuck each other." Brady looked at me.

25

———

"**W**hat are you saying?"

Brady looked at me like he could commit murder, but he didn't say anything more. He reminded me of his father at that moment.

I pressed again, "What are you saying?"

Still nothing.

I couldn't look away from him. He was about to say something neither of us could take back. I wasn't going to let that happen. No matter how angry, for whatever reason, he wasn't going to throw us away. No chance in hell so I demanded this time, "What. Are. You. Saying?"

He opened his mouth, but again no sound came out.

"Say it!" I screamed this time. "You're not going to do this to us, to me. You're not going to make me go away, so stop it. I'm never going to want to NOT see you again so stop trying to make me."

I forgot about Clarissa. I didn't care what she overheard.

"Brady, tell me what happened. You're going to have to. At the end of the day, it's you and me. Always you and me and you know it."

"Always you and me?" He gave me a crooked, mocking smile as he drank from the bottle again. One swallow. Two. Three. He didn't stop until half the bottle was gone. "Is that what you thought when you fucked me? Or when you thought I was your brother?"

Clarissa gasped.

"How's that for irony, Rayna? Do you get off on incest?"

"I'm...going to leave...," Clarissa muttered.

A second later her car was gone.

A shiver crossed my skin. My heart was racing, but that was normal now. "You knew Frank Stephens was your dad?"

"So did you!" Brady accused.

His words hurt me, but I pushed past it. This wasn't about who was right, who hurt worse. "How long have you known?"

"How long have *you* known?" he countered.

"For two days. They've been the worst two days I've ever experienced."

Brady looked away.

"It wasn't until Viola threw that fit when she found out about us. I realized more was going on. It didn't make sense to me why she was acting how she was unless, god forbid, we couldn't be together. Once I had that thought, things clicked in place. She always hated Frank Stephens. I didn't know who my dad was, we didn't know who your parents were and I guessed that Viola knew more than she admitted so I asked her whose father was Frank Stephens, yours or mine. It was a long shot, but I was right."

"And?"

My arm twitched. As I felt a softening from Brady, my entire body wanted to launch myself in his arms. "She doesn't know who my father is, but she knew he was yours. She's known since you were a baby."

He took another two swigs from the bottle. "She's known all my life? She's been lying to me all my life?"

"Brady," I started, but did he really want to hear this? It was so painful.

"I have to know all of it, Rayna. I'm tired of these secrets."

If the tables were turned, I'd want to know. So I told him everything. I didn't stop until I got to the part where Kid had confided in me.

Brady nodded. "Kid told me he knew at the hospital. I went there to ask Frank about your mom. You said at the jail that he and your mom knew each other. It makes sense. Your mom doesn't have the best reputation and he's a manwhore. I couldn't handle not knowing if you were my sister. I didn't care what hornet's nest I was going to stir up. I didn't care."

He did what I was too scared to.

"I couldn't handle the other option."

Some tears fell down my cheek. "I'm pretty sure he's not my dad. He was talking about someone else. A lot of it was gibberish, but that was the gist of it."

Brady sighed. "He's not your dad. Your dad is his old partner, Domitri Charisteaus. I think he just died or something. Frank was spewing a lot of crazy, but he said something about a funeral.'"

"He hates my mom now."

Brady nodded. "My dad's a psychopath."

Agreed. "Why are you mad at me?"

Brady ran a brisk hand through his wet hair and shook his head. "Because I thought you knew this whole time. I was hurt. I thought you weren't ever going to tell me and you were just going to let me look like a fool, running after you. That's how I felt today at your school. I felt like an idiot, coming after you, and you didn't have the time of day for me."

"I didn't know what to do. I didn't want to deal." I felt less of a person. All I wanted to do was run away and I had hurt Brady because of it. "I'm sorry for not saying anything."

"You needed time to figure things out. I see that now. I

should've figured that out when Frank told me you knew. I was so furious. I felt like you didn't care about me."

"God, no. The opposite." I wiped at some more tears.

"I get that now. I do." He looked at his bottle and sighed. "The thought of you playing me like a fool messed me up."

I bit my lip.

He finished the bottle and went to sit on the fence once more. This time I wasn't scared to sit beside him. I was a little fearful to take his hand, though my own was itching for it. Brady added, "I know I just flipped out thinking you were keeping a secret from me, but this is where I grovel for your forgiveness. I've known about my dad for three years."

The tattoo.

I traced it with my fingertips. "Is that when you got this?"

He flexed his bicep and the tattoo moved under my touch. "I was hurt and pissed. I wanted something permanent to show that I didn't care. I'm sorry for never telling you."

"What does it mean?" I always knew it meant something with him. I'd be lying if I said it didn't hurt he never confided in me.

"Nothing profound." Brady gave me a rakish grin. "Just means 'my own.' I come from my own, no one else except for you and your family. The Forresters helped, but they really just let me have a room there as long as I didn't mess up too much."

"The tattoo, it's beautiful." I meant it. "How'd you find out about him?"

"From my mom," Brady confessed. "Man, it feels good to say that. Finally someone else knows."

"Your mom?" I flinched when jealousy flared in me. This wasn't about me.

"She found me a while ago. Told me that she'd had an affair with Frank Stephens. She also told me a lot about him and your mom. Said he was in love with your mom and was devastated when she left. That's why he pursued my mom, I guess."

"Your mom was okay with that?"

"No, not in the beginning. She thought he loved her, but one night he raped her. Then he told her to fix the pregnancy. She didn't. She went back to her family and they disowned her. She brought me back because he said that he'd take care of me. We all know how that ended up. After a while, she wrote him a letter asking to meet me. When he never replied, she showed up at the house one day. He told her to take off and that I'd died all those years ago."

My eyes widened. "What?"

"She didn't believe him. She asked around if anyone knew a kid by my name. We were both lucky that he kept my name. She wanted that for me. I'm named after her father, my grandfather."

"People knew of you, of course."

"Yeah." He grinned proudly. "She was pretty shocked by that, but she said she liked knowing that her son was well-known. Said that it meant I'd been taken care of by someone and loved, too." He sighed. "I wish I could've told her about your grand-mother's involvement, but I didn't know. I just knew I'd been put into foster care."

"Where's your mom now?"

"She went back to where she lives in New York. That's where she was originally from. I'm still in touch with her. We e-mail back and forth."

I grabbed his hand. "Why didn't you go there?"

Brady looked at our joined hands and then met my eyes. "Because you're here, Rayna."

I melted at the tenderness in his eyes. "Really?"

He tucked a strand of hair behind my ear and cupped the side of my face. "Rayna, I could've gone to college last year. I stuck around because of you. Because..."

"Because...?"

When his phone rang, I closed my eyes. *'So close.'*

Brady reached into his jeans and silenced it before he touched underneath my chin and whispered, "Open your eyes. Look at me."

I did. Through tears, I saw something that Brady had always masked to me. I'd known it was there, but never really knew. Now I saw it, full and brimming to the top.

"I love you, Rayna. It's why I've never left and never wanted to leave."

My eyes closed with a snap. I burrowed into his chest. It's what I'd wanted for so long. I finally heard it and wrapped my arms around him.

He brushed my hair back and kissed my forehead. "I've just been waiting for you and I'm sorry that I haven't been a saint. When Kid came and said stuff about you, I went crazy for a moment. I thought he was going to try something with you and I couldn't lose you. It's why I made love to you after you got me out of jail. I was making you mine. Then I started thinking it wasn't fair to you. I wasn't sure if you were ready to deal with me, with everything I felt for you when you were going to go away to college. That's why I started to back away from you, but you got so mad at me. I thought for sure that meant you felt the same, but then Viola was there and everything got messed up. I didn't know what to think and then you were avoiding me."

I stopped him. "I love you, too!"

I met his mouth with mine and poured everything into that kiss. He lifted me in the air and climbed to the other side of the fence. As I entwined my legs around his waist, Brady walked backwards and gently lowered me to the front of his car. After that, I felt him surrender everything into our kiss, into me. I wanted nothing more than to be one with him.

We stayed like that, fused together, arms around each other, until both of our hearts slowed and reality filtered back in. Then he pulled away and groaned. "We can't stay here. I'm not going to do what I want to on the hood of my car. I want a bed and a week."

I rubbed a hand over my sensitized lips. "Might want to wait until after graduation."

"Graduation. Tomorrow." Brady grimaced. "I forgot about that. Clarissa's got a party tonight. Did you want to go?"

My mouth fell open.

He grinned and gently squeezed my hands. "I'm kidding. I want only to be with you tonight." Then he nipped my lips and deepened the kiss. It started out a gentle touch, but flared into more.

After he pulled away, I was reluctant to let him, but I couldn't ignore the real world. "I think we have other stuff to do tonight. You need to do damage control with Clarissa and everyone else who thought you were coming up here to jump off Highpoint Bridge. I need to explain to Viola why we might be getting sued by Frank Stephens."

"I doubt that." Brady laughed and pulled me off the car, back into his arms. "From what he was spewing, your mother has his balls in a nut-hold. There's a reason why he's scared of your grandmother too. Nah. You could've killed him and he wouldn't come back to haunt you."

"Really?"

"If he tries to hurt you, I'm going after him."

"God forbid." I grinned and looked up.

Brady met my gaze and kissed me lightly. "Much as I hate to admit this, I've had time to study Frank Stephens and I'm a lot like him in some ways. I know how he thinks. I won't let him hurt you. Ever."

"Ever forever?"

"Ever forever," Brady promised and kissed me again. He pulled away to rest his forehead against mine. "I want to take you home and then I want to do something for you."

"What?" My hands tugged on his shirt and pulled him down

for another kiss. He met my lips, softly and then harder. It wasn't long before we were short of breath. He ripped away again.

"I mean it. Let's get in the car now before I decide I don't care if we're in the back of a car or on top a car." His voice was hoarse, thick with desire, as he pulled me after him. He got in the passenger seat and I drove out of there.

26

It wasn't long before we had pulled up to my house. The lights were lit, then the door flew open and my grandparents stumbled out. I heard Viola shriek in laughter. Neil laughed in his baritone after.

"Rayna!" She swung her arms in the air and giggled. "Wait there, we'll come to you."

She fell at one point even with her arm draped over Neil's shoulder as they weaved their way towards us.

"Oh god," Brady groaned.

Viola fell again and her feet lifted in the air. I bit back a laugh.

Neil stood and looked down. He'd dropped her, but then bent with his arms outstretched to scoop her up. She grunted, rolled over and scrambled to her feet. Then she threw back her head, let a laugh bellow out, and ran around him. Her fists pumped in the air and her knees followed suit, higher and higher. Neil followed suit, but his coveralls tripped him. Down he went.

My mouth fell open. When had my grandparents become drunken teenagers?

Viola fell beside me first and patted my knee. "Are you okay, honey? What'd that bastard say to you?"

I looked at Brady with an eyebrow raised. He shrugged as he bit his lip, and then he couldn't hold back. He bent over and his shoulders shook in laughter.

"Why are you guys drunk?"

"Oh," she snorted and waved a hand in the air. It took her back to the ground.

Neil cleared his throat and tried to stand tall. Brady snorted and grabbed his arm to help him upright. "We heard the news, honey."

"We did," Viola said from the ground.

"You punched Frank Stephens."

"Yohoo!"

"And your mother stopped by."

Everything stopped. It ground to a halt and I sucked in my breath. "What? What did you say?"

"Yeppers," Viola punched the air. "She came by and told us everything. You two can be together."

"Who?" Brady questioned.

"You two, you two lovebirds. Rayna, your father isn't Frank Stephens."

Neil grunted, "We're going to church tomorrow to praise the Lord."

She kept on, "And your dad died. He left you a bunch of money." Then she shot to her feet and a sobering look filled her face. "You don't have to do anything with it, Rayna. We sent your mom away. She can come another night, but I wanted to tell you first."

"My mom's still here?"

They both nodded at the same time.

Brady narrowed his eyes. "She was here, at the house here?"

Viola sniffed. "We sent her away."

"But your real father died, Rayna. We're really sorry."

"And he left her an inheritance?" Brady looked at her.

I looked down at my hands. They were clenched together in front of me. I knew all of this, but I hadn't cared when Frank Stephens ranted about my inheritance. I didn't care then and I don't now. It was enough to know I wasn't related to Brady.

"You okay?"

I looked up and met Brady's eyes. "I'm good. I'm really good."

He walked over and pressed a kiss to my forehead. Then he whispered, "I'll be right back. Don't go to bed. Stay out here."

I nodded and smiled when his hand squeezed mine before he left.

"Where's he going?"

Viola turned all the way around. "I don't know."

I sighed, "He'll be back. He wants to do something for me."

Neil leaned against the car and shook his head. "We're sorry we're a bit inebriated right now, Rayna. It's not been an easy night for us."

Viola swung her arms around, her body followed suit. "Yeah, he's right. I was shaking so much from your momma that I needed a drink to calm down. I had a few too many, then I got my hubby to start with me. It reminded us of our honeymoon days. You remember those days, honey?"

"I sure do." He sounded gruff as he wiped at an eye.

"Look at that, he's still so in love with me that he sheds a tear. Just like you and Brady."

Neil wrapped an arm around his wife. "We both love you very much, Rayna."

I blinked back sudden tears. "I love you, too."

"And tomorrow is your graduation. We've got something special planned." She patted my knee. "Congratulations, honey. You and Brady deserve each other. You're soul mates. I always thought it, but I pissed myself when I didn't know whose daddy was whose." She twisted and looked at her husband. "Did you know that? I peed my pants that night."

Neil shook his head. "We should go to bed before we traumatize our granddaughter any more than we already have tonight."

She twisted back. "I love you. I guess that's all I've got to say. For now. Oh—and what a wallop you must've given to Frank Stephens. He deserved it. Good job, Rayna!" She threw a closed fist in the air and her body followed once more.

Neil caught her before she fell, then shook his head before he smiled at me. "Goodnight, honey. Congratulations on your graduation."

My throat was choked up again.

As he pulled Viola inside, I heard her say, "Frank Stephens deserves worse than that. I think Rayna is the best daughter I could ever have..."

Neil soothed her, "Yes, dear. I love you, too."

I took a deep breath after the door shut and muffled their voices. They might've been drunk, but they loved me. They would fight on my side. I didn't know what to think about all of that, but my grandfather was right. It was my graduation tomorrow. I should focus on that. There was nothing else I could control...

"Hey." Brady stood by the house with his hands stuffed in his pockets. He pulled me against his side once I drew near. "I figured those two kids wanted some time with you."

Those two kids, I grinned at that thought. Then he lifted me in the air and hoisted my legs around his waist.

"Brady!"

He chuckled and started to walk around the house, into the woods.

"Where are we going?" The path to his house went the other way.

He held me tighter and put a hand over my head to shield me. "I told you I wanted to do something for you."

"What?"

"You're already demanding in this relationship."

My head turned into the crook between his shoulder and I nipped him lightly.

"And I already know you like it rough," Brady chuckled and hoisted me higher. He turned from the path onto another path. I'd forgotten about the maze from when we were kids. The woods had been home to many never neverlands.

"Here we are." Brady put me back on the ground and I turned to look.

What I saw made me speechless. It was our tree house we built before seventh grade. Brady, Kid, and I had a lot of sleep-overs that summer.

"Wait a second." Brady climbed up the tree and ducked inside. Light shone through the windows a minute later and I was able to see that the tree house had new siding and new flooring. He'd been hard at work.

He stepped out on the tiny balcony, smiling. "Okay, come up."

My heart skipped a beat and I shook my head, wiping a tear from my cheek.

"Come on." His smile turned tender. "I want to hold you again."

My heart went into warp speed, but I took a deep breath and grabbed the bottom of the ladder. I could think about how dreamy Brady was later. He stepped aside when I got to the top and my eyes were wide when I saw the inside. Bedding was spread out across the floor with two pillows at one end. Mason jars hung from the ceiling with tea lights inside. They were lit and surrounded by sand. A few of them were in the corner, near the pillows.

Brady stepped around me. "I figure the jars are safe. If they fall or tip over, the sand will put out the candle."

My mouth had fallen open. I closed it now and turned to him. "When did you do this?"

"I did the tree house a while ago, but I grabbed everything real quick just now. I had it all set aside."

"This is so..." I was speechless.

The glow from the candles gave the room a romantic look. The bedding gave it a cozy look. He bent and opened the bed. Inside was a small black box, nestled among the covers. My eyes went even wider and my mouth fell open again. The tears spilled free now.

"It's not a ring, but I bought this a long time ago." He sat down and patted next to him. As I sat, he opened the box and I saw a bracelet made of colorful beads. A small heart hung from it. Brady took my hand and slipped it on. "I bought this last year when I decided to stay and wait for you."

"It has your heart," I teased. Then I looked up and saw how serious he was. My heart continued fluttering away.

Brady leaned down and kissed me softly. One of his hands cupped the side of my face and he deepened the kiss. We lay down slowly, still kissing. Brady rested on his elbow and lifted his head. Looking down on me, he then traced the side of my face and lingered over my lips.

I reached up and held the side of his face with my hand. Overcome with emotion, I barely managed out, "I love you so much. I don't think I'm going to get tired of telling you that. I finally can."

Brady caught my hand and kissed it. He closed his eyes for a moment. When they opened, I saw a small tear at the corner of one. "It's you and me, Rayna. Now. Forever. No matter what."

I leaned up and kissed away the tear. "Deal."

He smiled tenderly and then kissed me as we both lay down. We didn't speak the rest of the night. Later, when I curled in his arms and closed my eyes, I knew everything else would be okay.

The next chapter would start tomorrow.

If you enjoyed Brady and Rayna, please leave a review!
They help so much.
For more stories, head to www.tijansbooks.com

ACKNOWLEDGMENTS

Brady and Rayna's book was one of my first that I ever wrote, and to be honest, the readers who kept asking for me to continue Brady's story helped me keep writing in general. It was a time when I was in school and I could've gone another route.

Thank you to those for asking for more chapters of this story!

Thank you to everyone and all the continued support.

RICH PRICK

1

Everyone knew who Blaise DeVroe was.

It didn't matter that he'd come to Fallen Crest Academy late in the year—and FCA was *not* a school you showed up late to.

I knew this because I showed up shortly after this year—my senior year—began, and no one, I repeat *no one*, knew who I was. Since my parents decided to have a mid-life crisis and tried to make up for some of their wrongs and bring me back to Fallen Crest, my last year of high school had sucked. FCA was filled with rich, stuck-up people. That meant you had to speak their language to be in their groups, and I didn't. Not because I didn't have money. My parents were movie producers and directors. We had money, and I previously went to one of the most exclusive private schools in North America, *and* a stint in a boarding school in Europe.

I could be fluent in stuck-up-ese if I wanted to.

But I chose not to. I've never been that girl.

I was the library girl.

I was the book nerd girl.

I was the wallflower.

On the whole, I tended to avoid people. I didn't people well.

I had an affinity for blending into the background. It's a skill. I'd been perfecting it all my life.

But anyway, Blaise DeVroe was the opposite of that.

He may have moved to this school late in the year, but he walked in as if he already owned it. And to his credit, he kinda did.

The guy who ran the school before Blaise showed up was Zeke Allen. He's this wealthy jackass who's a bully, a muscular douchebag, and who slept with girls and then talked shit about them. He was king of the school by default, I guess—not because he was anything fantastic.

Then Blaise DeVroe walked in.

Guess who gave him a welcome-home hug? Zeke Allen did!

I was there, just coming out of the counselor's office, so I saw it all.

Blaise DeVroe strutted in with that cocky walk all the athletes had, and he was gorgeous. Like, seriously gorgeous. He had the high, arching cheekbones only the prettiest of the pretty-boy models had.

I knew this too because I'd done some reluctant gigs in the business.

But back to freaking stunning Blaise DeVroe. He had a chiseled, square jaw. He could have had his own waterfall off that jawline. Dark eyes. His hair was short, but long enough so he could rake his hands through it and let it be all adorably messy. And his body. Don't even get me started on his body—I was all crushing on it because it was *sick* and I mean that in the hot kind of sick way, not the real sick way. He was definitely not the real sick way at all.

He wasn't as big as Zeke, but he had these big, broad shoulders. Trim waist. And there were muscles everywhere. I swear I saw shape definition in his neck.

Blaise DeVroe: the *hottest* guy at Fallen Crest Academy.

One of the richest guys too.

I didn't hear the story of why he came here—not the real reason. Rumors circulated that his mom was going through a divorce, but there were also whispers about secret siblings. I wasn't on the up-and-up with anyone, so I never heard for sure if any of that was true. All I knew was Blaise DeVroe had walked into the hallowed and pretentious hallways of the private school in our town, and he was hailed like a long-lost son or something.

Or something, as it turned out.

Blaise and Zeke knew each other from childhood. Zeke considered him his long-lost best friend. So it was a coming home sort of situation.

Not that I could talk much about the history of FCA, because I was new myself, but I had been here almost a whole semester before Blaise. And full disclosure, I'd been here when I was much younger at the private elementary/middle school. That was before Mom and Pops decided they didn't like the influence my older brother's best friend was having on him, so they pulled both my brothers and me out of here.

But that's a whole different story.

The story for right now is that I'm being a total weirdo stalker and perving on Blaise DeVroe getting his dick sucked.

Like, right in front of me.

In hindsight, this was probably not the best idea I'd ever had. And I've had some doozy ideas. But this one takes the cake. I just couldn't help myself. As I've mentioned, I usually keep to myself, but something got into me this year. Every time I heard about a party, I couldn't make myself go, but I also couldn't *not* go.

So...I went.

But I stayed on the outskirts, so the people actually attending the party didn't realize I was there. There'd been a big bonfire that our town and the neighboring two towns had a while back. I was there, but I'd decided to make it a camping trip—just for me.

I was there, but not there. And that night had ended weird too, but nothing like this one.

This time the party was at Zeke Allen's lake cabin. Not that his cabin was a cabin. It was a mansion—a twenty-room *mega* log cabin, which no one even blinked at, because that's just normal for these people. Most everyone was staying at the cabin, not trekking back here into the woods like me. I'd set up my tent a bit away, doing my camping thing again (something I love, by the way), when I heard voices. They weren't down by the house, spilling out over the back patio, or even at the lake. Nope. These voices were up the hill, coming from farther into the woods.

I'd done my research. Zeke Allen's cabin was set a good ten miles away from the nearest neighbors. I should've been in the clear to sneak onto their land, do a little freestyle camping, and listen to the party sounds like the loser I was. But noooo. I was about to get company.

As I snuck out of my tent, and realized who it was, I almost crapped my pants.

It was Blaise DeVroe, holding hands with Mara Daniels.

As popular girls went, Mara Daniels was one of the nicer ones. She was on the dance team. Dark hair. Shorter, but athletic. The problem with Mara was that she was friends with the other popular girls. Some of them were nasty—hence the reason I wasn't friends with them. Not that they'd tried to get to know me. Not that I even registered on their radar. But then again, that's what I did.

I didn't engage. I didn't attend. I was on the edge. I was the invisible girl, and here I was, being the invisible girl once more, but man...

When I saw it was him, and then saw how his hand went from holding hers and guiding her to a tree to slipping around and grabbing her ass, something came over me. I couldn't retreat back to my tent. I couldn't even stay hidden behind a tree and just listen.

I know, I know. This was all sorts of wrong, but Blaise was Blaise.

He'd become the guy in my dreams, my weird schoolgirl fantasies. He was my high school crush. Everyone had one. If you didn't, you're even weirder than me, and that's saying something. So when I started salivating over Blaise DeVroe, I kinda just let myself go. I mean, nothing was ever going to happen. Guys like him didn't date girls like me. They didn't even notice girls like me.

I wasn't crazy. That'd make me all sorts of delusional.

I was a realist. I knew my place in life's hierarchy. I was at the bottom. I was not the very bottom—because of my family— but socially, I was barely one rung up the ladder.

Anyway, when Blaise started kissing Mara, when Mara knelt in front of him, when she opened his pants and took out his cock—I lost all train of thought.

I watched as she took his dick in her mouth, as her head began bobbing up and down over him.

And, oh my God.

My whole body was awash with sensations, and I was captivated. Captivated! Entranced. Mesmerized.

I could not look away.

Then I felt throbbing and a warm feeling between my legs, and it was game over. It was all I could do not to make a sound, because I wanted to. So bad. I wanted to moan. I wanted to touch myself, but I didn't. I kept myself reined in, but watch? Oh yeah. I watched.

I couldn't *not* watch.

I watched the whole thing.

I loved the whole thing.

And then at the end of it, I almost died.

BLAISE

I was getting my dick sucked while a weird chick watched us.

"Hmmm...Blaise." My girl moaned, readjusted, and took me in again. She reached up to stroke under, and damn, that felt good. My eyes almost rolled back, but I caught myself and held steady. My hands went to her head. Sometimes a little guidance went a long way, and as I applied gentle pressure, my girl was receptive. So I started to drive her mouth over me. All the while, I never stopped watching the other girl.

I couldn't place her.

I was pretty sure she hadn't been at Zeke's party, but who the fuck knew. He'd invited fifty people, way more than he needed to, but Zeke was a lovable bully idiot. He was mean. Some might say he had a slime effect on them, but he was my best friend. I couldn't judge. I had an attitude the size of fucking Alaska. Anyway, back to Zeke. He liked to go big, and that included his parties and his fuck-ups, and there were a lot of both.

That girl...

I liked her.

Fresh face. I could tell she was light on the makeup. Her face was one of those that would look jaded under a ton of crap, but without it, she looked the way she did right now: innocent and pure. Though the fact that she was watching my blowjob didn't fit either of those adjectives. She was tugging on her lip now, her hand lingering on her shorts.

Christ.

Her shorts.

My chick was wearing a bikini top and shredded jean shorts —and those shorts were hardly there. They were more decorative so she didn't get arrested for public indecency. All the girls at this party were like that. Bikinis, and anything else they wore was painted on their bodies. The old school way of thought might've labeled them sluts or whores, but since we were all liberal and progressive, we went with *sexually healthy appetites*.

I, currently, was enjoying my girl's appetite.

She opened her mouth wider, angled her head to the other side, and oooh yeah—I was in at a whole different depth now. Fuck it. I took hold of her hair and started moving. She moaned, but only widened her jaw and spread her knees a little more apart. She was bracing herself.

Fuuuuck yeah.

That meant I could go a little harder, which I did. I shoved her down a bit more, a better angle, and right there. I loved when they let me take over. But then I looked back up to watch Voyeur Girl. My friends and I did not hang out with girls like my voyeur. My dick got harder. I almost cursed, gritting my teeth. I had not expected that reaction, but I'd take it.

The girl watching wore a buttoned-up maroon shirt, the ends tied at her waist. She had a good rack. The shirt was bunched up to hide 'em, but I saw her girls. They would be a decent handful, almost perfect. And she wasn't wearing a bra. There was enough of a tease between the buttons that I could see just skin, just tits.

The rest of her... I had no words.

Khaki shorts that ended mid-thigh, and what a fucking thigh she had.

This girl could model.

Long. Lean. Legs meant to wrap around your waist—I thrust a little harder, and my girl groaned around me. I needed to ease up, but I was almost gone. Almost. Not quite.

Then Mara reached up and massaged my boys. That was enough.

I unloaded into her.

She swallowed like a champ and smiled up at me. She

wiped her mouth with the back of her hand, and for a second, the weird chick was forgotten. I grinned at Mara. I always liked Mara's blowjobs, and because I wasn't an asshole, I tugged her up and moved her farther behind the trees so she was hidden from view.

Now was my turn to make her feel good.

Kissing her, I slid my hand inside her shorts and inside her, and when she was done and moaning, I looked over my shoulder. The other girl was still there, still glued to her tree, her eyes still right on us, but this time, she saw me.

Her eyes bulged out, and she inhaled sharply. She jerked back, and I grinned, lifting my hand to my mouth. I tasted Mara on my fingers as I watched her. Then I winked.

She uttered a muffled scream.

Chuckling, I grabbed Mara as she tensed in my arms.

Her head snapped around. "What was that?"

"Nothing." I kept her tight to my side as she fixed her pants. "Come on. Let's go back to the party."

As we left, I glanced back.

The girl was gone.

Keep reading for the rest of Rich Prick here!

ALSO BY TIJAN

Sports Romance Standalones:

Enemies

Teardrop Shot

Hate To Love You

The Not-Outcast

Rich Prick

Latest books:

A Dirty Business (Mafia, Kings of New York Series)

A Cruel Arrangement (Mafia, Kings of New York Series)

Aveke (Fallen Crest novella, standalone)

Fallen Crest and Crew Universe

Fallen Crest/Roussou Universe

Fallen Crest Series

Crew Series

The Boy I Grew Up With (standalone)

Rich Prick (standalone)

Frisco

Series:

Broken and Screwed Series (YA/NA)

Jaded Series (YA/NA suspense)

Davy Harwood Series (paranormal)

Carter Reed Series (mafia)

The Insiders

Mafia Standalones:

Cole

Bennett Mafia

Jonah Bennett

Canary

Paranormal Standalones and Series:

Evil

Micaela's Big Bad

The Tracker

Davy Harwood Series (paranormal)

Young Adult Standalones:

Ryan's Bed

A Whole New Crowd

Brady Remington Landed Me in Jail

College Standalones:

Antistepbrother

Kian

Enemies

Contemporary Romances:

Bad Boy Brody

Home Tears

Fighter

Rockstar Romance Standalone:

Sustain

More books to come!